Christmas in Flanders Fields

By Chris Waddington

Dedicated to my beautiful daughter, Chantelle. You have bestowed upon me enough love and joy to sustain a thousand lifetimes, leaving me owing you a debt of gratitude I can never hope to fully repay.

IBSN – 979-8-89965-577-7

Trench Life

'Lice rats, barbed wire, fleas, shells, bombs, underground caves, corpses, blood, liquor, mice, cats, artillery, filth, bullets, mortars, fire, steel: that's what war is. It is the work of the devil.'

German Expressionist artist, Otto Dix.

So bereft of hope and devoid of dreams, empty human vessels strewn across a boggy mire dominate the grisly landscape I perilously survey. Stricken with sadness and fear, I duck swiftly beneath the parapet. The dangerous terrain ahead cruelly denies them the dignified burial they richly deserve; easy fodder for the portly rats that scurry through the deep, gaping chasms of no mans land. So called distinguished gentlemen destined to never taste the brutality of battle are callously using the blood of decent men as ink to write history. All the while, my slowly hardening heart aches for home, having already endured far too much tragedy. Merry bloody Christmas, Private Crosby!

It's in stark contrast to the balmy late summers day when I arrived at the makeshift recruitment office with my best mate, Davy Frost, to a rousing ovation. Raucous cheers intermingled with exuberantly played trumpets created a carnival style atmosphere that did little to dampen the hedonistic haze descending over the pair of us. With our dazed heads held high we were swiftly answering Lord Kitchener's rally cry, an impassioned plea to stand tall and gallantly serve ones King and country. Ironworkers by trade, we'd spent our youth in scorching factories, now the promise of travel, celebratory beers in Berlin and home in time for Christmas decorated with medals and cloaked in glory is proving irresistible…

With all the enthusiasm of a group of fellows on a charabanc trip to the lights, we marched briskly, our bulging chests swollen with pride. Oblivious to the elements of a fresh autumnal day and armed with a naïve eagerness to reach our destination, we made good time singing heartily all the way. The buoyant mood rapidly dissipated on arrival at the Western front when we were confronted with the dawning realization that there was no glory to be had on the blood soaked fields of the Flanders region. The sight of a ghostly German soldier impaled on barbed wire in front of your trench will do that. It's hard to fathom, that in the not too distant past, unbridled ambition flowed freely through the veins of his now frozen corpse. No amount of basic training prepares you for this reality. Inaugural feelings for my own mortality rush violently to the surface, I might never get to cradle my sweetheart Rose again, become a doting father or lay eyes on my beloved Blighty once more. *Snap out of it man, there isn't a jot of time to dwell on ones circumstances, the bullets are already ringing around your ears!*

I've known Frosty for most of my days; schoolmates dragged up on the same drab council estate. We've smoked many a fag behind the bike shed, downed our first pints at The Dirty Duck, heck we even lost our virginity together (same night but different girls, thankfully). Yet I've never witnessed such emptiness in his eyes before, without a semblance of colour and laced with fear. It's all too evident that the barbarity before us bared no resemblance to the heroic fairytale we'd cooked up in our minds. I muster an awkward smile in his direction, but my futile efforts of reassurance are no match for the horrific realism engulfing us. Bathed in the shadow of death, our fate now rests in the lap of the God's for the foreseeable future.

Over the next two months, I settled into trench life as best as one could, a daily diet of bullets, billets and bully beef that bordered on the bizarre became routine. The practice of breathing, sleeping and eating within yards of men intent on killing me inexplicably morphed into normality. As a patriotic Tommy I've been subtly conditioned to despise the average Jerry, but the human heart isn't designed to carry hatred so comfortably and with every passing hour it's proving impossible to not feel empathy for young men suffering indignity in equally squalid conditions. The propaganda machine keeps mercilessly spreading it's poison, consequently we're all pawns trapped in a sadistic game, sharing the same pain and misery, our lives wholly dispensable.

Each day a battle rages within as I desperately strive for sanity and survival amidst an array of formidable foes, if only it was just Jerry's bluster I had to contend with! December has brought with it a harsh Belgian winter, every bit as unrelenting as the ferocious German shelling I've sadly become accustomed to. Falling asleep now requires the accompanying and somewhat soothing crackle of enemy fire. The flat landscape does not lend itself to the torrential downpours that rain viciously upon my weary head, each drop fuels a growing sense of embitterment that threatens to consume me, but I daren't succumb.

The torment, now simmering between my ears, will forever be my daily penance, that's if I'm lucky enough to make it out of this godforsaken Belgian hellhole. Life's most caustic memories will obliterate the euphoric ones, leaving behind an indelible imprint scorched on my mind that affords no prospect of escape. Ultimately, these will manifest themselves as dreams, the dark and disturbing kind that come for you in the dead of night. Chilling images of war that can never be unseen will rebound around my head like a tennis ball caught up in a gladiatorial rally as beads of cold sweat pour from my brow. Trapped in a torture that I'll never conqueror or even tame, my forlorn hopes rest with a dulling of my demons over time. That's the bleak future I'm fighting for, me and all these other poor bastards sharing this desolate patch of soil. There will be no winners, that much is painfully apparent.

God's fury has been battering down for what feels like an eternity, causing a dramatic deterioration in what's now beginning to feel like the palatial surroundings once enjoyed in pleasant autumnal sunshine. Frostbite, gangrene and the dreaded trench foot have infested and depleted our ranks, claiming more young lives than conflict in the last few months, as both sides incur Mother Nature's wrath. Fellow comrades on sentry duty through the night have tragically perished, despite what I can only imagine were frantic efforts to claw their way out, sinking into muddy graves. The land is rich in sand and clay which is a deadly combination when it comes to absorbing water. Our hastily built drainage channels are no match for the unrepentant torrents of rain and desperate attempts to bail out the trench have become a long, exhausting daily ritual that provides precious little respite from the elements.

As water pours in, it swirls around the ankles meandering effortlessly through the trench, bringing with it the pungent stench of death. Body parts intermingle with rats and slushy mud facilitating the inevitable spread of disease. Extra pairs of socks and puttees put up a staunch defence, but ultimately have to give up the ghost in conditions I can only describe as atrocious. If it is a choice between a prolonged opening of the heavens or a biting winter chill then I'll happily take the cold, all night long. Each four day rotation in the trenches is its own individual war, made all the more arduous when spent in soggy boots and a sodden uniform. I hold no strong religious beliefs, but I've recently turned to prayer-the last refuge of a scoundrel! *I'll take my chances with the shells and bullets Lord, but please I beg of you to let the rain relent for a short while.* My appetite for medals has long diminished, but it would be grand to wake to a clear blue sky and patrol at night beneath a bevy of stars. As the December deluge rumbled on I could be forgiven for thinking my impassioned pleas had fallen on deaf ears, but finally on the 24th day God showed up.

Christmas Eve delivers all the weak and weary battalions, situated in close proximity, an early present in the form of a beautiful winter's day. The dark lingering clouds that blighted us remorselessly have given way to a piercing blue sky accompanied by a hint of frost which cools the hands, but warms my heart. The sharp crunchy sound made underfoot as I stomp through the frontline is quite frankly exhilarating, it's making me feel positively giddy and that's before the thick heavenly aroma of sizzling bacon wafting through the trench assaults my senses! One comes to appreciate and enjoy the simple luxuries in these extraordinary times and it doesn't get much better than indulging in a steaming mug of coffee and a warm greasy bacon sandwich. The queue forming around the sizzling pan bears testament to the fact it is a sentiment shared by my fellow comrades. My rumbling stomach's timid gurgling has evolved into angry growling as I patiently inch towards a taste of paradise. *Great, there is mustard available!* I long to spread it lavishly across the bread, but adopt a more conservative approach mindful of the hungry chaps in line behind me. The moments following first light tend to be a more sedate affair and I exploit the opportunity to savour every moreish mouthful of my breakfast whilst mustering up the necessary enthusiasm for another bruising day of battle. However, this morning feels different, lively chatter reverberates around the trench and the mood seems distinctly chipper. That's not to say we're normally a miserable bunch of sods, just mere mortals subdued by the weight of waging war.

It's Christmas, well at least that's what I keep telling myself, but it's a notion that's tough to digest given the dire circumstances I find thrust upon me. Its significance has been underestimated, especially by the Generals tucked up in their cosy winter hideouts, even if I try my damndest to ignore it , one suspects Christmas will find me. Thoughts of home and loved ones left behind are never far from my mind, but must be expunged during prolonged periods of intense battle; any loss of concentration can serve as a death sentence so one must be on his mettle! If there is a fate worse than dying then it's living on with the knowledge that your ineptness cost one of your muckers their life, a prisoner to the heavy conscience simmering inside. My responsibilities run deeper than just my precarious existence. I'm fighting for Frosty and all the other magnificent men in this battalion. I'm willing to die for them, no other mentality is acceptable. Reuniting as many men as possible with their sweethearts, that's the perennial sense of purpose that keeps me stumbling through the darkness. Sentimental thoughts gnaw away at the crumbling walls of my conscious mind incessantly, like a mental cancer, but my resolve must remain steadfast. Nostalgic musings are an indulgent pastime and are strictly reserved for sacred moments of recuperation, but today they appear more prevalent than ever given the time of year and therefore harder to shake.

Prior to my tasty breakfast, our daily stand to arms ceremony had taken place at dawn's first light. Comrades standing shoulder to shoulder, packed in like sardines and listening intently to Sergeant Bevan's forthright address. An impressive man that commands respect, Mike Bevan is a bank clerk by trade with designs on becoming a branch manager. I imagine in his pre-war incarnation he lived a rather studious existence, but war moulds a second character with its predecessor often lost forever. Inevitably, the heat of combat brings vices that are paramount if one wants to absorb the pressures of war whilst retaining the faintest slither of sanity. Like most, poor old Sergeant Bevan has succumbed, sobriety and the soldier rarely make for good bed fellows. Liquor is readily available in the trenches, particularly whisky and rum to fight the cold. It settles the nerves and silences the old grey matter, helping keep the demons at bay, so partaking of it is pretty much universal. The war has made a hard drinker out of Sergeant Bevan and he's developed a penchant for American whisky. On occasion, I'm summoned to his quarters to discuss anything from covert missions after dark to the Tottenham Hotspur back four, but whatever the time of day, we drink bourbon from some rather grand crystal cut tumblers and enjoy a smoke. Certain civilians during this war have been known to go power crazy when given a taste of authority, revelling in their new found status to the point of becoming intolerable, but not Sergeant Bevan and the men admire him for it. In the main he speaks softly, but with a comforting assurance and we take him at his word without question. Some men are born to lead whilst others are willing to bleed, but possession of both attributes is as rare as smooth custard.

"Good morning, chaps, and a Merry Christmas to each and every one of you, I only wish we could be spending it under different circumstances, but mercifully at the very least we have better conditions today." The men smile and nod in unison, Sergeant Bevan warmly reciprocates before continuing.

"Naturally, at this time of year our thoughts will drift towards home and the festivities we'd be partaking in as a matter of course." He pauses momentarily, a sombre expression spreads across his face. "There will be a host of empty chairs at dinner tables as our loved ones sit down to enjoy their Christmas lunch. They are sharing the immense burden war affords us and we owe it to them to remain vigilant, keep alert and above all else men, stay alive. Not more than eighty yards away, Jerry may well be concocting all manner of fiendish plans designed to catch us off our guard, but we shan't gift them the opportunity. Make no mistake gentlemen, the threat of imminent attack remains our constant companion, Christmas or no Christmas we mustn't allow ourselves to lose focus."

His voice now exudes a much more serious tone, which is not lost on me or any other man given the intent way we're listening, while the eloquence of his address in no way disguises the severity of its message. Sergeant Bevan concludes his impassioned plea in familiar fashion.

"Let us all remain unscathed today by the scourge of battle and may Godspeed our hearts and minds to glorious sanctuary."

This is met with defiant cries of "hear, hear" from the majority of quarters as his sobering words began to sink in, it's to be business as usual, another day of deathly duelling beckons!

The day's events dance to a familiar worn out tune as a steady flow of enemy fire crackles all around me, any careless raising of the head will be met with the uncompromising cold steel of a snipers bullet. I stand with my back to the trench wall, trusty rifle in hand and mentally prepare to retaliate. This callous war makes murderers out of the mildest mannered men and I'm yet to derive any satisfaction from the barbaric act of taking a human life. Despite having several months to become accustomed to this kill or be killed environment, I still experience an abrupt shudder each time my index finger hovers over the trigger. Some men develop a taste for bloodlust, thriving on the adrenalin fuelled state that only the threat of imminent death can deliver, but not me. The repercussions of my daily indiscretions will be devastating for all those who hold affection for the poor victims whose fresh blood stains my weathered hands, but my crimes are committed out of necessity and that is the justification I cling to whilst slowly coming to terms with my deplorable actions. Every single kill leaves a permanent scar across my deeply troubled mind, emitting disturbing thoughts I must bury within some dark and forgiving crevice. I'm a dead man walking, habitually haunted by the ghosts of every young service man I've ever slayed, may God bestow solace upon me and spare my dishevelled soul!

The trench I begrudgingly inhabit can be a curse or a comfort. It is undeniably susceptible to the elements, bringing untold misery to its occupants, but the barbed wire lined borders and towering walls of mud provide substantial protection. This sorry state of affairs has created a stalemate which serves to prolong the agony as both sides bed in for the long haul, neither relishing the prospect of engaging in open warfare. It's giving political leaders ample time to get round the table and end this madness, but there seems precious little appetite for that either. It's traditionally the time to offer goodwill to all men, but try telling that to the German sniper who's making full use of his aerial vantage point to enthusiastically discharge his weapon. It's severely limiting any opportunity I have to wrestle the initiative away by lunging above the trench wall and returning the compliment. Daring forays of this nature are more palatable when conducted under a blanket of darkness, but needs must whence embroiled in the art of conflict. A sudden silence jolts me into action, with a racing heart I unleash a flurry of ill-directed bullets in his vicinity, before throwing myself back in readiness for his violent reciprocation. Slumped against the clay, I breathe heavily as the adrenaline slowly dissipates from my body. Acutely aware my actions haven't proved fatal on this occasion, fleeting feelings of disappointment are tinged with relief.

So far, today qualifies as a success, despite heavy shelling and a generous spray of bullets being fired in my direction, I'm still in one piece and blessed with a beating heart. At this rate I'll get to enjoy a warm mince pie once the sun goes down. Festive treats started arriving long before December graced us with its ugly presence, apart from the aforementioned mince pies; biscuits, chocolates, cake, Christmas pudding, sherry, socks and knitted blankets amongst other goodies have been gleefully received into the trenches. This isn't the handy work of our loved ones alone, the British public have been very generous and their kindness has touched our homesick hearts. We have not been forgotten this Christmas time and there appears to be a real determination from all the folks back home to make things as joyous as possible for us. To know we haven't strayed too far from their thoughts makes this wretched struggle all the more bearable. Its mid-afternoon and the crazed conflict rages on unabated, delightful daydreams of turkey dinners and Christmas pudding have no business infiltrating my mental armoury and must wait…

A single silver bullet offers a chilling destiny, but my ongoing desire to dodge death keeps my head below the precipice as much as possible. If it wasn't for this blasted shelling, another sunset would dangle precariously within my grasp. It's a different beast, wholly indefensible and absolutely terrifying, those pesky exploding steel balls possess the capability to create carnage on landing, blowing anything in close proximity to smithereens. I've seen arms and legs end up in trees as body parts are strewn far and wide. In the immediate aftermath of executing a successful strike or tragic hit, it's hard to feel any sense of jubilation at causing such catastrophic devastation. I'm out here rain or shine gambling with my own mortality, it's a game that's cloaked with a tragic inevitability. Thankfully, today the dice of death has fallen in my favour, but one day as the law of averages allude to, my luck is going to run out. With the exception of charging headlong across no-mans-land into a storm of steel, this feeling is never more prevalent than when enduring a sustained period of shelling. I'm helpless, a sitting duck waiting patiently for death to come knocking, with only a light sprinkling of hope as my cowering companion. Each bombardment sends streams of soil spurting violently into the air, leaving huge craters which will, in time, double as watery graves across the decimated terrain that separates its perpetrators.

"There goes a whiz-bang," cries Frosty, as the all too familiar screeching sound peppers the sky, "thank God it's not another woolly bear!"

I crouch down, clasp my helmet with both hands and close my eyes for what may be the last time. Travelling quicker than the speed of sound, this missile offers scant warning and barely enough time to die. If it lands in close proximity my goose is cooked, only if it's then revealed as a dud will I be spared eternal damnation. Suddenly, the whistling sound I yearn to hear blazes out above my motionless bowed head as the shell finds land well beyond our fretful ditch. An almighty bang delivers a deafening crescendo which sends tremors ripping through the earth. Clumps of mud blended with tiny metal molecules shower my head like confetti, feverish with relief, I allow myself a breath.

Undisturbed by painful screams, a golden silence ensues, suggesting my compatriots have come to no harm. It garnishes my scrambled mind with hope, but at this point it's nothing more than wishful thinking. My heart still races, pounding out of my chest as I nervously swivel my head left and right in search of confirmation. I see traumatized bodies shaking profusely, young heads buried in hands, silently praying for it all to stop, their youth viscously pillaged from them by this wretched war. By the grace of God everybody seems ok and even if it doesn't feel like it, this is a small win. The once majestic blue sky is now besmirched with thick dark lumps of smoke which gradually clears to reveal a huge crater, the last remnant of an ill directed strike. I've witnessed the devastation that exploding shrapnel wreaks first hand, such as a piece lethally embedded in a crumbling skull and another gouging out a poor fellows eye, one man's fatality is another man's fortune!

The desperate moans of the dying reverberate around a trench like no other sound, ever so sadly endured when the agonising spectacle of a slow death plays out. I've cradled men in my arms, their ravaged bodies punctured with horrific flesh wounds gushing blood, yet still granted one last glorious moment of terminal lucidity. The ghastly pain they're so bravely baring freezes momentarily, allowing them to converse with a fluent clarity that belies their condition, often to declare their love for a sweetheart and beg for assurances that their last words will be passed on. The faintest sign of recognition, be it a word or gentle nod is enough to send them to their final rest with a smile. Amidst such heinous moments emerges the power to make a man's final seconds tolerable, who knew tragedy can be tinged with such beauty?

Here Comes Santa Claus

'If I had my way some person in authority would proclaim that Christmas will not be celebrated this year. The simplicity of Christmas, with the laughter of children, the joy of giving little things; this is as it should be when it appears alone. But when it enters the list with a war it is out of place. Enemy, death and a Christmas tree – they cannot live so close together.'

German Cavalry Master, Rudolf Binding – December 1914.

Up until 5 years ago, my life could hardly have been considered the stuff of Hollywood legend. Largely uneventful and played out in black and white, but then I met Rose, she brought the colour and has been painting my world beautiful shades ever since. The inaugural moment I cast my eyes upon her in a smoky palatial dance hall was the first I knew of loves existence, the deeply intoxicating kind, rich in passion and unashamedly exhilarating. Sure, I'd experienced desire before which more often than not manifested itself in frenetic fumbles with the lights out, I was a testosterone fuelled young man after all, but this felt different. The way her silky dark locks bounced off her shoulders when she moved made my heart dance, so laden with beauty Rose possessed the graceful poise of an angel, she was mesmerizing. Her lacey white dress teased of the deliciousness beneath, highlighting perfectly the contours of her slender body. I couldn't tear my eyes away from her, nor did I want to…

When it comes to chatting up young ladies I'm no smooth operator by any stretch, but this hasn't proved a hindrance with my faithful buddy riding shotgun, Frosty is one silver tongued devil and I'm more than happy to hitch a ride on his coattails. Eager to concoct a foolproof plan, I turn to brief my trusty partner in crime, but much to my dismay the randy bugger has already had it away on his toes! I spot him at a nearby table unloading his considerable arsenal of roguish charms on a very pretty and somewhat petite blonde girl. Judging by the size of her beaming smile and attentive nature one can safely assume he is doing rather well. Despite being stone cold sober, the jammy sod oozes confidence and charisma and I can't help but marvel at the size of his spuds, but my unstinting admiration comes with a thinly veiled coating of envy. Without the razzle dazzle Frosty delivers in spades, I'm left to my own devices and ill prepared to navigate the rocky romantic wilderness that dauntingly lies between me and a shot at crazy beautiful love. I seek immediate solace in the form of a frothy beer; hopefully the goddess in the white dress will still be here when I've built up enough Dutch courage to approach her. *I wonder when's closing time?*

Three clarets of ale later, I find myself lost in a period of deep contemplation. Frosty is long gone and no doubt enjoying the fruits of his labour, leaving me to fly solo with only a fragile ego for cargo. Whilst slumped on this barstool, I've witnessed half a dozen dapper looking suitors attempt to woo the lady I find so captivating, each sent skulking off into the unforgiving night with their short lived dreams politely scuppered. Maybe her much coveted heart belongs to another? Some ridiculously handsome athletic type one imagines, with biceps like boulders and a cracking sense of humour to boot. I swiftly order another drink, this wallowing is thirsty work. The crowd is beginning to thin out as another night soon to be etched in history gradually ebbs away.

For God sake man, my internal voice screams, *at least give it a bloody go*! I can feel myself grimace in disgust at the cowardly approach I'm adopting, my raging conscience has found me out and no amount of alcohol will silence it.

I'm off my stool, legs feel a little shaky and beads of cold sweat are forming, but progress nevertheless. All I have to focus on now is getting the buggers to move in the right direction. My pulsating heart gives credence to the fact that this is a now or never moment, but at the very least I can console myself with the knowledge that failure doesn't taste as bitter as regret. It's definitely not cool or stylish by any standards, but by Jove I'm moving alright! *How can a journey be this terrifying when the goal is so irresistible?* I ask myself, whilst sauntering with intent amidst a deluge of self-doubt that's suddenly raining down on me.

You have no business breathing the same air as this woman Crosby; she's going to laugh in your face before sending you on your sad little way. The voices get louder, but I boldly persevere, maybe ungovernable desire is quashing my mental monsters or the alcohol is finally kicking in. I try to recall the famous proverb about a faint heart never winning something or other, but alas my fretful mind has been reduced to mire. Indulging in one last defiant act of betrayal, it silently begs for procrastination. I persist, inching ever closer, but a debilitating sensation grips me, it's as if every molecule in my quivering body has been impregnated with fear. Suddenly, I'm acutely aware of how dry my mouth feels. Even if the old grey matter can cobble together a plausible arrangement of words, *am I capable of delivering them with a modicum of cohesion?* I yearn to escape this torture, but I'm too far gone to back out now, my throbbing heart is caught in the eye of a seductive storm.

Entrapped in a daze, I somehow summon up the foresight to stop a few steps shy of her table. As a prelude to my ill-fated charm offensive, I despairingly attempt to gather my thoughts, but the urge to vomit is ubiquitous. I take a deep breath, one final quest for calmness designed to disguise the fact that this is my seminal moment. Needless to say, it fails miserably but persevere I must, everything I've ever dreamed of and more sits so tantalizingly close.

I'm standing, or rather quaking, at the hallowed gates of utopia with a gormless grin embossed across my face, excruciatingly conspicuous by my silence. My goodness, it's hard to fathom, but she's even more beautiful close up and blissfully unaware of my presence. Whilst engaged in conversation she ever so gently runs her right hand through her thick mop of hair, stopping at the back to adorably twist a strand around her fingertips, richly textured and the colour of dark chocolate, it crackles with sensuality. Her hazel shaded eyes double as deep pools of enchantment that beg to be explored and I long to dive in, armed with a mischievous glint they seductively shimmer in the flickering candlelight. Subjected to such a barrage of intense beauty I willingly succumb, floating into the most splendid paradisiacal state. Joyfully incarcerated in my hypnotic heaven for God knows how long, I'm oblivious to the fact that the woman, whose spell I dreamily idle under, is now sat alone and looking in my direction. The stark realization sends my poor old heart somersaulting as reality crashes all around me.

The growing silence weighs heavy on my shoulders, but fails to elicit any action as I remain tight-lipped. If I don't pipe up soon, this could become extremely awkward, talk about keeping your powder dry, the poor lass will need to be telepathic at this rate! I contemplate instigating an embarrassingly hasty retreat, but when all seems lost the most beautiful thing happens. It lasts for the briefest of moments, but will resonate within for a lifetime, she smiles at me. It is so much more than my efforts, or lack thereof deserve, but I'll graciously accept it! I'm not talking about a simple token of recognition either, this smile is as bewitching as it's unexpected and capable of melting the hardest heart. I'm reeling in a bizarre state of wondrous shock, the gorgeous girl in the white dress just smiled at me. It's all my Christmases in an instant, if ever a situation demanded action this was it and yet I still maintain the status quo, drowning languidly in a sea of silence, too scared to grab the rubber ring I've just been tossed.

One's life is ultimately defined by a handful of moments and I'm pretty sure I'll still be agonising over this one when I take a stern look in the bathroom mirror later tonight and for many thereafter. The coward inside me begs for her to walk away, putting me out of my misery, yet angelically she remains, enticingly close, but hopelessly out of reach.

"Hi," I nervously blurt out, backing it up with a strenuous smile, I'm a right little charmer when I get going! She looks up and lays her beguiling eyes upon me, they're warm and inviting. It's like being struck by a bolt of luscious lighting, my legs turn to jelly. I steady myself by grabbing the back of a nearby chair and smile back, desperately trying to exude a touch of coolness, *who am I kidding?*

"Well, hello there, Sir," she replies with an endearing sweetness that embellishes her soft tone.

I gaze briefly upon her perfectly proportioned heart shaped lips and imagine how amazing it must feel to kiss them, before expunging such delusions of grandeur from my mind. I've uttered one measly word; it hardly makes a romantic union a fait accompli!

"Hi," I say once more, it's all I can feebly muster, a paltry return for such a beautiful smile.

It's excruciating, I've never felt so pathetic in all my life, but to my immense surprise it elicits a playful giggle. Unwittingly, I've prised the door open, but still blighted by a fear that refuses to thaw, walking through it will be something else entirely. As the conductor of ones own shambolic masquerade it's imperative that I come to the party at some point, the opulent jewel of opportunity waits for no man. It's time to cast my bread upon love's tumultuous waters and see where the tide takes me.

"Good evening, Madam, apologies for the impertinence of my intrusion, but I just wondered if you would care for some company and perhaps another drink?"

On delivering a perfectly formed piece of coherent grammar I instantly feel a palpable sense of relief, but this is no time to sit back and admire ones eloquence, I must tussle tirelessly to win her cherished heart, improbable maybe, but impossible, surely not. Delicate strands of hope rest on this reply, the next word that flows from her sweet lips may determine the life I'll get to live. The pause is debilitating, seconds feel like hours as the unsuspecting perpetrator of the pain contemplates my fate. Is she orchestrating this dramatic interlude to delight in my silent anguish or simply weighing up her options? Dark clouds of doubt hover menacingly; I feel the weight of their impending fury, but mask my torment with a smile, just a tiny little 'yes' is all that's needed to scupper damnation. I'm doing my best to project a picture of composure, but mentally I'm on my knees begging for clemency.

"Champagne," she replies, "I'll have a glass of pink champagne, please, Sir. It goes straight to my head, but it's utterly divine, wouldn't you agree?"

"Quite, quite," I mumble back, contemplating what meagre resources fester within my beleaguered wallet, fretful that I'll be unable to fulfil her decadent desires. "One glass of pink champagne coming right up, my lady."

"You are a sweetheart," she gushes and with a sense of foreboding I scurry off to the bar.

Maybe, upon my return I could declare they're all out of champagne and slide a warm half of stout across the table. I fear it doesn't quite pack the same panache and order the conveniently stocked pink champagne, waiting with breath suitably bated.

"That will be two shillings and threepence, my love," says the cheery lady, outstretching her palm of doom.

I smile before frantically checking every crevice of my tatty wallet. *You have got to be kidding me,* the realization I can't muster up the required funds makes my blood run cold. I'm hammering at the door of destiny, but could be denied admission for a lousy tuppence. I quickly survey a somewhat sparce bar and weigh up my options, returning to the table to hastily arrange a loan is a huge romantic faux pas and scrounging opportunities appear somewhat limited. I opt to put on my best smile and appeal to her sense of leniency.

"I'm frightfully sorry, but I seem to be tuppence short," I exclaim in disbelief with a wry smile.

"Oh I see, well I guess I'll have to put this back then, Sir."

"Of course, but please Madam, can you find it in your heart to make an exception just this once?" I plead, "I can drop by with the money tomorrow."

"I'm not sure I'm allowed to do that, Sir."

Her cheery disposition is fading amidst the uncomfortable position I'm thrusting upon her, causing pangs of guilt to start subtly gnawing away at me, but in the name of true love I feel compelled to persist.

"This is not just a glass of pink champagne, Madam," I declare.

"Isn't it, Sir?"

"Good heavens no, it is infinitely so much more."

"Erm, ok," her puzzled expression cries out for some elaboration, I duly oblige in a matter of sorts.

"This, glass of fizz, is the gateway to every romantic notion I've ever dreamed coming true a hundred times over. This is my moment, a shot at everlasting love and a glass of milk stout just won't cut it."

"Milk stout? I'm not following you."

"Tonight in your fine establishment, I have met the most beautiful woman and somehow manged to engage her in a brief bout of conversation. Well basically it was one sentence offering her a drink."

"Ah I see, and she has asked for pink champagne."

"Precisely."

"And you don't believe she is a stout drinker?"

"I fear so, yes."

She smiles and pushes the champagne glass towards me.

"Are you sure?"

"Who am I to stand in the way of everlasting love? Enjoy your evening Sir."

I hurriedly drop all my coins into her hand and gratefully clasp it with both my hands. "May God bless you my dear, you are an angel. I won't forget this."

She smiles and I depart with my fingers tightly squeezing the stem of the champagne flute, one final foray before the music dies…

"Your Champagne, my lady," I declare proudly, setting it down carefully in front of her.

"Why thank you sir, are you not joining me in a drink?"

"Erm, no, I've had more than enough this evening."

"To self-control," she says raising her glass,

"alcohol's greatest contradiction."

She takes a long lingering sip from the glass and holds it momentarily to relish the sensation of bubbles dancing around her tongue before swallowing. The pleasure she derives from this palatable experience is etched all over her joyous face, glowing gloriously with contentment, it only serves to enhance her radiant features. I yearn to move closer and bathe within the stream of beauty flowing so endlessly.

"Isn't champagne simply marvellous? Heavenly on the lips and delivering a taste so far removed from the drudgery of everyday life. It's like existing in a dream that survives, but for a moment." She smiles, "we all need more bubbles."

"Yes, I suppose so. What is life without a few luxuries?"

"Arduously long and wholly uneventful I imagine," she sighs, "and that simply won't do. To life's luxuries," she proclaims with a raised glass before enjoying another diminutive mouthful. She seems intent on savouring every last drop which is just as well given my delicate financial predicament.

"Please sit down, Sir and feel free to introduce yourself."

"Well, only if you're sure, Madam." I reply while unceremoniously plonking myself down. A silent interlude ensues as I gaze adoringly across the table

"And your name?"

"Oh yes, erm it's Jack, Jack Crosby. Delighted to make your acquaintance, Madam." I extend out my arm in a regimented fashion to offer a firm handshake.

My formality amuses her, but she has the good grace to reciprocate, cordially placing her dainty hand within mine. I feel her soft skin brush against my rugged palm and wrap my fingertips gently around. The sweet sensation of our flesh being pressed together sends a current of excitement coursing through my quivering body. The feeling is beyond the realms of comprehension, enveloping me in a cocoon of elation and it persists once her hand is slowly eased from my tender grasp. I fear she senses my reluctance, but maybe that's not a bad thing.

"I'm Rose, by the way."

"How delightful, a beautiful name for a beautiful lady."

She giggles again and fixes her warm eyes upon me, rich with enticement they render my senses oblivious to all but her charm. The crackling of conversation dissipates as the music fades to grey, leaving me deeply embroiled in the moment. We may as well be the last two people on God's earth, kindred souls clinging to the impossible dream.

"Oh Jack, flattery will get you everywhere, almost. Tell me handsome, is there currently a potential Mrs. Crosby out there?"

"Heavens no, I'm very much footloose and fancy free, but remain open to the notion of a romantic liaison, just haven't found that someone who… well, you know."

"Sets your heart ablaze?"

"I couldn't have put it so poetically, but yes. Love has so far eluded me, I'm afraid. That's not to say I haven't had my moments, far from it but nothing lasting or meaningful. Anyway, that's enough about me, lets talk about you Rose."

She raises her eyebrows suggestively, "ok Jack, what would you like to know?"

What's the name of the lucky blighter who has captured your heart? That's the burning question racing through my mind, the notion she could somehow be available feels preposterous, but I plump for a gentler tact.

"It's getting late, do you have a sweetheart waiting for you at home?"

"Are you kidding, there's an army of them!"

"Ah, I see," I mumble solemnly.

"I'm joking you daft apeth, what kind of girl do you take me for? I'm as lost in the romantic wilderness as you, Jack."

"Sorry, it's just hard to believe."

"Why?"

"Because, erm, because you're so damn beautiful."

And there it was, fate has dealt me some promising cards tonight and I've rashly thrown them all in. Only lady luck can now drag me from the wreckage of inevitability.

"Thank you Jack, that's awfully sweet of you to say," she smiles somewhat coyly and touches my arm. Her eyes dullen alluding to a past marred by heartache. "But, no sweetheart waiting for me, not anymore."

Her cryptic reply spikes my curiosity, but I'm wary of attempting to dissect it for fear of unearthing any painful memories. "Perhaps you've been looking for love in the wrong places?"

"Maybe, who knows? Love eh, practically impossible to find and even harder to hold on to. Life's greatest, yet most beautiful, enigma. Let's drink to that." With a rueful smile she raises her glass one more time. "To love, the perfect conundrum."

"To love indeed."

With a more pronounced swig the bubbly disappears leaving behind the daunting image of an empty champagne flute gleaming pristinely in front of me, it serves as a brutal reminder of my paltry existence. Amongst all the exhilaration I've relinquished my grasp on time, hopefully the bar has closed! A quick glance confirms its wishful thinking, but judging by the barren landscape we appear to have entered the precarious realms of last knockings. I look at Rose and picture a life without ever seeing her again, it provokes a nasty sensation in the pit of my stomach. Without her there is no tomorrow and just the merest contemplation of this scenario sickens me. I want her, I need her, For God sake I think I love her!

"Erm, Rose, I was just wondering..." I pause, in desperate pursuit of the right words, but my blasted mind has been reduced to an infertile chasm of total nothingness.

"Wonder what, Jack, what is it?"

"I was wondering if perhaps, erm..." Sensing my agonising struggle, Rose throws me another lifeline.

"Well Mr Crosby, are you ever going to get round to asking me to dance?"

"I beg your pardon, dance? Well why of course, it will be my honour."

She smiles, takes my hand and I walk her proudly on to the dancefloor. I feel elated, like I'm king of the world and joyfully bask in the unbridled jubilation of the moment. We turn and face each other, she steps towards me, our lips separated by inches! I can feel my body start to tremble under the influence of a heady cocktail of emotions. Rose takes my hands and delicately places them on her hips before wrapping hers around my neck. The scenario I wouldn't dare to dream a matter of hours ago, an alternative reality built on fantasy and steeped in desire has inexplicably materialised. My thumping heart builds to a glorious crescendo as our bodies gently sway to the rhythm of the soft music. Rose inches closer and instinctively I hold her more tightly. She rests her head against my shoulder, causing hot breath to caress my neck. Good lord, it's driving me wild, I feel so alive yet gloriously out of control. I'm suddenly aware that this moment, like all others, is finite and painfully fleeting. I absorb every last sensation, knowing the music will die when the lights come on, pleasures of the heart are so wickedly temporary. My desire to kiss her is insatiable, I pray for one last song and unceasing darkness. The daylight is coming to steal my dream and I'm ill equipped to relinquish the beauty held within my arms.

Wretched time, please let me exist only in this moment, forever. I clasp my arm around her torso and ease her head onto my heart, cradling it tenderly whilst stroking her hair. Even if this is all we'll ever be, the cherished memory will be indelible. The fading music paints a picture of grim inevitability as our swaying ceases to reveal two poor souls desperately clinging on to the precious remnants of a sublime night.

"I'm scared Rose," I whisper in her ear.

"Scared of what, Jack?" she murmurs back.

"The music ending, I don't want to ever let you go."

She raises her head and with a subtle smile gazes lovingly in to my eyes. "Kiss me Jack Crosby, just shut up and kiss me."

In the trenches amidst all the sorrow and squalor, chinks of light are a rarity seldom experienced, but for one daily ritual. With today being Christmas Eve, it feels even more significant and in keeping with the excitement shared by children around the globe tonight as I eagerly await the post. My solitary link to normality and the warmth of loved ones, it evokes stirring thoughts of the sweetheart I've left behind and the perfect world I now grieve for. The bittersweet effect of this correspondence puts me through the emotional ringer as I devour every last paragraph. Crafted with care and littered with love, the words leap from the page before resonating so profoundly within me. Each new letter from Rose will be read over and over again, in a deliberate fashion, in order to absorb every priceless drop of heartfelt emotion. For a few sacred moments, I allow myself to be transported back to the beautiful life I've created, now seemingly forever out of reach. Every reading sends a warm fuzzy feeling pervading through my body, but ultimately leaves a bitter taste of regret. Each sweet reminder agonisingly magnifies my sense of loss, but the craving for literary nourishment remains steadfast.

It is hard to look past the fact that this war turns kids in to killers, but sustained periods apart from family hasn't half stimulated the creativity within me, unleashing my inner Shakespeare by committing to paper the careful composition of inner musings contained within a troubled mind. When inking these ramblings, I'm mindful not to project a tirade of fretfulness or desperation on to the page, particularly when writing to Rose. One can only imagine the immense toll this wretched war is taking on her and naturally I want to protect her as best I can. It is a fine line to tread, but I must suppress the desire to unload in order to shield my darling from the most harrowing heartache. All wars are not fought on battlefields and hers is one of painful patience entwined with endless worry. Each rattle from the letterbox is greeted anxiously as she wonders what lies on the mat. Is this going to be the day that the dreaded telegram arrives? One can only imagine how excruciating those moments must be knowing tomorrow she will relive the wretched torture all over again. The penance cruelly inflicted on Rose is a foreboding sense of hopelessness and her suffering breaks my heart, give me shell and shrapnel any day over the tempestuous ticking of time.

The arrival of a burly fellow, dragging a trolley briming with sacks of post, is greeted with a spontaneous burst of jingle bells, it seems appropriate given the impressive beard he is sporting. Like excited children outside the grotto, we hurriedly form a line in anticipation of meeting 'Santa' or Bill as he is more commonly known. I wonder what goodies he has in store for me! The wait is reminiscent of past Christmas mornings on the landing with my mother and siblings while dad nips down to check if he has been. Once we were informed 'not yet' and trudged back despondently to our beds, while our parents enjoyed a lie-in. God bless them, it was well deserved, given all the effort they poured in to making Christmas special for us. It has always been my favourite time of year, but this will be the first one away from home, I'll miss them terribly.

Bill graciously enters into the spirit of the occasion, handing out the parcels in a jovial manner and enthusiastically throwing in the odd "ho, ho, ho." The light relief is manna from heaven, what a trouper! I emerge with a tidy haul of 3 parcels and retreat to a quiet corner in order to enjoy them. The first gift has been sent by royal approval, a shiny embossed brass tin bearing an image of the head of Princess Mary. Inside there is tobacco and cigarettes, a portrait photograph of Princess Mary and Christmas cards from herself, King George & Queen Mary. Each serving man has received one, a gift from the nation that will be hastily sent home for safekeeping, minus the tobacco, of course. Each brave soul along this trench has answered their countries call, human fodder perhaps, but at least they haven't forgotten us. There is some comfort to be had in that and God knows I need all I can get. The next parcel is not so grand, but warmly received, a Christmas card from my parents and a generous slab of my mother's homemade Christmas cake. The pungent smell of rum blended with whisky has my stomach rumbling, but I'll resist this exquisite taste of home until after supper. It will make the coming hours a fraction more bearable. That leaves just one gift… a Christmas present and letter from my beloved, Rose. I pause and contemplate leaving this for later too, maybe even Christmas morning. It's a nice sentiment, but war offers no guarantee of a tomorrow and I can feel flames of curiosity rapidly engulfing me.

A letter from Rose is always something to delight in, her avidly anticipated words serve as nourishment for my soul and as a consequence of being privy to her thoughts I feel closer to her. My eagerness to dissect the contents isn't reflected in the way I gently tease them apart from the scarlet red and gold paper. Wrapped lovingly, the finish exudes luxury and deserves a better fate than being ferociously torn to shreds. It also happens to be the highlight of my Christmas, so I make no excuses for wanting to prolong the experience. Once inside, I find a box and lift the lid to reveal a cut glass bottle of cognac encased in black satin. Momentarily, the bottle glints in the winter sun, it is both spectacular and fitting. I smile to myself, no matter what the predicament Rose never fails to bring the sunshine! Underneath the box is an envelope doused in perfume. I put it to my face, close my eyes and breathe deeply to experience a fragment of her beautiful scent. The heavenly aroma is overwhelming, I reluctantly drop my hands for fear it might drive me insane. Whilst carefully prising open the envelope, flutters of excitement build to waves crashing against my stomach walls. With a shaking hand I remove a lilac coloured sheet of paper and cast my eyes upon it…

My dearest Jack,

My great hope is that this letter finds you safe and well, my darling.

This was to be our first Christmas as a married couple celebrating in our new home, but without you here it doesn't feel like Christmas at all. The house looks a picture all lit up and sparkly, but it takes your heart beating next to mine to make it a home. I must sound terribly ungrateful given the harrowing reality you face on a daily basis, but I miss you so much Jack and long to have you home.

Are you eating well and taking care of yourself? I can't imagine what kind of Christmas you'll endure, but I pray you find a modicum of peace and contentment, however fleeting that may be. In body, I'll spend Christmas with our parents, but my heart and mind will be many miles away in Flanders Fields. I love you, Jack Crosby, you consume my thoughts, both waking and otherwise.

I have deliberated long in to the night about mentioning this, but your leave is some months off and by no means guaranteed. I have one final Christmas present for you, Jack and it's big so please, sit down. I so wanted to share this with you in person, but I'll simply burst if I don't tell you. The doctor confirmed on Tuesday that I'm pregnant, almost 4 months. You're going to be a dad Jack, isn't it simply marvellous! It's everything we've ever wanted. I know how much this means to you and wish I could see your face lighting up right now. We're going to have the biggest family celebration when you get home my darling, I promise you.

So listen here, Private Jack Crosby, and take heed, don't go being some brave bloody hero out there. I need you back here raising this bundle of joy with me, do you hear me? You're going to be a daddy, Jack and a brilliant one at that, just like you are as a husband. Come home to us Jack, all I want is to see you walk through our door wearing the hugest smile and have you gather me up in your arms.

I love you Jack, yes I'm repeating myself, but I'll never tire of saying it. You're my world and life doesn't work without you. I pray God will grant you safe passage back to me and the cherished life we share.

Merry Christmas Jack.

With love, always and forever,

Your Rose

The paper is now moist with my sobbing, but its tears of unadulterated joy flowing down my cheeks. I have a gorgeous wife waiting for me, utterly devoted and I'm going to be a father too, goodness gracious. A warm sense of gratitude radiates through my body, all of my deepest desires are coming to fruition. If only I could hold Rose in my arms and tell her everything will be ok. Sadly, reassurance isn't something I'm able to offer, it's a bit thin on the ground among all this death and desolation. Will I ever get to hold my newborn son or daughter? By hook or by crook I have to make it out of here for my beautiful Rose, she needs me now more than ever and I need her.

Darkness is rapidly descending and I'm still digesting the words written across the damp piece of paper I clutch in my hand. A few neat squiggles of a fountain pen have changed the life I know forever, I'm reeling. Having enjoyed the gift of being raised in a close-knit unit, I've naturally always longed for a family to call my own. Kicking a ball with my son in the park or walking my daughter down the aisle on the biggest day of her life and best of all, getting to share it with the person I love more than life itself. Some men crave money and gold, but this is my treasure, there isn't a richer man alive!

Staring at a blank piece of paper for what feels like an age, how do I begin to reply to this letter? A forlorn search to find the words to justify the emotions scurrying through my scrambled mind is wisely abandoned. I'll get through Christmas day before attempting the impossible again. There is nothing like a fresh sprinkling of friendly fire to restore one's clarity, but peculiarly as day bleeds into night the guns have fell silent…

<u>Madness in the Moonlight</u>

'Christmas in the trenches! It must have been sad, do you say? Well, I am not sorry to have spent it there, and the recollection of it will ever be one of imperishable beauty.'

Extract from a translated letter written by an anonymous Belgian solider, published in the Dublin Evening News on the 4th January 1915.

It's hard to fathom, but beauty can manifest itself in the most absurd places, this mass graveyard of ambition being a casing point. Bands of homesick men living out the dying embers of Christmas Eve in the furthest thing from a traditional setting. Their hearts stationed many miles away. A showering of steel has bought us to our knees, but the one thing this brutal Belgian winter has failed to claim is our spirit. If anything, it has fostered an even greater desire within our ranks to not allow Christmas to quietly pass by, a season that champions peace and goodwill to all men.. If we have Christmas then we have hope, even if that is all we have. Unbeknown to every lost soul encamped in muddy ditches, all the elements are conspiring to make this night immortal, the stuff of legend…

Operating under a cloak of darkness brings opportunity, but one must guard against complacency, a mistake that many a good fellow has paid for with his life. A snipers bullet never sleeps, the slightest rustling incurring a flurry of fire, any foray into no-man's-land must be conducted with ghost like movement. Going where angels fear to tread plays havoc with the old ticker, but if an advantage can be gleaned then needs must. Equally, if Jerry is in the mood to spring an attack at close quarters, we must be ready because a failure to anticipate often proves fatal, so when night falls my state of alertness intensifies. It's a prerequisite if I harbour any desire to gaze adoringly upon another sunrise. Any thoughts of impending fatherhood must be eradicated, easier said than done when the news cascading through my mind remains so fresh. Rumours of a surprise enemy offensive are rife, leaving no time for plum pudding and pleasantries. Jerry isn't going to catch us with our pants down, not on my watch.

The air fell silent some hours ago, giving way to the most blissful state of sereneness. No-mans-land is coated with a light dusting of frost that glistens when caressed by the moonlight. Labouring under a blanket of stars, one can't help but be swept away by its intrinsic beauty. The calm conditions give me the courage to gingerly raise my eyeballs above the parapet. Whilst marvelling at such picturesque majesty, ones mind can easily stray from the dark tangled roots of reality. This ravaged land, having borne witness to untold bloodshed through the needless dying of embittered men, incredulously depicts a Christmas card. *How can I cultivate such feelings of hate towards young men equally embroiled in this enchanting winter wonderland?*

The gentle soothing ripple of placidness meanders gracefully through the trench, mellowly infecting our hope starved souls with fragile promises of Christmas peace. Like the hopeless romantic I dare to dream, albeit in a far-flung corner of my mind, before quickly berating myself for entertaining such foolish notions. We are engaged in a bloody war and our mantra remains, kill or be killed, but the calmness is beginning to feel all too comfortable. It is a luxury I mustn't become accustomed to, but my staunch defence is proving itself an unworthy adversary for such blatant irresistibility.

Slowly seduced by benign beauty, I find myself imprisoned in a storm of tranquillity, it feels wonderful. My professional façade crumbles under the weight of salty tears, streaming uncontrollably down my cheeks as I deliriously dwell in a state of unadulterated joy. Quelling any desire to check this emotion, my troubled mind waves the white flag with reckless abandon. I close my eyes and deeply breathe in the frosty night air, savouring every last morsel of silence. My senses are heightened, contentedly languishing in the stillness of the night. Temporarily liberated from the shackles of a miserable existence, my once depleted soul rejoices in the fruits of rejuvenation. Inexplicably, whilst inhabiting the frosty fields of Flanders on the eve of Christmas, I've unwittingly stumbled on nirvana.

Whilst a sentimental ballad continues to play within the borders of a blown mind, my eyes remain locked on the German trenches situated a mere hundred yards away. Living precariously in such close proximity, I can almost hear them breathe. Unfortunately, I'm unable to decipher their many audible conversations as my linguistic skills don't stretch to fluent German. It remains eerily quiet with little sign of life, but rifle in hand I'm primed for action. They're just young men hankering for home and one assumes that they, too, are absorbing the sheer grandeur of this moonlit winters night. Another explanation for this seemingly diminished appetite for battle could stem from an overriding desire to keep the sanctity of Christmas intact. This is, after all, the evening when Germans traditionally exchange gifts.

I have always loved Christmas Eve growing up, a day layered in anticipation and brimming with excitement.

After supper, along with my brothers and sisters, we'd hang our stockings above the fire, looking on giddily as mum left out a delicious homemade mince pie and a small sherry for Santa. Rudolph wasn't forgotten either, his reward for pulling and guiding the sleigh all night was a modest carrot. I can't honestly recall ever noticing an empty plate the following morning amongst all the festive hullabaloo, but I assume our hospitality was heartily received given the gravity of the task.

My father is blessed with a well of creativity and can concoct the most wonderful bedtime stories on demand, hence Christmas Eve being his crowning glory. Prior to being dispatched up the jolly old dancers, we'd hurriedly gather around the tree, eagerly awaiting the telling of his latest masterpiece. There were no notes and I'd since often wondered if he made the whole thing up on the spot, but to this day I've never asked, preferring to preserve the magic.

My favourite festive tale involved us all being elves, naturally we resided at the North Pole and had a jolly old time making presents and testing them in Santa's workshop. Mrs Claus would pop in regularly with steaming hot batches of the most dreamy melt-in-the-mouth chocolate chip cookies. I'd wash them down with a delicious chocolate fudge milkshake, it's a hard life! As you'd expect, it was a frenetic place prior to the big day, but sadly on this particular Christmas time disaster struck. Santa was out sledging with Jack Frost on Christmas Eve morning and took a nasty tumble, putting his back out. Well, you can imagine the commotion this caused, the very existence of Christmas for boys and girls was in jeopardy as the prospect of waking up to no presents loomed large. This statement alone drew audible gasps around the living room, we were hanging on to my dad's every word. Line after line was delivered with unwavering enthusiasm, at key points he'd leap to his feet and start moving around the room, arms flaying. *My goodness, that man was wasted as a civil servant!* Each spellbinding adventure took us on an emotional rollercoaster, jam packed with twists and turns, this riveting yarn was no exception. Santa was caught up in a race against time to save Christmas and turned to us, his trusty elves for help. In no condition to climb up and down chimneys, it was decided that we would accompany him on the trip of a lifetime and deliver the presents. Loud cheers erupted across the living room as we embarked on a thrilling sleigh ride with Santa at the reigns. Within moments, like a comet, we were blazing our trail across a starry sky. In one night, we raced across the rooftops of the world and saved Christmas, *how on earth am I meant to sleep after that?*

"Don't forget to listen out for those sleigh bells," my Dad beams as I head for the stairs. God love him, as parting shots go it's an absolute corker!

Fortunately, my passion for the festive season is shared by Rose and as a consequence Christmas Eve has retained its wonder. I'd always work a half day, longing for the sound of the buzzer. On hearing it we'd all pile down the pub to enjoy several refreshing beverages. Loud jovial chatter reverberated around the saloon bar of The Dirty Duck, as honest working lads herald in a well-deserved Christmas break. Hearty handshakes exchanged amidst a sea of smiling faces, there was no better place to be. After some frantic last minute shopping, Rose would join me mid-afternoon for a tipple, by which time I'd transformed in to a pie-eyed romantic. Repeating slurred declarations of love hardly passes for coherent conversation, but she endured it with good grace and at times even seemed to enjoy my loved up offerings. The poor lass had the unenviable task of coaxing me out of the pub, but she made light work of it with some gentle persuasion. In truth she couldn't fail, I'd follow that girl to the ends of the earth. I'm not a big drinker, but there is something about this day that makes me want to soak everything in, that's Christmas spirit I suppose.

It was during one of these fabled early evening walks from the pub on a snowy Christmas Eve that a beautiful moment of spontaneity occurred. Despite being wrapped up in her favourite chunky duffle coat, Rose was clinging affectionately to me to combat the cold as we strolled through the town square. Large snowflakes were floating in the chilly December air, but as I gazed at the twinkling lights adorning a magnificent tree, all I could feel was warmth. Wide eyed children were playfully, tossing snowballs in the direction of any adults brave enough to cross their path. Chivalrously, I shielded Rose and for my troubles I copped a fluffy missile full in the face. I couldn't help but smile as the cheeky rascal scampered off home in delight, armed with a tail of victory ripe for retelling. Rose brushed the snow away with her furry pink gloves before ever so delicately planting a soft kiss on my lips. My feeling of merriment, in part alcohol induced, now bordered on euphoric. I experienced a flashbulb moment, the stark realization that there will never be a more perfect time than this, not ever. Life is a succession of moments, but the one we find ourselves in is all we ever really have. Melting snowflakes caused Rose's hair to glisten under the Christmas lights and she had a smile as wide as the ocean, I'd never seen her look more beautiful. I may be peering through beer goggled eyes, but everything suddenly appeared so clear. I want to wake up each morning and see her angelic face on the pillow next to mine, have her fall asleep in my arms every night of my life. A world without her didn't bare contemplating, the mere thought sent pain surging into every chamber of my heart. I adore this woman snuggled in close to me and crave nothing more than a life devoted to loving her uncontrollably. Instinctively, I sink to one knee, the crisp snow crunches under its weight and I take Rose's left hand.

"Oh my goodness, Jack," she gasps, "whatever are you doing?"

Fortunately, the snow is providing a steady platform, affording me the privilege of looking intently into her gorgeous eyes once more. Temporarily I lose myself, the snowflakes aren't the only thing melting.

"Rose, ever since the first moment I saw you, in that smoky dancehall, I've been hopelessly in love with you."

"I love you too, Jack," she whispers, now gazing through tear filled eyes.

"It's always been you Rose, it always will be, I promise, darling. Please allow me the great privilege of building my dreams around yours, to mould an unforgettable life together."

Choked with emotion I pause, silently praying for a final shred of composure.

"Rose."

"Yes, Jack."

"Will you do me the upmost honour of consenting to be my wife?"

"Oh, Jack."

"Rose Elizabeth Thornton, will you marry me?" I wait patiently whilst my beloved Rose sobs her heart out, *I do hope they're tears of joy.* The pause is plentiful without being excruciating and I suppress the urge to comfort her, choosing to remain kneeled until she offers an answer.

"Oh, Jack," she wails, "of course I will marry you my darling, in a heartbeat. You're my everything."

She drops to the ground and throws her arms around me, causing us to both fall into a bed of fluffy snow. Lost in the magic of a momentous moment, we kiss passionately whilst rolling around joyously. This draws a chorus of cheers and whistles from passing bystanders, serving to claw us back into reality. Desperate to restore a little decorum, we struggle to our feet and scurry off rather sheepishly to Rose's parents to share our good news, giggling all the way.

Just beyond the stroke of midnight on Rose's porch, I wish her a merry Christmas, kiss her goodnight and begin the short walk home. I arrive back with scant recollection of the journey, the world goes about its business whilst I remain splendidly entrapped in a beautiful fantasy.

In the scared early hours of Christmas morn, I lay down in what feels like fields of gold, heart still throbbing with pangs of exultation. A glut of possibilities race through my mind, as I dream of a Rose filled limitless future, a rich tapestry woven out of rollicking adventures extravagantly littered with precious moments. We have the opportunity to write our own story and sculpt memories destined to be etched across our entwined hearts forever. How on earth did life get so beautiful, I'm the luckiest bugger alive, hang on, is that bells I hear?

Suddenly, I spy a hint of movement in the German trenches, jolting my body in to action. This uneasy feeling intensifies, but I can't tear my eyes away as heads keep randomly bobbing above the parapet, *what is Jerry up to now?* A bullet has still not been fired since late afternoon, but amidst a hive of activity I sense something peculiar is afoot. Collectively we lean forward, jittery fingers hover over cold triggers at the peculiar sight of our foes lifting items out of their trench.

“Hold your fire men,” cries Sergeant Bevan, no doubt as curious as the rest of us to discover what the devil is going on.

It appears they are attaching things to the trench walls, but what? I can scarcely believe my eyes as flickering lights appear across the length of the trench, Christmas trees no less, each one now illuminated by glowing candlelight. Against all odds, Christmas has come to Flanders fields, what a glorious sight to behold.

“Oh my God, it’s beautiful,” I gasp in disbelief, can this really be happening?

I look across the trench at the battle hardened men who carry my life within their hands, softened features frozen in an hypnotic state provide vindication that we have indeed entered this bizarre alternate reality. The sea of light embodied more than the spirit for Christmas, it showcased the very best of humanity, exposing fragile strands of hope where once only darkness existed. We lay down our rifles and vigorously applaud, causing our foes to reply in kind with a salvo of rapturous cheers. This unprecedented flourish of candlelit camaraderie unleashes a plethora of emotions, tough men smile through misty eyes whilst embracing wholeheartedly. Frosty lunges forward with a beaming smile, hugging me with all the exuberance of a randy teenager on the back row of the Roxy. It’s the first physical contact I’ve had in months and I must admit to rather enjoying it, thank heavens for the absence of mistletoe!

These hedonistic moments have no business being played out on a field of war, but for men courageously carrying hearts riddled with unbridled misery, this momentary lapse can surely be forgiven. In conjunction with a thickening frost, the darkness has conspired to hide a multitude of sins, but the fact remains and shouldn’t be forgotten, that fallen comrades lay rotting just yards away. In the still moments of solitude, I can hear the rats gnawing mercilessly at their decaying carcasses, serving as a brutal reminder that there's no dignity in a so called hero's death. Therefore, it is only fit and proper that Sergeant Bevan brings our sporadic outpouring of sentimentality to a swift conclusion.

"Ok now gentleman, please settle down and focus," he calls out.

His tone is far from berating, but nevertheless quickly restores a sense of decorum amongst the men. Thank goodness we can all rely on his level headed thinking, many a man in our troop owes his life to it. The appetite to dispense with war and mark Christmas is clearly evident on both sides, but any fanciful thought that peace will exist as long as Christmas is celebrated is both dangerous and delusional.

A break from sentry duty affords me the opportunity to grab some dinner. Due to the influx of parcels, the obligatory fayre of corned beef and stew has made way for some splendid festive treats. Roast beef is accompanied by sprouts and potatoes with ample gravy on offer and it doesn't stop there, plum pudding and custard for afters alongside a nice drop of red. Talk is minimal, as myself and Frosty gratefully tuck in, it's delicious and cutlery is scrapping across our plates in no time at all. I imagine this is a small taste of how life is for the bastards who've left us here to slug it out Generals encamped in grand country residences, a world away from this godforsaken terrain. My total distain for these gentleman is a hatred universally shared by all soldiers, regardless of rank or nationality. Cowards waging war with waiter service, *I don't know how they sleep at night wrapped up in their Egyptian cotton sheets.* If these decision makers and life takers had to get their own blood stained hands dirty there would be no wars. Our valour is rewarded with squalor, while they languish in splendour, possessing the gall to declare we're all in it together. Why not throw the rotten blighters in a ring together to fight it out, sparing the needless bloodshed of decent young men? I hope the caviar truffles choke the whole ghastly lot of them. I shouldn't complain though, this plum pudding is exceedingly succulent.

"David."

"David? Blimey, this sounds serious."

"I heard from Rose today," I say sternly.

"And... is everything ok?"

"Yes, yes splendid thanks, but it seems I'm going to be a father."

"Crickey!" Frosty yells while choking on his dessert. "Congratulations Jacko, that's wonderful news. You must be over the moon, mate."

"I am, of course I am, but it scares me."

"Don't worry, mate, you'll make a brilliant dad."

"No, it's not impending fatherhood, daunting as the prospect is, that's bothering me."

"Then what?" Frosty enquires concerningly.

"It's the thought of not making it home."

"Ah, I see," Frosty sighs.

"Remember Fun-Time-Frankie who perished last week? Blown to bits, the poor bugger. Within an hour, the jacket was unceremoniously stripped from his still warm lifeless body, label removed and dispatched back to Blighty, in readiness for the next poor bastard who's currently being spoon-fed a diet of propaganda. The very next day, we were tucking in to the birthday cake his sister sent."

"Look, this is an emotional time for you mate, for all of us in fact, given the time of year, but you mustn't let the fear defeat you. Otherwise you're dead before you lace your boots up."

"But, what if I never get to hold my son or daughter?"

"You bloody will mate, if I've got anything to do with it. We embarked on this wretched journey side by side and we'll be going home together. I'm not leaving you behind for the rats, I promise. So cheer up, you miserable sod. It's Christmas, for Christ sake, and you're going to be a daddy. Not to mention that little chap is going to need a godfather, too."

Frosty smiles and suddenly life feels a touch more bearable. We have been through our fair share of scrapes and he's never let me down, he'd fight to the death for me, but I pray it never comes to that.

"If it makes you feel any better, we all get scared mate."

"Even Lionheart? The guy is fearless and built like an adonis."

"Don't be so sure, Joker slipped a rat in his kit bag the other day and the big, daft lug ran a mile."

"Really?" I gasp in astonishment.

Frosty laughs, "of course not, the bloody guys fearless, but poor old Joker scarpered for his life when he discovered it, I kid you not."

I shake my head, *Danny 'Joker' Hirst, when will that boy learn? Hopefully never.*

"Promise me one thing, Jacko," says Frosty, adopting a slightly more serious tone.

"Anything, Davy."

"Please, don't tell Lionheart I referred to him as a big daft lug."

"You have my word."

Another two hours of sentry duty beckons, one tiny segment of this gruelling three day marathon of the mind. My perception of time has been skewed by such an enjoyable a meal break and subsequently I'm left feeling cheated once more. My rational brain accepts that each tour of trepidation is divided into even chunks, but in reality it feels like one big ugly slab of trench time perforated with fleeting moments of rest. Thankfully, within minutes of taking up my post, I'm summoned to Sergeant Bevan's makeshift office which is situated in a nearby section of trench wall. I arrive promptly to find a nice glass of whisky waiting for me and a rather bemused looking superior officer.

"Ah Jack, good to see you old man, please sit down have a drink by all means."

"Thank you, Sir," I say before treating myself to a sip of rather fine deep rich bourbon.

"I've been speaking to a few of the men regarding this nonsense with the trees and so forth. Much as I welcome this rather peculiar period of silence, we must remain vigilant."

"I quite agree, Sir."

"Don't get me wrong, I'm not averse to a bit of good old Christmas cheer and Lord knows we can use it, but we simply can't allow Jerry to lure us into a false sense of security. Contrary to the usual noise emanating from headquarters, I'm sure there are decent chaps amongst them. Of course there are, but they remain the enemy and should be treated accordingly, do you understand Private?"

"Indeed I do, Sir."

"Good, lets not allow ourselves to get distracted by Christmas lights or grow complacent during this precarious ceasefire. Make no mistake about it, those men have been sent to kill us, let's not give them the satisfaction."

"Should we take the initiative, Sergeant, and fire off a few rounds?"

"No Jack, let's keep our powder dry and see where this thing goes. A break from combat will be good for morale and the men's sanity, just let's not allow ourselves to grow accustomed to it. We must maintain a high state of alertness at all times, can you please impress that forthrightly upon the men?"

"Yes, of course, Sir."

"Good man." He takes a swig of whisky and sighs, the burden of leadership painfully etched across his tortured features.

"Do you know Jack," he says wistfully, "I've never fully appreciated Christmas, that is until now, especially the effort my long suffering wife, Elizabeth, puts into it, God bless her. You know, making the house sparkle so it's perfect for the children, buying and wrapping gifts and so forth. She bakes the most delicious mince pies filled with all manner of winter spices, simply exquisite. I, on the other hand, barely pay the season lip service, too much faff and bother." Eluding to a deep sense of regret, he ruefully shakes his head. "I know that I can't rely on a visit from the ghost of Christmas past to right my many discretions, but I do hope that one day I get the opportunity to make it up to her, it's the very least that she deserves."

"I'm sure you will, Sir," are the only crumbs of comfort I can muster to counter his deep rooted dejection.

"But, you know what the saddest thing is?"

"No, Sir."

"The saddest thing is, that now I'm ever so far away, it's the one place I desperately want to be. All it took is this bloody war for me to realize the abundance of beauty in my life I have to be grateful for."

I've always viewed Sergeant Bevan as a strong individual, almost indestructible and maybe it is the whisky talking, but at this moment all I can see is a suffering soul gravely in need of solace.

"It's never too late Sir, perhaps write her a letter."

"I wouldn't know where to start old boy, affairs of the heart aren't exactly my forte."

"Well, if I could be so bold as to suggest sir..."

"Please, by all means."

"You can start by telling her exactly what you've told me."

"Do you really think so?"

"Yes, Sir, just tell her how you feel and how much you're missing her. She'll really appreciate that."

His face lights up, invigorated with renewed hope. "I can certainly give it a go, thank you Jack."

"My pleasure, Sir."

"Not a word to the men about this mind you," he says, somewhat sheepishly.

"Of course not, Sir."

He nods and smiles warmly. "Now then, what the blazes is going on with that Tottenham back four?"

"Well, how long have you got, Sir?"

Undisturbed by the bluster of bullets, the new found tranquillity of trench life lingers on late into the evening. Wild rumours, of a more formal Christmas truce, have been circulating for a few days, but given the current status quo they are gaining more traction. There is even talk the war may be ending, but I fear the men perpetrating this particular brand of balderdash still leave milk and cookies out on Christmas Eve. Nevertheless, I can't deny that this day of conflict is like nothing I've experienced before. I'm staring across a glistening field bathed in moonlight at a row of illuminated Christmas trees for goodness sake, I suppose at this point anything feels possible. Maybe jolly old St. Nick might fly by on his sleigh and sprinkle some seasonal magic over the forlorn fields of Flanders, tis the season after all!

Following the sobering directive laid out by Sergeant Bevan, my scrutiny of the German trenches remains resolute. This fledgling *'live and let live'* mentality, while both welcome and morally acceptable, goes against every rule of engagement, therefore leaving an uneasy feeling in the pit of my stomach. Sadly, I've been conditioned to kill and that isn't something that simply dissipates.

"Merry Christmas, Englander," shouts out a lone German voice, abruptly breaking the silence in the most unexpected fashion.

The bullets don't baffle me, it's business as usual, but this friendly voice calling out in to the chilly night air has me dumbfounded. A few short hours ago they were battling like blood thirsty barbarians, now it's compliments of the season! I arrived at the Western Front fresh faced and full of ideals, but quickly learned this den of despair and desolation is no place for the dreamer. Wholly preoccupied with the preservation of life, one can quickly loose their sense of identity. Waking thoughts, once so fertile with seeds of possibility, slowly decompose and darken within a mind besieged by the impregnation of fear. Battle resolutely as I may against the unrelenting beast, this ghastly mental turmoil provides the perfect breeding ground for my inner cynic. As much as I want to believe this seasonal greeting will herald the beginning of a burgeoning friendship borne out of brutality, the annoying little bugger won't allow it. Merrily chiselling away at my desecrated dreams, it's constant chirping offers precious little escape from this heinous reality. Regrettably, I'll take this torment to my grave, regardless of when death finds me. Nothing more than another tool in Jerry's armoury, it's the only way I can begin to decipher this madness. Disingenuously engaging us in the act of fraternisation in order to sneakily initiate a lowering of our defences, the bastards are plundering us with pleasantries!

"Merry Christmas, Englander," the voice cries out again, but more fervently.

The tonality, so rich with cheerfulness infuses me with an absurd promise of jollification. Every last shred of humanity, laying dormant in my beaten down soul, inexplicitly crackles with hope as excitement surges through arteries furred up with hateful discontentment. Seduced by this act of human kindness, I fiercely suppress the urge to bellow out "Merry Christmas" at the top of my lungs. Ransacked by thoughts so ludicrously steeped in fantasy, they briefly liberate my mind to ponder the art of the possible. My battle ready body has been infected with a potentially fatal dose of warmth and goodwill to all men, even Jerry. It's the disease every Commander or General dreads and fiercely guards against through the deployment of fear and propaganda. The desire to converse with my foes is surprisingly strong, stirring up a cocktail of complex emotions that defy comprehension. I've invested so much energy into hating an enemy I don't really know. Perhaps these feelings stem from a need to feel once more like a compassionate human being, downright decent with the capacity to forgive. They, too, must share my utter indignation for this callous war, having suffered untold misery at our blood soaked hands. Too many lacerations have been inflicted across the wounded hearts of all who inhabit these living graves for healing to transpire, but armed with civil tongues, can we cast grudges aside and come together? Even if it's only for one glorious day? This magnificent full moon must be driving me crazy, but it feels like a night where all manner of scenarios seem plausible. I shake my head, this utopian thinking will be the death of me.

"Shouldn't we shout something back?" Asks Frosty, "feels rude not too."

In light of Sergeant Bevan's earlier instruction, I'm hesitant to engage in conversation, but struggle to see what harm it will do. Frosty is right, us British folk pride ourselves on our exemplary manners, if nothing else. We wouldn't want to come across as impertinent, that simply wouldn't do.

"I agree," adds Joker, "he does sound an awfully friendly chap and 'tis the season' after all."

"Don't be fooled," warns Lionheart, "that's Jerry over there and I wouldn't trust him as far as I could throw him."

"Which is quite some distance I imagine," quips Joker, earning himself a scolding look in the process.

"All I'm saying is there's always an ulterior motive with that crafty lot, we need to keep our eyes peeled and guns at the ready. We are at war and lest we forget, they are the enemy."

"Of course," I reply, "and we shan't, it goes without saying, but I see no reason for refusing to extend them a little goodwill and courtesy."

"Good man, Jacko," replies Frosty, "that's the spirit."

"Here, here," cries Joker in staunch agreement.

"Ok good, but lets not appear too over familiar. Lionheart is right to be wary, we'll proceed with the upmost caution and keep our heads out of the clouds."

Lionheart sighs, "I've said my piece and will utter no more, but I don't like it."

"Let's just wish them a Happy Christmas and then we can get back to hating them," suggests Frosty, ever the pragmatist.

To hate is such an ugly trait, the mention of it turns me cold. Callously bred into the make-up of decent young fellows, seduced by patriotic persuasion to facilitate the tragedy of war. I weep for the waves of young, untainted souls that will sadly follow, transported like sardines from the bosom of civilisation to the tyranny of battle, their rosy futures cruelly dispensed with.

"There will be no hate tonight gentlemen," I pronounce authoritatively, "is that understood?"

I'm a lowly Private, with no superiority to speak of, but a few of the chaps seem to look up to me and subsequently I've garnished a degree of respect that belies my lowly position. No doubt, as exhausted as me, with purveying hatred and taking heed of my conviction, they nod in agreement. This is Christmas, albeit in a hopeless place, but its unlikely observation grants me the opportunity to behave in a manner that bears some semblance of decency. This war has remorselessly pillaged so much of my character, reducing me to this, pinning the last remnants of hope for the salvation of my dark soul on a simple greeting. The sheer preposterousness of the notion is enough to force an incredulous smile from the most fervent dough eyed dreamer.

"Merry Christmas to you, too," I cast out exuberantly upon night skies, decorated with the faintest shade of optimism.

My rhapsodic tone causes an eruption of gasps among men thrust into the insidious realms of fraternisation. Nibbling on the forbidden fruit tastes of sweet liberation, I feel neither guilt nor regret. On eliciting a positive response, cheers ring out among the well lit enemy ranks. The audible elation pouring out from across no-mans-land lends credence to how significant this moment feels. Keen to share in the unbridled joy, we launch our own impressive salvo of cheers in a united display of spontaneous reciprocation. The commotion is enough to bring an exasperated Sergeant Bevan, dashing out of hibernation.

"What's the meaning of all this?"

Big, burly blokes stare sheepishly at the ground, mirroring naughty school children summoned to the headmasters office, as joviality quickly descends in to stoney silence.

"Hurst, Frost, does anybody care to enlighten me?"

Unwittingly, with gazes swiftly averted in my vicinity, *my muckers have ratted me out, all Sergeant Bevan has to do is follow the eyes, bugger!*

"Well Crosby, is there something you want to tell me?"

"Erm, yes, Sir..."

"What is it man" he snaps impatiently, "spit it out."

"It's Jerry, Sir."

"What about them?"

"They've been talking to us, Sir," I mumble.

"Really?" He replies sounding more intrigued the angry. "In English?"

"Yes, Sir, good English."

"How odd, and what on earth have they been saying?"

"Well, Sir, they wished us a Merry Christmas."

"Good gracious, how queer."

"Quite, Sir, most unexpected, but jolly decent all the same."

"Did you respond, Private Crosby?"

This is one of those moments in life which crystalise a man's thinking. Two clear paths present themselves with the route being taken determined by the next thing to leave his lips. It's an uncomfortable choice, admit the truth or lie through ones teeth. It's unlikely to garnish favour in this instant, but I've always been partial to a bit of honesty.

"Yes, I did Sir, following consultation with the men."

There's no bloody way I'm taking all the flack for this one. Some rather nasty scowls assure me they'll find a way to express their appreciation later.

"Is that so, Private?"

I nod grimly, in readiness for a right rollicking.

"Good man, it doesn't hurt to be polite."

"Pardon, Sir?" I reply, my head spinning in a whirlwind of bemusement.

"We're not savages, Jack and I suppose it's Christmas for those poor bastards too." He smiles and as if by magic the worry lines that appeared permanently engraved on his face vanish, it lifts years off him. Christmas spirit seemingly works wonders, or maybe the whisky is responsible, for his mellow demeanour. Either way, his touching sentiment exhibits empathy and a genuine sense of compassion. It's enough to melt the coldest heart.

"I couldn't agree more, Sir, thank you."

"That being said men, remain wary at all times. Much as this passage of peace is pleasing for ones soul, recognise it is finite and incapable of derailing the business of war. When the time invariably comes to recommence hostilities, we must be ready. Trust only in ones valour and the men you stand shoulder to shoulder with, it's our only escape to victory."

My goodness, when it comes to imparting wisdom then Sergeant Bevan possesses a distinct turn of phrase, but there's barely time to digest his sobering words before, binoculars in hand, he lets out a startled cry.

"Positions men, as quick as you can, Jerry is on the move!"

I throw myself into the trench wall and ready my weapon. With my face moulded in to a cold slab of mud, God only knows what's happening, but the skies remain silent. Without a crumb of hesitation, Lionheart bravely scales the trench wall to peer across the barricades.

"What the hell?" He cries, leaping back down trembling.

Crikey, it takes an awful lot to frighten that big bugger!

"What is it man?", I enquire furiously.

"It's Jerry, they're all climbing out of the trench."

"Good lord," I exclaim, "the bloody bastards have tricked us, they're mounting an all-out attack!"

"Prepare to fire men!" ,Sergeant Bevan screams.

This is it, my initial flush of fear is replaced by a river of adrenalin. It's time to stare down the spectre of death.

"Good luck boys and may God be with us…"

"Englander, Englander."

"Hold your fire," is Sergeant Bevan's hastily screeched instruction.

"We don't want to fight, it's Christmas."

The words, beggaring belief, pander perfectly to each soldier's overriding desire. The communication, unprecedented in nature, is met with a wall of silence. I search in vain for a shred of validity amongst a gallery of bemused faces. The temptation to trust and dispense with this abhorrent hostility feels tantalising, but history is littered with a fistful of cautionary tales, beware the thinly vailed promises of devils disguised as angels!

"We will not fire if you don't Englander. Tonight we are friends!"

These outlandish sentiments paint an idyllic picture of paradise in the moonlight. I'm itching to climb out of the trench and stretch my legs without fear of reprisal. It's the type of fanciful freedom that can make a young soldier's heart sing. I'm not the only one desperate to escape our mud lined cell judging by the size of Frosty's gormless grin.

"Come and join us Englander, we will not hurt you."

That's as damn near an invitation as we're going to get to this impromptu jamboree, but I don't envisage Sergeant Bevan reaching for his dancing shoes just yet. The call has to be his alone, anyone with greater seniority is safely ensconced in the land of nod many a mile away. I'm sure they wouldn't welcome being awoken, from their alcohol induced slumber, to ask if it's ok for us to partake in some friendly fraternisation with the Germans! His tortured expression shows it's a call that weighs heavy. This isn't a scenario one envisages when drawing up battle plans. Despite sympathising with his predicament, I feel powerless to lighten the burden. It's hard to remain impartial whilst craving a breath of civility.

"Well, men," he begins, "these certainly are unchartered waters we find ourselves in. I don't quite know what to make of all this nonsense."

"It's extraordinary, Sir." I reply.

"Quite, Private Crosby, extraordinary indeed. Frankly men, I'm at a loss. This isn't the kind of situation one stumbles across in the pages of an army training manual," he scoffs.

His candour is admirable, and to be fair, he's right to be hesitant. This is an honourable and decent man whose decisions have the capability to send good men to early graves. One can never truly comprehend the enormity of pressure that resides upon his shoulders, not until they've walked a mile in his shoes. It's an unenviable path to tread, offering scant reward and a hefty conscience.

"Gentlemen, in war bravery and foolishness are often two sides of the same coin, one draws praise whilst the other invites nothing but scorn. It's easy to cast judgement from within the thick walls of a Belgian chateau, but we don't get the luxury of pontificating under a blanket of relative safety. For months, we have admirably bared the consequences borne out of the decisions of others, but this one is ours alone. Make no mistake men, this is completely bonkers and nobody needs to go up there, but wouldn't it be something?"

"I'll say," I reply, "incredible."

"Let's do it!" Shouts Frosty eagerly. His eyes portray all the traits of a dog begging to be let off his leash. Joker's already started scaling the trench wall!

"Hold your horses men," instructs Sergeant Bevan, "this is on me. I'll climb up top first to ensure this isn't a trap. If God forbid it is, reply in kind men and tell my darling wife and children that I love them, dearly."

"Are you absolutely sure, Sir?" I enquire, "I'm more than happy to test the water."

He smiles and rests his hand on my shoulder. "God bless you, Jack," he whispers before placing down his rifle and climbing out of the trench.

This selfless act is typical of the man and I'd expect nothing less, but part of me wonders if these are the actions of an exhausted soul who just wants to be done with this wretched war. Mercifully, his appearance draws nothing but cheers. His face bathed in moonlight, Sergeant Bevan stretches and breathes in a precious gulp of fleeting freedom.

"Good evening, Englander, we wish you a Merry Christmas."

"Thank you," replies Sergeant Bevan gracefully with a wave, "Merry Christmas, chaps."

"Thank you, kind Sir," shouts a cheery German voice, no doubt buoyed at eliciting a positive response. His distant tone can barely be heard above a fresh wave of raucous cheers. The carnival atmosphere adds fuel to an already raging fire of anticipation sweeping through the trench. Excitement suddenly flows freely through veins clogged with dejection, as we contemplate the enticing prospect of clambering out of our mud lined cell. Sergeant Bevan turns back to discover a vast array of puppy dog eyes, gaping hopefully, incarcerated hearts aching to be free.

"Isn't it a wonderful evening," he teases, "simply splendid." Clearly revelling in leaving us dangling, he takes a couple of leisurely paces before spinning on his heels, "well men, what on earth are you waiting for?"

Que the most beautiful bedlam imaginable! On mass men enthusiastically scurry out of the trench, their scarlet faces portraying the first flush of freedom. Some are quick to drag fellow comrades up, while others are rendered motionless by the magnitude of the moment. No-mans-land bares the stricken symbols of sacrifice and no amount of darkness can hide the ugly truth, but it's crowded fringes are soon bustling with spirited conversation. Men constantly shackled by the imminent threat of death, adjust seamlessly to this sweet state of liberation, appearing animated, but relaxed. The night air crackles with laughter as smiling comrades share jokes, labouring deliriously under a blessed blanket of relief. I'm acutely aware that it's a fantasy steeped in fragility, but that's what makes it all the more seductive. Moments like this scarcely grace one's lifetime and beg to be lived in. This heady cocktail of elation and relief is whipping up the most surreal emotions, it's a feeling I'll cherish for the remainder of my days. My burdened heart is a vessel besieged with pain, but this memory will be borne with eternal gladness. *Oh Lord, freeze the constant ticking of time and let me languish in the majesty of this peaceful paradise forevermore.*

Across the glistening plain, our foes appear to be embracing the joyous interlude with comparable gusto, gathering in large clusters that exude cheerfulness. Chiselled out of forlorn hope, this utopian landscape denies hatred the necessary oxygen to breathe. Amongst the frontlines, a lack of desire for war constantly nibbles away at ones determination to do their duty for King and country, and now this desire appears to have all but drained from weary bodies. *Let's shake hands, call this regrettable bloody mess a draw and bugger off home. Fanciful thinking indeed, Private Crosby!*

Christmas is dominating the conservation, lots of hankering for home as one would expect, but festive menus are also being meticulously drawn up for a tomorrow that suddenly appears much brighter. It may be built on glass foundations, but confidence in this truce is growing. With talk of roast turkey smothered in gravy, rich puddings and fine wine it's easy to get carried away on this flight of fancy. I've always been partial to a bit of sage and onion stuffing, just the thought of it is making my stomach grumble with anticipation. I wonder what Rose will be tucking into tomorrow? Spending time apart is always difficult, but Christmas day adds an extra layer of sadness to a mind busily mourning the loss of her infectious presence. *What more can this deplorable conflict take from me? Only the dead escape war.*

A stocky figure emerges from within the enemy ranks, rifle on shoulder and carrying a tree. His walk across the beat up and blood soaked terrain quickly wrestles our attention as merry bands of men on both sides fall silent. Eyes transfixed, all thoughts cease, allowing me to exist entirely in the moment. His courageous strides, though short, remain purposeful and undeniably huge in magnitude. Halfway across he stops and pauses, you could hear a pin drop. My heart beats with authority amidst this electric atmosphere, intensifying with every thump. The solider slips the rifle from his shoulder and places the tree on the ground. Using the butt of his weapon he proceeds to hammer the tree into the crunchy surface. A task made simple by the saturated ground beneath the frosty veneer. Once in place, he draws a box of matches from the side pocket of his tunic and begins to light the adorning candles. He nods in our direction before retiring to German shores. Mercifully, the elements can't muster up enough breath to extinguish a solitary flame, allowing this glorious beacon of hope to burn brightly across rugged land soiled with tragedy. The simple gesture feels symbolic, like driving a stake through the beating heart of evil. Light flickers in the tired eyes of simple men, craving nothing more than peace and the warm comforting sanctuary of their own beds. Arms thrown across comrades shoulders, I'm rendered motionless in quiet contemplation observing and absorbing history. Through teary mist, I can barely make out the glowing outline of dancing flames. Hopefully, one fine day I'll get to say I was there when harmony descended on the war-torn fields of Flanders, proudly recounting to my child the extraordinary events that unfolded, one fabled Christmas Eve night.

A lone voice breaks the silence, as golden dulcet tones carried across no-mans-land on the wings of angels caress my cold, ravaged ears. Blessed with the talent of a tenor, this young German chaps sublime offering quickly seduces souls swollen with pain. The traditional song still nacht, despite its lyrics, sounds reassuringly familiar. Naturally, I think of Rose and everything that makes Christmas so intrinsically beautiful. Mellow musings so tangible, I can taste sherry wetting my lips. Her hand rests upon mine as I run my thumb tenderly across her delicate skin, my racing heart, so laden with love that it's liable to explode. Seeing my destiny, reflected in her deeply alluring auburn eyes, I'm hopelessly beyond paradise. My whole wonderful world resides within these four walls, silently I beg to be imprisoned forever in this fantasy…

A plethora of exuberant applause disturb my idyllic daydream, though one can't argue that they're thoroughly deserved. A performance of such stature will be a tough act to follow, but we British are nothing if not resourceful.

"Come on lads," shouts Frosty, "let's give 'em something back."

God only knows where this is going!

"God save our gracious King, long live our noble King..." he bellows.

In unison, we heartily sing along, standing tall, chests proudly pushed out. Our grand display of pageantry may have lacked their finesse, but the German's watch on admirably, a few of them even sing along. Patriotism is a trait that resonates deeply among both sides, for heaven's sake, we slay each other in the name of it! It's conclusion is greeted with a fresh wave of adulation, courtesy of the old enemy, their good grace fills me with satisfaction. This harmonious state is tentative at best, but nevertheless devilishly addictive, my elevated mood now teeters on the cusp of elation.

During all the pandemonium, midnight's passing goes unnoticed. In the most wondrous fashion, Christmas had broken across the unforgiving fields of Flanders. A land starved of hope, it's presence has never been more welcome or needed. The eventual realization that the 25th had dawned is commemorated with handshakes and hugs the length and breadth of both lines. The emotion is evident during more subdued celebrations, out of respect for those lying nearby who never got to witness another Christmas. I quietly say a prayer to myself, begging for the safe passage of their souls, whilst remembering the sweethearts they left behind. *How many cherished dreams lie unfulfilled within this graveyard of potential?*

I softly mouth the words, "Merry Christmas my darling, hope to see you soon."

"Right gentleman," says Sergeant Bevan, "it has been quite the evening, remarkable indeed, but we should be returning to our posts now. Tomorrow affords no guarantees and God only knows what it will bring, but we must guard against complacency and be ready for it. Merry Christmas, men, may God bless you."

It appears the German's are out for the duration, but our moment in the moonlight is over. With not a single word of complaint uttered, we cheerfully file back into our disease ridden ditch, despite tonight's jollification, the business of war must be respected at all costs. When I finally retire for some rest, my usual foreboding sense of dread has been replaced by a more welcome bedfellow, excitement, albeit tinged with apprehension. My heart, so congested with pain, has been infiltrated with brittle fragments of hope.

It has been the most beautifully absurd evening imaginable, merrily conversing with men I wilfully attempted to kill only hours earlier. Precious particles of peace lived out joyfully within the confides of a bloody war. This very morning, not a single fellow wanted to be anywhere near this blood stained land, but surely not one soul would have missed this for the world. One can only wonder what gifts Christmas morning has in store…

Sombre Solidarity

'We spent the morning burying the dead, killed in the battle of the 19th, as we had not previously been able to. Some of them were nasty sights, I can tell you, and for the first time I saw what a human body looks like when it is half blown away. I felt quite sick for some time after it, but it is good for us to try and get used to it, as we shall no doubt see plenty more. But if some of the glib talkers could have come and looked at that field strewn with corpses they would talk less airily about wars. I tell you it made me feel what an awful crime against humanity war is.'

Capt. John Robert Somers-Smith, 5th City of London Bn, London Rifle Brigade.

The first slither of Christmas light seeps through the narrowest of cracks in my bedroom curtains, causing my eyes to squint, but this is no rude awakening. My whirling mind scuppered any hope of a decent night's sleep some hours ago. The culprit, an act of snow-clad spontaneity, exposing it to a treasure chest full of possibilities. For so long, the chest has been guarded by this big rusty padlock, appearing unbreakable, but in Rose I have found the key. To adore so completely is an utterly divine experience and, of course, I love her more than life itself, but my feelings for Rose stretch beyond this simmering cauldron of emotions. She possesses an effervescent personality that's thrillingly addictive and so much fun to be around, consequently time melts away. My mind harbours an impossible desire to preserve the memory of every precious second absorbed in her presence. Outside of Rose, it all feels like a bit of a pantomime. As if I'm playing at living, being with her is the only time I truly connect with the moment, when all feels exactly how it should be. Her glorious strands of pure unadulterated joy, coated generously with love, now delicately woven through the fabric of my swollen heart. My whole world begins and ends in the majesty of her eyes. Who needs sleep anyway, it's Christmas!

The drunken haze has now lifted, but thankfully my euphoric state shows little sign of abating. Remarkably, given the hearty amount of alcohol I threw down my neck, my head feels clear and pain-free. Whilst embarking on the short walk back to Rose's parents, where a sumptuous feast awaits, I revel in the joy of strangers. The winter sunshine has enticed both young and old to wrap up warm and brave the cold crisp air. People trudge merrily, through the slushy snow, offering compliments of the season as they pass. Santa Claus has been busy, judging by the amount of shiny new bikes and scooters being rode gleefully by children displaying scant regard for the slippery terrain. This sublime state of happiness appears infectious, with beaming smiles evident throughout the journey. Christmas brings out the beauty in people, it's an agonisingly short, but wondrous fantasy to behold.

I'm back on the wooden porch, the place I last kissed my sweetheart. I'm now sober and have to admit to a tinge of trepidation, pausing prior to knocking on the front door. Last night we were two loved up sweethearts, swept away in the splendour of the moment, but now in the cold light of day, reality lurks menacingly beyond that big blue door. Rose has had time to think, mull things over and contemplate her future. She's either walking on sunshine, caught up in a quandary or haplessly drifting somewhere in between. I'm annoyed at briefly giving credence to thoughts so utterly ridiculous and duly banish them from my mind. I always experience flutters of excitement prior to seeing Rose, a delicious anticipation that builds from a gentle stream to a smouldering river of molten lava flowing through my veins. Each romantic rendezvous feels like a new beginning, fresh and flourishing with passion. A brand new opportunity to cast my eyes upon the breadth of her beauty, lovingly gather her up in my arms and kiss her tenderly. On the back of our abrupt engagement, those feelings have magnified and my desperation to kiss her again is palpable. I've kissed other woman before, well one or two, but with Rose the act of coupling lips is incomparable. It's an electric experience, lavishly riddled with pulsating emotion and capable of whisking me into the most exhilarating world. A place inhabited by two entwined souls, hopelessly bound by love and a common destiny. It's somewhere only we know, our piece of heaven, and Rose is the only person who can take me there. I raise my right hand in readiness for executing a brisk, sharp knock, but the door flies open, and there stands Rose. Effortlessly stunning in wool and beaming outrageously, sunshine it is then.

Our daily call to arms ritual finds Sergeant Bevan in rather a pensive mood, hardly surprising given the freakish events which transpired a few short hours earlier. He's not the only one struggling to come to terms with our new found reality, I barely slept a wink. Eventually nodding off whilst nursing a racing mind beset with excitement, only to wake up in the throes of bewilderment.

"Good morning men, and a very merry Christmas to each and every one of you."

"Merry Christmas, Sir" is the greeting enthusiastically delivered back, well as enthusiastic as one can be at this godforsaken hour. Sergeant Bevan nods and smiles warmly in recognition.

"I often wondered, over the course of the last few months, if I'd live to see the dawn of another Christmas," he says wistfully. "We are the lucky ones gentleman, and we must never forget that. Too much blood has been spilt on both sides, so I want to take a quiet moment on this special day to remember the poor souls who tragically succumbed to the tyranny of war. I'm not talking specifically about our own, but all the brave soldiers who paid the ultimate price; husbands, fathers, sons and brothers who'll never go home again."

Heads lower throughout the trench in tribute to the dearly departed. I take the opportunity to remember the stricken comrades who touched my life. All that wasted potential, it brings tears to my eyes. A young, brave solider brings the respectful silence to an end with some slow clapping, we eagerly join in to provide a fitting conclusion to a poignant period of contemplation. Cruelly, war does not afford one the luxury to grieve, but the dead will never be forgotten. Their earthly shells will naturally decompose, but the human spirit cannot be contained by earth nor man, ghosts walking beside us forevermore.

"Last night was something to behold gentleman, quite the spectacle and wholly out of character with the business of war. Any thoughts we harbour of this harmonious state becoming the status quo must be expunged from our minds. Regardless of how wonderful it feels, they're riddled with danger and breed complacency. So, lets consign them to the realms of fantasy and move on, forever in hope of a swift, but peaceful conclusion."

"Here, here," chimes out emphatically in to the chilly morning air. Sergeant Bevan nods and smiles, satisfied his sobering words of warning have been heeded.

"This isn't the Christmas any of us envisaged, but we have the makings of a splendid morning and provisions aplenty to enjoy. Keep a watchful eye on Jerry and stay safe out there men, we owe it to each other and our families to remain vigilant. We tread amongst heroes, and our sacrifice will not go unnoticed or be forgotten. God bless you all, those you hold dear and God bless the King."

"The King," we cry triumphantly, before dispersing to crack on with the duties of the day.

Each morning, the rising sun brings with it fresh hope of a new dawn. Criminal acts perpetrated under a blanket of darkness give way to welcome, but unspoken, breakfast truces. A time for weary heads to rest, refuel and summon up the energy to dance once more within the valley of death. Despite the growing number of casualties, neither side seem to be gaining much ground. Nevertheless, meetings are held and plans dissected in the forlorn hope of gaining an advantage. This desperate situation is the definition of hopelessness, but I must find a way to persevere, especially when all thoughts allude to its futility. I'm doing my damnedest to adopt the mind of a mercenary, but this morning feels unique and cloaked in unfamiliarity. A smattering of Germans have already emerged from their trenches, mingling carefreely across the bloody borders of battle. Clearly unperturbed by the prospect of enemy assault, coffee and conversation appears to be the order of the day. A hasty resumption of hostilities seems unlikely, but with Sergeant Bevan's stark warning still resonating stoutly within my ears, I'm reluctant to breakout the Christmas crackers just yet.

After a slurp of coffee and with pen in hand, I'm primed for action. A blank canvas lies across the table, patiently awaiting the words that will bring it to life. Conveying all the emotions that reside within my heart in a handful of sentences is an unenviable task, but I feel compelled to portray my love in prose. I rest the nib on the paper, and with a swoosh of the wrist I'm off to the races. Blessed with a rare moment of clarity, I exploit it and the words come easy.

My dearest darling Rose,

Bizarrely, as I pen this, it's Christmas morning, and we should be waking up together in our cosy new home. This wretched war has denied us so much happiness and I pray constantly for its swift demise. You're all that consumes my mind, well, you and now the thought of impending fatherhood!

When I read the blessed news, all I wanted to do was gather you up in my arms and hold you close. You and a little family to call our own, it's more than I could ever dream of. The last perfect fragment of our forever, I couldn't be happier or more excited at the thought of becoming a daddy!

Thanks for your wonderful gifts (Frosty's already eying up the cake) and loving sentiments, they're sustenance for my soul. I beg of you not to fret, my sweetheart, I'm eating well and staying strong.

Possessing a heart brimming with love for you and a mind harbouring a steely determination to get home, I will find a way back to you, my darling. You're not getting rid of me that easily!

I must mention, experiencing what I can only describe as the most incredible Christmas Eve imaginable. It beggars belief, but I can assure you these extraordinary words are the workings of a sober mind. In late afternoon, mercifully the guns fell silent, and within a few hours the Germans were shouting over compliments of the season. Isn't it incredible? Bullets after breakfast followed by well wishes before supper, it's incomprehensible. They all climbed out of the trenches and casually chatted without a care, prior to beckoning us to do the same. Initially, we were dubious about their motives, but eventually followed suit and had a jolly good time. Both sides were singing songs to each other across the barricades, truly remarkable. I have to say, those German chaps appear to be a splendid bunch of fellows. Just to walk around without fear of reprisal, it felt so liberating. Maybe I'll get to enjoy a peaceful Christmas after all!

On the subject of that Rose, I want you to enjoy your Christmas without a shred of guilt or worry. This isn't the day either of us would wish for, but we must endeavour to make the best of it. The thought you can find some snatches of happiness makes me feel warm inside, you deserve it and so much more. I'll be there in spirit and will today, as always, carry you in my heart.

Thank you for loving me Rose, I can't and won't contemplate a world without you. We're going to grow old and grey together surrounded by hordes of great grandchildren! I miss you too, my darling, and inexplicably fall in love with you a little bit more with every passing day. Being separated is sheer hell, but we have forever.

Merry Christmas, my darling Rose.

My undying love, now and always.

Your Jack

I smile, satisfied with my efforts. They're only words, but until God knows when, it's all we have. I've lovingly stored all of Rose's letters in a small wooden box, which I keep close to wherever I'm sleeping. Strong emotions expressed so eloquently, they are my most treasured possession and well-travelled companion. Other than Rose's face, they're the last thing I see before retiring for the night. It's hard to go to sleep happy, under a blazing crimson sky, but her beautifully crafted correspondence offers the chance to drift off into unconsciousness with a smile on my face. Equally, upon waking, I tend to reach for the box almost immediately. There is also a lock of Rose's hair in there and a tiny bottle containing a few drops of her favourite perfume. It's the fuel that drives me on when everything in my weary body is begging to be put out of this turgid misery. Even on the battlefield, Rose is with me, and I couldn't survive a day without her. Whatever it takes, I must forge a way back to her.

The sun is now slowly creeping over the frozen fields of Flanders, causing the thick film of frost to glisten rather exquisitely. If there was ever a time when the world needed Christmas, then this is it. Unsurprisingly, given Sergeant Bevan's earlier directive, I return to the front line to find our boys adopting a more cautionary approach than our German counterparts. Encamped in trenches once more, but in good spirits. I spy an abundance of sweet treats being enjoyed and the odd tot of rum, if I'm not mistaken, as men pass the time reminiscing about bygone Christmas times. It's an art I've struggled to master, some men read while others write copiously to fill the void created by father time. It's more of an issue outside of sentry duty, once the adrenalin dissipates. Battle is many things, but it's never boring. On arriving at my regular patch of dirt, I'm greeted with the rather unpleasant sight of Frosty devouring a mince pie, the last mouthful is scarcely digested when he reaches for another one.

"Steady on mate, we're barely past breakfast time," I implore.

"Bugger off" he shouts with a grin, "it's Christmas, and these are delicious!"

"Really?"

"Aye, my mother has a secret recipe, passed down by generations."

"Is that so?" I reply, whilst peering into his half empty tin.

"Are you sure I can't tempt you Jacko" he says laughing, clearly revelling in my weakening resolve.

"Well, tis the season and all that."

"Go on lad, fill ya boots," he says, thrusting the tin in my direction. I gladly reach out and grab myself a piece of pastry clad paradise.

"Thanks mate, and Merry Christmas."

"Happy Christmas, let's hope it's our last away from dear old Blighty," he replies before sighing heavily, "and the Dirty Duck!"

"Indeed my friend," I concur, "there is nothing quite like it is there?"

"Home or the Dirty Duck?"

I laugh, "both, they're equally splendid."

He chuckles too, but within this smattering of laughter I sense an underlying sadness lurking. Bless him, he's always been a homebird and devoted to his dear, old mum. Beyond the brash Jack-the-lad facade there beats a heart of gold. In time, once he's done sowing his wild oats, he'll make a wonderful husband and father. He always plays down the notion of settling down, but eventually love will render him powerless to do anything else. It finds us all, even lotharios like Frosty.

"I'll drink to that me, old mate," he cries, passing me a tot of dark rum.

Its early, but what the hell. "Cheers," we clink beakers with ardour and swig it back.

"Goodness gracious, that hits the spot!" I exclaim, taken aback by the intense heat enveloping my chest.

"Packs a punch, doesn't it? That's Caribbean export rum for you, not for the faint hearted," he says with a grin.

I can't help but smile. It's typical Frosty, he has a marvellous knack of extracting the joy from life's most simple pleasures. It's an indispensable skill to possess whilst inhabiting the forlorn fields of Flanders, and instrumental in keeping me on the preferred side of sanity. When somebody has always been there, its easy to start taking them for granted, but I'm forever grateful for his ensuing presence in my life. When the demons are menacingly knocking down the door, it's great to have someone who can make light of the most dire situations in my corner. If Rose is my motivation, then Davy Frost is my rock, the three of us against the tyrants of terror, the bluster of bombs and bullets don't stand a chance!

"Have you seen Jerry up there?" Asks Frosty, "swanning about without a care in the world?"

"Yes," I nod, "they seem very relaxed."

"Good on 'em, I say," injects Lionheart, while cheekily helping himself to one of Frosty's cherished mince pies. Frosty shakes his head disapprovingly, but wisely stays quiet. "They seem a decent bunch of men," he adds whilst munching away.

"You've changed your tune," barks Frosty with raised eyebrows.

Lionheart nods, "It's this war, makes ya think."

"You're a philosopher now," scoffs Frosty, but his smirk proves short lived when met with a fearsome scowl from his burly counterpart.

"In what way?" I ask intriguingly, given that Lionheart is usually a man of few words.

"It's Jerry."

"What about them?"

"We use up all that energy trying to kill the buggers, then you realise…"

"Realise what?" Shouts Frosty impatiently.

"Realise that they're just ordinary blokes, skin and bone like us, frightened young men with hopes and dreams, desperate to get back home."

"Quite," I add sombrely, "this wretched war is an unforgiving business."

"Aye," nods Frosty with a sigh, "we're all in the shit for sure. Lord, grant us redemption from this pitiful existence," he adds ruefully to nods of agreement.

I look over at Lionheart, and for the first time all I can see is fragility, a prisoner to his thoughts, he appears almost tearful. The cloak of invincibility, ever so prominent in my eyes has been shed, blimey! If this war of attrition can infiltrate his herculean defences, then what hope do the rest of us mere mortals have? Wars are fought as much in the mind as on the battlefield, if not more so and, I guess poor Lionheart is, as susceptible as the rest of us to its enduring misery.

"Come on boys," I howl, "lets get another rum down us."

"Now you're talking Jacko!"

Several tots later and I've been summoned to Sergeant Bevan's quarters as a matter of urgency. Given the relaxed nature of this surreal Christmas morning, I'm slightly apprehensive and not to mention a few sheets to the wind. The agitated expression that greets me does little to dampen my pangs of anxiety.

"Ah, good morning, Private Crosby, please take a seat by all means."

"Good morning, Sir, is everything ok?"

"To tell you the truth old pal, I'm not quite sure, the most peculiar thing has just happened, its Jerry."

"Ok," I say, my curiosity pricked.

"They've been in touch, sent a chap over with a message, young slip of a boy, looked terrified."

"I can imagine, the poor lad."

"Quite, his hand was trembling by all accounts as he handed one of our boys the note." Much as I sympathised with his predicament, my curiosity is now burning. "It's…"

"Yes, Sir?"

"Its hard to fathom, but they've requested a meeting."

"I see, Sir, when?"

"At zero nine hundred hours, in the middle of no-man's-land."

I check my watch, it's almost quarter to. "Crikey Sir."

"My thoughts exactly old boy, relations have mellowed somewhat in the last day or so, but can we trust them to play with a straight bat?"

"Given the spirit of the season and all we've shared, I'd like to think so, Sir."

"Indeed Jack, and in a perfect world I'd be inclined to agree, but it's an incredible leap of faith."

"Absolutely, Sir, it's both courageous and crazy, but without the courage of decent men, what hope is there? Under the directive of evil minds, good folk toil, something has to change."

Sergeant Bevan looks into my eyes, awash with foolhardy optimism, smiles and nods. "You make a compelling case Jack, maybe now is the time for brave hearts to burn brightly. Come on my dear friend, let's go and serve up some history."

"Yes, Sir," I boom, standing bolt upright, my chest protruding proudly.

"Before we do though, a quick nip of whisky to help fight the cold" he says with a wink.

"Don't mind if I do, Sir."

As I accompany Sergeant Bevan across the clumpy terrain, littered with the stricken corpses of men I've had the privilege to stand shoulder to shoulder with, I feel no bravery, but instead an uneasy sense of foreboding. In a gesture of good faith, we've left our guns behind, but I do have a bayonet concealed about my person, just in case. Despite the best efforts of the winter sunshine, the ground remains rock solid, with each gingerly taken stride producing a crunchy snap as we inch closer to our date with destiny. This hastily arranged foray, at the polite request of the enemy, is unprecedented to the best of my knowledge, I can feel my legs shaking. Within minutes we'll stand face to face with our foes and look them square in the eye. Warmth, hate, even emptiness, one wonders what will be staring back at us? Their motives remain unclear, but I hope for the former emotion. In the distance, I spy two figures walking towards us, a short studious

looking fellow of mature age and apparent authority flanked by a
strapping young man with thick blonde hair. It would be the first time that I meet the imposing, Wilhelm Becker.

In the heart of no-mans-land all parties come to stop and immediately salute.

"Good morning gentleman, my name is General Bernhard Muller and this is Private Wilhelm Becker," he announces in perfect English.

"Good morning, General Muller and Private Becker, my name is Sergeant Michael Bevan and this is Private Jack Crosby, Merry Christmas to both of you."

"Merry Christmas, gentleman," he replies, and a faint smile breaks out across his softening features. Cordial handshakes are respectfully exchanged and Wilhelm gives me a heartwarming grin while gripping my hand firmly.

"May I say, General Muller, your English is quite exemplary," comments Sergeant Bevan.

"Thank you, Sir, I have spent many happy summers at your beautiful seaside with relatives in Scarborough," he says with fondness. "Regrettably, this barbaric war is not of my choosing and offers such horrid circumstances to meet under."

"I couldn't agree more, Sir," replies Sergeant Bevan, "I'd rather be anywhere but here today, "he adds ruefully.

Sergeant Bevan's candour is met with slow nods of agreement by myself and both opposing soldiers. Strip away the accents and slightly smarter unforms and there is no discernible difference, it's evident they too derive nothing more than misery from this poisonous predicament. It's a healthy hatred that transcends the barricades, uniting us all.

“It is how you say, bloody awful, yes?” Replies General Muller, we all laugh.

I was expecting a far more tense exchange, but both men seem thoroughly amiable chaps. In a different moment, we could be good friends, but given this reality it feels highly improbable. Despite the so far pleasant nature of this exchange, I’m trying to apply a sense of realism to my surging emotions. Humanising the enemy can wreak havoc with a soldiers mindset, and sadly these decent young men, though likeable, remain just that. In the coming days, if not hours, battle will inevitably recommence and the more I befriend them, the harder it will be. Up until now I’ve fought against a faceless foe, but recent events have allowed ambiguity to breed, causing my interpretation of the enemy to crumble. I’ve seen desperate hope in tired German eyes and heard the warmth in their tone, rendering them faceless no more. It will go against everything that makes me human, but prior to that next shot ringing out, I must master the art of suppression. Easier said than done, with Wilhelm’s beaming smile dominating the landscape.

“It is indeed, frightfully bad show for all concerned,” adds Sergeant Bevan. “What is it you wanted to specifically talk about?”

“I would like to suggest an official ceasefire to allow us to give our fallen comrades a dignified burial.”

“Yes, of course,” replies Sergeant Bevan without hesitation,

“Thank you, Sir.”

“Please, please, no thanks are necessary. It is the very least our brave chaps deserve.”

“Shall we say until noon?”

“Perhaps we can hold a joint burial service,” suggests a nodding Sergeant Bevan, “I’ll arrange for a

Chaplin to say a few prayers, does ten hundred hours suit you?"

"That will be splendid, thank you, Sir."

"Excellent, I'll make the arrangements. It's a ghastly business, but those poor souls deserve to rest in peace."

"On that we can all agree," adds the General.

"Indeed," replies Sergeant Bevan with a heavy sigh.

"Well, I believe that concludes our business gentleman," says General Muller with a salute, "good luck to both of you for whatever remains of this ungentlemanly war."

"Farewell," replies Sergeant Bevan, "may Godspeed you both."

Before parting, handshakes are again respectfully exchanged with an accompaniment of warm smiles, and just like that it was over. The briefest of civil interludes amidst the ironclad grip of a cold callous conflict, but it will stay with me until the end of days.

Father Peters has the unenviable task of deputising as our battalion Chaplin. A practicing catholic priest, now serving as a fully-fledged solider in the most ungodly of places is enough to test anyone's faith. How he squares off the despicable act of taking lives with the big guy, I'm not quite sure, but he's been spared up to now, so maybe someone up there likes him. He often gets called to the most heinous situations such as to hold a dying mans hand, offer solace and administer last rites for those of a religious persuasion. He's an extremely likable fellow, who does a wonderful job, but religion for me remains a bit of a mystery. The thought that we all go on to a better place is a nice one, particularly at this moment and I'm envious of the people who derive considerable comfort from this belief, but I'm unsure what lies beyond that final curtain. Hopefully there is a utopian paradise hiding behind those pearly gates, but I can't seem to shake the belief that this is it and all that awaits us is the ground we now walk on. I really hope I'm wrong and will keep murmuring the odd prayer, just in case! Given the gravity of our current predicament, it's hard for any solider to resist the lure of prayer and you're never far from a bible…

The chatter and joviality has respectfully subsided, as both armies ceremoniously flank either side of no-man's-land. A tranquillity, possessed solely by nature, surrounds sombrely bowed heads beset with grief. Between us, destroyed and dismembered, lie the tragic consequences of our deplorable actions. In the cold light of day it's the bitterest pill to swallow and in the absence of pride, there is only guilt ridden shame. Thoughts of death letters landing on the mats of unsuspecting families, their worlds about to shatter and change forever, that could be Rose one day. I may be able to bury the dead, but not the darkness.

Father Peters, now joined by an interpreter, has taken up a central position in readiness.

"Let us pray, gentlemen. Lord, on this your only Sons birthday, please bless the stricken souls of the brave men who lay before you. Born of you and without sin, we now return them to your care in the hope they can take their rightful place in the kingdom of Heaven."

"Amen," I mutter.

"Lord, may you offer them forgiveness and safe passage. We also pray for the loved ones, who now mourn their tragic passing, may they be granted solace, a sense of serenity and the strength to carry on and live fruitful lives. Please join me in saying the Lord's prayer, Our Father who art in heaven…"

I pick up a spade and edge forward with my fellow comrades, combining with a small band of soldiers to commence the dour task of digging graves. Our group is a mix of both British and Germans working together, happily this practice is replicated across the battlefield. A respectful silence is maintained whilst digging, prior to the careful lowering of bodies into crowded graves. Piles of decaying corpses ravaged by war. It paints a heartbreaking indelible image, cruelly denied the opportunity to live contently to a grand old age and achieve great things, prior to being laid to rest at home amongst family. Despite our best efforts, it's an undignified ending for young lives that deserve a whole lot more. Dropping soil on to their dishevelled faces, I watch them slowly disappear into a dark abyss. On all sides of the grave, tough men plagued by regret filled emptiness fight back tears, I'm no different. After banging a wooden cross in to the earth, it's on to the next plot.

"Our dear Lord, we commit our brothers to the ground and ask you to bless their souls. In death, may they find joy and peace in the glory of everlasting life. Amen."

"Amen," is echoed loudly by all parties.

"Please Lord, watch over all of the brave men here who toil under your sky and shower them with your love and peace. We pray for a swift and permanent conclusion to this war without the need for further bloodshed. Amen."

This time the word is repeated even more vigorously and followed by subdued applause to signify the closing of the ceremony. Their battered and bloodied bodies now belong to the unforgiving fields of Flanders for evermore.

Joyous Fraternisation

'We paid each other visits at the halfway line and exchanged Christmas gifts and buried the dead. Tomorrow we shall continue the old game of killing as the truce cannot last forever.'

Pte Joshua Kelsall, 3rd Battalion, Rifle Brigade.

The festive fayre served up at Rose's house was delicious and could have fed an army. Subsequently, as a result of one's overindulgence, I'm feeling slightly lethargic. By early evening I'm seriously flagging, my eyelids feel like lead.

"Come on sleepy head," says Rose with a firm slap on my knee, "lets go and blow the cobwebs away with a nice brisk walk."

I jolt my weary head up and give her a tipsy smile. "A stroll," I say. It's a lovely idea in theory, but I'm not sure how willing or able my bloated belly and shaky legs are.

"Yes, a stroll. Come on, I'll grab the coats."

"Okey-doke, my darling," I reply while gingerly getting to my feet with all the grace of a dazed boxer dragging himself off the canvas.

Once the cold winter air brushes against my rosy cheeks, I'm swiftly transported back in to the land of the living. It's the first flush of evening, but we're already enveloped by darkness which adds a dash of mystique to proceedings. As we walk, arm in arm, through now near deserted streets, I feel waves of contentment crashing against a barrier of blissful happiness. There is a beautiful silence between us as we sweetly surrender to the moment. The day has been a trifle of joyous layers, with this tender instant being the sumptuous cream topping. If I had the power to freeze time, this precise second wouldn't be a bad choice. I never want this feeling to end, but with Rose I know they'll be an abundance of champagne sunrises on the horizon. Every new day with her is a gorgeous gift, begging to be unwrapped and explored, unique and precious in its own right, now that's a future I can't wait to live.

"Do you think it will always be like this, Jack?"

"What, cold, dark and icy?" I reply jokingly.

"No silly, between us?"

"How do you mean, Rose?"

"You know, this happiness. It's almost too perfect, sometimes it scares me."

"In what way?"

"It's so idyllic, this life we're building, but it frightens me to think there's only one way to go."

I stop, turn to her and smile. "Rose, my darling, there is nothing to be scared of."

"Couples fall out of love, Jack, it happens."

"Maybe, but not to us."

"How can you be so sure?"

"Because we're soulmates, it's just meant to be, nothing can stop us."

"Do you promise, Jack?"

"With all my heart, darling." I clasp my rough hands on her cool cheeks and plant a delicate kiss on her soft lips. "The only direction this relationship is going, Rose, is to the moon. We're going to get married, raise children and buy a big old country house with a veranda."

"A veranda?" She says quizzically.

"Yep, with matching rocking chairs."

"That sounds cute."

"We're going to hold hands and watch sunsets whilst growing old together."

"How blissful, please tell me more Jack," she begs.

"There's going to be an orchard and lots of space for the great grandchildren to play. It will have a tyre swing and a seesaw, maybe even a slide."

"Oh, Jack, it sounds like a dream."

"Rose, it's all been a dream, since the moment I first saw you. I love you darling, just keep dreaming."

She smiles and places her arms around me. "Jack."

"Yes, Rose."

"Let's always be in love." A solitary tear rolls down her cheek and I tenderly brush it away with the back of my hand.

"Let's, forever…"

The mass funeral has given us all much food for thought, a painful blast of cold, hard reality. The mood in the trenches since returning has been much more subdued as a result. Digging death holes for my muckers isn't something I contemplated last summer when the carrot of heroic victory was tantalisingly dangled before me. I can never unsee those congested graves, so much for glory. Even the steady flow of liquor is failing miserably to lift our dampened spirits. I sit quietly among a group of men, sharing a feeling of remorseful numbness. It's not inconceivable I had a hand in killing some of the German soldiers I've just buried, complicit in tearing the gift of life from their warm bodies. *Where's the gallantry in that?* Sadly, soon this precarious truce will be nothing more than a faded memory and I'll transgress all over again. In time, I may be able to forgive myself, but I'll never forget my deeds or their ashen faces. If I am fortunate enough to make it back to dear old Blighty, they'll be no normal life waiting for me. The brutal scars of war run deep and they're agonizingly permanent.

The afternoon is approaching with disconcerting speed, signalling the end of our hastily arranged truce. A gratifying oasis in a desert of destruction, and all too fleeting. I can't help wondering which side possesses the appetite to fire the first shot. There seems a distinct lack of energy in our trench and I can't imagine things been much different across the way. Given the amount of booze that's been consumed through the morning, I doubt anybody's capable, regardless of their persuasion and there's Christmas dinner to consider. It would be terribly inconvenient to get interrupted when tucking into one's roast turkey! Hopefully, a shared desire to enjoy Christmas as much as the circumstances allow will see peace reign until Boxing day, at the very least. After spotting Frosty grabbing forty winks, I glance around hoping to locate his magical tin of delights, *where's the crafty bugger hid 'em?* I contemplate waking him to begin my interrogation when I spot Sergeant Bevan striding briskly in our direction.

"Good afternoon men," he says authoritatively, promptly waking Frosty from his slumber.

"Good afternoon, Sir," we reply, standing to attention.

"As you were men. Private Crosby?"

"Yes, Sir."

"I'll need you to come with me again, but firstly there have been murmuring's amongst the men about some rather splendid mince pies," he says looking hopefully in Frosty's direction.

Davy is blessed with a silver tongue, but I'm not sure even he can talk his way out of this one. Frosty smiles and pulls out the elusive tin from under his crumpled overcoat.

"There you go, Sir," he says, "you can have the last one." There is a collective groan around the trench, but Sergeant Bevan looks as pleased as punch.

"That's very gracious of you, David, thank you, looks like I arrived in the nick of time," he beams, like the proverbial cat who got the cream.

"There's some whisky here too, if you'd like a wee tot to wash it down," Frosty adds.

"That would be smashing, thanks."

Frosty pours our band of now merry men, all huddled together, another dram and hands them out.

"Well gentlemen," says Sergeant Bevan raising his drink, "a Merry Christmas to each and every one of you."

"Merry Christmas, Sir," we reply clinking our glasses, before knocking them back. Just like the drop of whisky, he makes light work of consuming the mince pie and it's clearly a pleasurable experience.

"My Lord, that was exquisite, absolutely first rate."

"Thank you, Sir."

"No, thank you David, that was a treat, a real taste of home," he says exuberantly, but then following a brief pause, he sighs adding softly "It makes one feel quite nostalgic."

Following his short-lived state of satisfaction, he slumps back somewhat dejectedly and shakes his head.. It seems even the mention of home is enough to stir up a cauldron of sadness and regret that lies within, simmering away. "Sitting here, in squalor, toasting the Christmas season, isn't it the most bizarre business chaps?"

"I suppose it is, Sir," I reply, unsure if it was a rhetorical question.

"A savage stalemate bequeathed to us by less than honourable men, conspicuous by their absence."

"Quite, Sir," adds Frosty.

"Has left us," he continues, "left us scratching around for hope, when there is precious little to speak of. Yet here we are, drinking to each other's health and making merry." He smiles, "quite a testament to the human spirit, wouldn't you agree?"

"One does what one can," I reply resolutely, "in spite of one's circumstances."

Sergeant Bevan nods, "indeed you do men and I'm immensely proud of each and everyone of you. In a garden beset with nettles, you are the fresh shoots of optimism that attract the sunshine, making me believe there is hope after all, thank you."

Taken aback by his candidness, there is a collective silence as we digest Sergeant Bevan's honest outpouring. I guess he puts his trousers on one leg at a time just like the rest of us.

"Anyway," he says abruptly, adopting a more professional demeanour, "please follow me, Private Crosby."

"Yes, Sir, where are we heading?"

"Over the top."

"But, Sir, it's gone midday, the truce has now ended."

"Better go and negotiate another one then Private, I haven't had my Christmas dinner yet!"

Nursing a niggling case of trepidation, I hang back as Sergeant Bevan climbs out of the trench.

"Come along then boy, they're expecting us…"

My second foray into the heart of no-mans-land seems to have pricked the curiosity of our men, who're clambering out en masse to observe proceedings. The German fringes are also heavily populated, mercifully there isn't a rifle in sight, instilling a calming sense of confidence within me. The same two men are walking towards us with broad smiles, it feels like meeting up with old friends! The salutes are familiar, but the handshakes feel a shade warmer this time.

"Thank you for coming out to meet us again," says Sergeant Bevan. "Can I please begin by passing on the sincere thanks of all my men for the respect shown and help given when burying our dead."

General Muller nods and smiles. "I would like to pass our thanks on too, for the dignified and helpful manner in which your men conducted themselves. They are a credit to you and your country."

"Thank you General, their souls are at peace now."

General Muller nods solemnly, "may God bless them all." There is a respectful pause and silence observed by all four of us, it feels deeply poignant and wholly appropriate. "How can I help Sergeant Bevan?"

"Well, it's after midday and the truce we agreed earlier has now expired."

"Yes, that is correct," confirms General Muller. "I guess that makes us enemies at war once more."

"Yet, here we are," states Sergeant Bevan, "conversing as apposed to bombing each other to blazes."

"Yes, it is a peculiar state of affairs," the General concedes.

"Indeed, most strange, but where do we go from here?"

General Muller sighs, "our superiors will be very keen for the fighting to continue. I can only assume they believe it is carrying on now unabated."

"Yes, that's what I also fear. I could probably be shot for just talking to you. The bloody bastards."

"But," says General Muller with a hint of optimism, "today they will be preoccupied with feasting on turkey and fine wines in the type of comfortable surroundings we can only dream about, without a thought spared for us poor beggars, bloody bastards indeed!"

Sergeant Bevan nods, "precisely, so let's not give them the satisfaction."

"What do you have in mind, Sergeant?"

"I think all of the men on both sides should be given the opportunity to enjoy what's left of Christmas as best they can. Given all we've endured, it's the very least we deserve."

"That seems a very reasonable request, wouldn't you agree, Private Becker?"

"Yes, Sir, wholeheartedly."

"I'm in full agreement with Wilhelm, it is important we mark the feast of Christmas and celebrate to the best of our ability, mindless bloodshed can wait for another day."

As a passive bystander, I'm struggling to keep my professional persona in check. These words are manna from heaven and I can't stop smiling. Sergeant Bevan has understandably perked up too.

"Thank you General Muller, it's most gracious of you."

"It is my pleasure, Sergeant Bevan. May you allow me to make one further suggestion?"

"Yes, by all means."

"Perhaps we can allow the men to celebrate together. Not in the trenches, of course, but maybe out here in the middle."

Sergeant Bevan smiles and nods, "That's a splendid idea."

General Muller turns to his army of men and with an historic wave of the arm beckons them forward. Within seconds, they are streaming on o the rugged plains of no-mans-land in droves of delirium. Instinctively, our men follow suit with equal verve, spilling out on mass at breakneck speed. To stand in the middle, watching these armies of once weary men tearing towards each other with such wild abandonment is the most joyous sight I've ever witnessed. Heavy legs, now charged with adrenalin and faces etched with childlike excitement, revel in this new found freedom. Men of a more senior standing are blazing across the clumpy terrain at speeds that belie their mature years. After months of confinement in the most miserable conditions, the shackles are well and truly off and it paints a glorious picture. For as long as I breathe gulps of God's glorious air, this cherished moment will reside deep within. Now, following the frenetic dash, we stand shoulder to shoulder, staring in to the eyes of our tormentors…armed with nothing more than a smile.

Hearty handshakes are exchanged the length of the line, as smaller groups form naturally to facilitate conversation. The language seems predominantly English with a fair few Germans seeming to have a good grasp of it. Some of the more well versed are acting as interpreter's, while others are getting by with hand gestures. There is bound to be a bit of a language barrier, we have some Geordies and the odd Glaswegian amongst our ranks, and I struggle to understand them at the best of times! Nevertheless, people are gleefully conversing, regardless of rank or uniform, no doubt grateful for the opportunity to shed their satchel's of hate and feel civilised. Wholly understandable, given it's such an ugly and cumbersome load to bear. Whilst others mingle, I find myself rooted to the same spot, bathed in the shadow of one of Wilhelm's infectious grins. It's impossible to feel anything else but happy and I gladly reciprocate. He does appear to be a thoroughly amiable young fellow and I'm curious to learn more about the man behind the beaming persona.

"Hello again, Wilhelm isn't it?" He nods and we shake hands again.

"Jack, if I'm not mistaken," he replies.

"That's correct, Sir, and may I say, you speak the King's English quite beautifully."

"Thank you, I picked up bits and pieces while at Law school in North London, Camden as I recall."

"Law school," I say raising my eyebrows, "Goodness gracious, that is impressive, do you still reside in London?"

"No, it was a place I very much enjoyed, especially all the pie and mash, but after qualifying I moved back to Lubeck to marry my sweetheart, Freya."

"Lubeck?"

"Yes, it's about fifty miles from Hamburg, very pretty, the kind of place that never leaves you. No matter how far I roam, it will always drag me back, it's where my heart lives." Upon speaking of his homeland with great fondness his eyes well up, he quickly rubs them, almost with a sense of embarrassment.

"It's ok, Wilhelm," I say, patting him on the shoulder, "being so far from loved ones, particularly today, it's the cruellest penance."

"It's tougher than I ever imagined, my heart, it hurts," he admits, sighs and smiles wryly, "but what can you do?"

I nod and grimace, feeling his pain and anguish. "Carry on I suppose, and pray for it all to end. It isn't quite the glorious adventure we were promised at the outset, is it?"

"No," replies Wilhelm solemnly, "not at all."

"Cheer up, old boy," I reply jovially. "Common sense must prevail at some point, then we can all return home safe and sound."

"Do you really believe that?"

"I have to Wilhelm, otherwise the day will never end."

He smiles, not his usual beaming expression, but I'll take it.

"Anyway, did you get to marry your sweetheart, Freya is it?"

Instantly his facial features illuminate and he nods. "I certainly did, on a gorgeous sun kissed day back in nineteen twelve. My Freya, she looked so beautiful. Seeing her walk down the aisle, I felt so nervous, but it was the best moment of my life."

"It sounds splendid, you're a lucky man."

"I am, very blessed indeed. I never thought we'd ever spend a night apart, but now nights have become months…and there's Anna, too."

"Anna?"

"Our daughter, she turned one only yesterday, the greatest Christmas present one could ever wish for." He reaches in to his tunic and pulls out a crumpled photo from the inside pocket. "This is Freya and Anna," he says proudly, passing me the well-worn photograph. "Anna's only a few weeks old in that picture, she's changed so much already."

It's a beautiful shot depicting a young woman, clearly revelling in the first flush of motherhood. Gazing at the photo, I begin to picture Rose lovingly cradling our first born, her soft eyes steeped in adoration, remain locked on the baby sleeping contently in her arms. Unexpectedly, the image whips up a frenzy of unbridled emotion, I can feel myself melting as my hand begins to shake.

"Are you ok, Jack?"

"Yes," I mumble, jolted by the sheer ferocity of the experience. Everything I have to look forward to and lose is represented in this photo. Pangs of hope, love, joy and despair violently manifest as I continue to stare at the simple portrait.

"Sorry, Wilhelm, it's a lovely picture" I say handing it back.

"Thank you, they're my world," he says proudly, whilst carefully restoring his prized possession to its rightful place, close to his heart. Once safely ensconced, he tenderly pats his tunic and smiles. I smile back, now that's real love. I do hope this fine young man makes it home to happily live the idyllic life he's carved out for himself, that little girl needs her daddy.

"How about you, Jack, is there someone special waiting back home?"

I nod and smile, reaching for my pocket as Wilhelm looks on in anticipation.

"This is my darling, Rose, the absolute love of my life," I proclaim, gushing with pride as I pass over a photo with great care.

This cherished 6 by 4 inch piece of paper provides the emotional sustenance to get me through each day. Snapped on a gorgeous summers day and capable of conjuring up a myriad of memories, the picture captures the majesty of the moment perfectly. Rose is sat on a bench with a boating lake in the distance. Wearing a white linen dress and straw hat, she giggles playfully in the midday heat, effortlessly beautiful and carefree. It was taken earlier this year on her birthday, what a difference a summer makes! Pork pies in the park, it felt like the sun would never stop shinning…

"What a beautiful girl, is this your wife?"

"It's hard to believe, but yes, she is indeed."

Wilhelm laughs. "You are also a very fortunate man I think!"

"I know, she's a diamond. Today would have been our first Christmas together as a married couple." I add ruefully. "This blasted war has stolen so much, time we'll never get back."

Wilhelm nods with a pained expression. "I'm sorry, my friend, but don't lose heart, hopefully this truce can lead to something remarkable, beginning of the end."

"I bloody hope so and not a moment too soon, I'm going to become a Dad next year!"

"Really?"

"I found out yesterday by letter, quite the shock, but magical nevertheless."

"Wow, congratulations Jack," he bellows, embracing me enthusiastically. "That is some Christmas present too."

"I'll say, but it's got me thinking."

"I'll bet, your head must be swirling."

"Not half, still taking it all in. What's it like Wilhelm, being a father?"

"Oh my friend, it's like nothing that's ever gone before."

"How do you mean?"

"It's the moments Jack, the beautiful moments. They change you and not just you, your life and how you look at the world." He smiles, "you'll never be the same again, I promise you."

"Crickey, it sounds incredible."

"Like you wouldn't believe, you have it all to come. The first time you cradle your baby and gaze into their eyes, I'm not ashamed to say, I crumbled. The realization this new tiny being is wholly dependent on you, it's scary, but exciting too. They're part of you forever, you'll never stop protecting and loving them. Never before had I felt so elated and terrified at the same time, but it's a beautiful journey so far, so, so beautiful. Anna brings us so much joy each day, from that first smile in the morning to kissing her goodnight. That's fatherhood my good friend, God's greatest blessing." His smile suddenly sours as a tinge of sadness flickers in his eyes.

"What's wrong, old boy?"

"Anna took her first steps a week ago, I should have been there to share that moment. I was so excited to find out, but when I stopped reading the letter I, well I, cried my eyes out," he says sheepishly. "Me, a grown man, I just couldn't stop myself."

"Hey, come on, that's nothing to feel embarrassed about. It's what makes you a jolly decent human being. I've shed more than my fair share of tears across Rose's correspondence, the letters are barely legible by the time I stop crying."

"Legible, what is that?"

"Oh, it means easy to read or make out. Honestly, ink running everywhere!"

Wilhelm laughs. "Good to know I'm not the only big softie around here."

I chuckle. "Not a word to the other men though, I have my tough guy image to think of."

"My lips are sealed, Jack."

"Good man."

Listening to Wilhelm, and in particular how passionately he talked about fatherhood, is a joy to hear. The pain he's enduring while being parted must be unbearable. Yet on first glance this morning, I'd had never guessed the magnitude of the cross he bears. His deep sorrow hides behind the most infectious grin, that's commendable. If I turn out to be half the father he is, I'll be delighted. What a fine fellow I've stumbled across, a fine fellow indeed. We met as enemies, but will part as friends, war provides precious little reliability, but this much I'm certain of.

The conversation has been thoroughly engrossing, as a result I've become somewhat oblivious to the goings on around me. As Wilhelm lights up a smoke, I take the opportunity to gaze across the bustling plains of no-man's-land. To my great delight, the fields of Flanders remain an idyllic scene of much merriment. This once baron land, radiated with the warmth of human spirit has burst into life, with activities ranging from the basic to the bizarre. The conversation remains lively and good willed with plenty of laughter being shared. There isn't a cross word to be had between two bands of downtrodden men flourishing in the face of friendship. Instant cameras are clicking, as smiling soldiers pose with arms around their foes and not a weapon in site. A small group of men hurtle past me chasing a wild hare that's running for its life. Like children enjoying the first flurry of snow, they're yelping with delight. A despairing dive finally seals the poor hares fate, igniting raucous cheers from the band of merry hunters. The captor, delighted with his efforts, proudly raises the squirming hare above his head like a prize trophy. Moments later, with the aid of a large rock, the terrified animal is put out of his misery. There's nothing like a spot of brutality to taint a once joyous moment, but I guess it's inevitable given how good it will taste later.

To my left one of our soldiers is sat on a chair while a German solider skilfully cuts his hair! One only has to observe how gracefully he manoeuvres his comb and scissors to realise he's a master of his craft. His artistry has grabbed the attention of others too, with a steady que forming, eager to benefit from his talent. In other areas there are clear signs of friendships forging as men exchange souvenirs in the form of cards, belt buckles and buttons cut from tunics. Addresses are being scribbled down, in the forlorn hope of facilitating post war rendezvous, as fragile promises are made with the best of intentions. Any thoughts about a life beyond this war belong in an indulgent world, but under a dark sun emitting its constant rays of death, it's a land troubled minds will occasionally inhabit. Nothing screams hope like making plans, however tenuous.

"Would you care for a cigarette Jack?" Asks Wilhelm politely with an outstretched arm.
Ah, worry sticks, a staple of the soldier's diet.

"Thank you," I reply, gratefully slipping one out of his shiny silver case. "Do you know, Wilhelm, I never used to touch these," I state while taking a big drag before exhaling slowly, instilling contentment and a fleeting feeling of calmness, its heaven in a heartbeat. I smile at Wilhem. "Now I'm hooked, it's breakfast, lunch and supper."

"I know what you mean," scoffs Wilhelm, "I smoke far more than I used to, but good for settling the old nerves."

"Quite," I reply, "they're crucial if one hopes to maintain their sanity."

"A godsend, and the whisky too," proclaims Wilhelm.

"Both necessary vices in a soldiers armoury and an effective way to control the masses."

Wilhelm looks puzzled. "How do you mean, Jack?"

"Well, if the cigarettes stop burning and the rivers of whisky run dry, never mind the war, those bastard generals will have a mutiny on their blood stained hands."

Wilhelm chuckles and nods, he takes a final drag of delight and casually tosses the butt upon the deathly ground. His expression turns more pensive.

"I wonder, what it must be like?"

"What's that, Wilhelm?"

“How it feels to make decisions, for which no consequences will be personally felt, but actions that will nevertheless send young men, decent men at that, to their untimely deaths.”

“Now, there’s a question. One can only imagine old boy, I guess it takes a certain type of character, thankfully that isn’t me. I don’t know how they sleep at night.”

“Comfortably,” adds Wilhelm ruefully.

“ I bet, but it can’t last.”

“What can’t?”

“Their carefree existences, the transgressions of man will always come back to haunt him, once the mind grows idle. With time to dwell, the demons will only get louder. Trust me Wilhelm, with the exception of an early death, there’s no escape. In a weird way, it’s quite comforting to know they’ll suffer.”

“Hmm, I’ve never thought of it like that, it’s the least they deserve.”

“I couldn’t agree more, absolute rotter’s, the lot of them. Perpetrators of cowardly deeds disguised as courageous acts.” I’m not quite sure how much of my eloquent vocabulary Wilhelm understands, but he nods along gainfully, God bless him.

“I joined up for service as soon as I could, Wilhelm, couldn’t wait to go and fight for the cause.”

“Me too, our nation made us feel like heroes. I wanted to play my part, but it all feels so hopeless now. My best friend, Gerhard, he died in my arms after only a few days in the trenches.”

“I am bitterly sorry, Wilhelm.”

“Holding his limp body as he exhaled his final breath, it makes you question everything. We were the same age, I’ve never known life without him. Some of my fresh faced comrades were still talking of medals and glory, but I’d just buried my best friend. All it took was an instant, a solitary snipers bullet and life changed forever." Wilhelm begins to weep, but stoutly continues. "He was a smashing lad, full of kindness and big dreams."

"Dreams?"

"Yes, he wanted to make a real difference, leave his mark on the world. He was training in medicine and dreamed of being a surgeon."

He pauses to wipe the tears from his eyes, I pass him my hankie, thankfully it's clean.

"Thank you, Jack. He really loved helping people," he adds with a smile "and detested violence, but he just wanted to help his country and serve with his mates. Now he lies under blood-stained soil, it's ever so sad and such a waste. I think about him every single day, his sweetheart and family, riddled with pain and with the absence of his body, unable to mourn properly."

I shake my head and put my arms round him. Sometimes words feel meaningless and just aren't enough, the tears need to flow.

Wilhelm's heart wrenching admission, so beset with tragedy, is a sorrowful epitaph that epitomizes war perfectly. Knowing the pain he's been through, that still besieges him, leaves me in awe and I have an abundance of admiration for him. I might moan about Frosty every now and then, but to lose him in those circumstances, it's more than I can bear to think of. To still face the world every day with a smile whilst harbouring the heaviest of hearts, my God, that takes some guts. He's one of the bravest and thoroughly decent fellows I've ever had the privilege to meet and remarkably, he bats for the other side! A few short hours ago, the very notion of forming a meaningful friendship under these circumstances would seem preposterous.

The sun is beginning to set on what has been the most astonishing Christmas day and regrettably our truce too. It's mid-afternoon, but not a solitary soul has vacated our spontaneous gathering. I'm conscious, however, that the impending darkness coupled with the lure of Christmas dinner will hasten an end to proceedings. I've exchanged details with Wilhelm and made tentative plans to meet up one fine day, but we both know the very notion is pie in the sky. If even one of us makes it home, we'll be bloody lucky. The real truth for me, or any solider of war for that matter, is all we have is the fretful moment, beyond that is God's domain. When I say goodbye to Wilhelm today, it will almost definitely be the last time I ever speak to him. That is the cruel reality seeping in to my mind as we continue to chat frankly. Tomorrow we will be firing bullets at each other as if today never existed, but to forget isn't that easy. The powers that be may succeed in forcing us to fight again, but they can't expunge our memories. Empathising with our foes, sharing laughter, that's real and it means something. We're not cold hearted killers, just ordinary blokes desperate for compassion and human kindness. Regardless of what the future brings, today matters and it will never be forgotten. The bastards may from time to time break our will, but not our bleeding hearts, often downtrodden, but defeated, not on today's evidence.

I'm just in the middle of explaining to Wilhelm the importance of deploying a straight bat and strong forward defensive stroke when I see an excitable Frosty bounding towards me.

"Cor blimey, are you two lovebirds still chatting away?" He quips with a grin.

"Wilhelm, please allow me to introduce to you my best friend, the legend that is Mr David Frost or Frosty to his friends."

"Good afternoon squire, pleasure to meet you."

"You too, David," replies Wilhelm, shaking his hand warmly.

"Please pal, call me Frosty. Jacko hasn't been boring you with his love of cricket?"

"Not at all Frosty, it's actually quite interesting," replies Wilhelm with a cheeky wink. Frosty's in stitches, I can't help but laugh too.

"What a day," he exclaims, "it's been bloody brilliant. Who'd have known these German blokes would be such a good laugh!"

"Who indeed," adds a smirking Wilhelm.

"I've had a blinding time and it's about to get even better," Frosty declares giddily.

"Whys that?" I ask curiously.

"Football me old mate, football."

I exchange puzzled glances with Wilhelm. "Football?"

"Yes, football."

"What about it?"

"It's Heinz, a guy I've been chatting to."

"Ok," I reply, none the wiser.

"He's gone off to get one."

"What?"

"A football."

"Oh, I see."

"We're going to have a game, England versus Germany."

"Are we?" I say nervously. "I may sit this one out mate."

"What, you're joking, this is going to be epic. Are you up for it Wilhelm?"

"I guess, it could be fun."

"That's the spirit, and relax, I know we invented the game, but I'll ask our chaps to go easy on you."

"Thanks Frosty, but that won't be necessary, we have some pretty decent players" he states confidently.

"Oh, that sounds like a challenge, come on Jacko, lets show them how it's done."

I'm sure Frosty senses my reluctance, but he's in no mood to take no for an answer. It's not that I don't like football, not at all, but I'm just not that good at it. I'm one of those people that has to work hard and practice incessantly to achieve any level of competency when it comes to sport. Frosty on the other hand is so naturally gifted, the jammy sod can turn his hand to anything. He was the captain of our school football team, a marauding midfielder with magic in his muddy boots. Observing him dribbling a football was frightfully captivating, like watching art. We won every cup under the sun under his stewardship, the guy was a God at our school. He never got in to cricket, barely played it at all, but one day due to our side being blighted by a bout of food poisoning, he played his one and only competitive match. A cup final, against St Bartholomew's, defending champions and the best team in the county. Frosty batted his way to a hundred with the minimum of fuss and then proceeded to rip through their top order, finishing with a seven wicket haul! *When it comes to sport, he's a freaking legend, not that I'm jealous, not a bit of it!*

Rows of men line the borders of the bumpy pitch, eagerly anticipating a battle royale. A handful of brave souls have dispensed with their tunics, which are now doubling as makeshift goalposts. Heinz strides out into the middle with the ball under his arm closely followed by the referee, Sergeant Bevan no less, flanked by a pair of German linesman. I jog onto the dishevelled playing surface in my heavy boots, either are hardly conducive to a high quality game of football, and take my place on the right side of defence. Frosty is in the middle shaking hands with his German counterpart and receiving some final instruction from Sergeant Bevan. I spot Wilhelm slotting in at centre forward, for now we're on opposing teams once more. The crowd are getting more boisterous as kick off approaches, causing the butterflies in my stomach to flutter violently. I've never experienced such an atmosphere before, more carnival like than hostile, but deafening nevertheless. Frosty turns round and claps his hands loudly, he's fired up and chomping at the bit.

"Come on chaps, let's do this for England," he bellows, "let's have it!" That seems to rile the crowd up even more, then the whistle blows and…carnage.

I don't know the exact number of people on the pitch, but it was more than the regulation 22 players. Who cares, I find myself swept up in a whirlwind of chaos and it's glorious. Adrenaline fuelled men in heavy overcoats are defying logic, giving the game a frantic pace. There's no real order to proceedings, men are chasing the ball in packs and tackles are flying in. Bodies are tumbling all over the place, consequently Sergeant Bevan's whistle is going ten to the dozen in a gainful attempt to keep order. The game has afforded us the opportunity to release months of pent up energy and all over the pitch players are unleashing their inner competitive beast. It's giving the exchanges added spice, but determined faces are peppered with the widest smiles.

My body has relinquished all its niggling aches and pains, I've never run so fast or far in years, its invigorating. My mind, too, has succumbed, floating in a blissful state of frenetic freedom, awash with only sensations of sheer joy. I've forgotten how good it feels, to exist in a moment filled with pure happiness, free from the worries of war that blight my fatigued mind mercilessly. The unforgivingly rugged turf feels like a carpet beneath my feet and my big heavy boots like ballet shoes. It's the most beautiful intoxification imaginable, I've transcended the pinnacle of pleasure and haven't even touched the ball yet!

Frosty loves to sparkle in the spotlight, whereas I prefer to skulk in the shadows whilst quietly going about my business. To that end, playing in defence suits me perfectly. Let the strikers and attacking midfielders grab all the glory, allowing me to fade into the scenery on the back of a workmanlike performance. Don't get me wrong, who doesn't want to shine once in a while, but a man has to know his limitations. I'll get my moment in the sunshine, but it's unlikely to occur in a sporting arena. Nevertheless this day has been anything but predictable, so who knows?

My first opportunity to dazzle comes courtesy of a rapid German counter attack. *Bloody hell, there's three of them charging towards the area and they're getting bigger!* My fellow comrade has failed to cut off the cross, leaving me one on one with a surging Wilhelm. Our goal is dangerously exposed, so I make one last desperate lunge for salvation, but I'm late and poor Wilhelm tumbles to the ground, his legs swept from under him. Sergeant Bevan has no hesitation in pointing to the spot. Frosty protests, more out of hope than anything, but Sergeant Bevan's having none of it and rightfully waves him away. Wilhelm places the ball on the spot and the crowd fall silent. My teammates are graciously consoling me, but all is not lost. Between the sticks, well tunics, stands the imposing figure of Lionheart, he's so huge, there's barely any of the goal visible. Good luck, Wilhelm in threading the ball past that man mountain. The whistle blows and Wilhelm begins his run up, Lionheart is poised as the crowd watch on. It's a good penalty, struck well towards the right hand corner, but the big guy is equal to it and parry's the ball away. British cheers ring out, but the ball is loose and Wilhelm is the first to react, slotting it neatly past a despairing Lionheart. It's now German cheers drowning out British groans as the players celebrate. Despite a sprinkling of Frosty magic, in the form of a mazy run down the right wing, the Germans get to half time with their lead intact. Time for some words of encouragement from our skipper.

"Right lads, we're in a bit of a pickle here" admits Frosty. "These chaps can play a bit."
Hmm, not the most inspiring words I've ever heard, but an honest assessment.

"We're only one goal down men, so don't let your heads drop. It just takes one special moment and we're right back in this. We need to look after the ball and utilise the flanks to get in behind their defence. This is our time gentlemen, so muster up every last bit of effort and give everything to win this thing for England. We can do this boys, we can bloody well do this!"

Frosty's impassioned plea proves the perfect tonic, it even has a sceptic like me believing.

"You heard the man," roars Lionheart, "let's get out there and give them hell."

Walking back on to the pitch, I feel ten feet tall, like a gladiator. My mind is contemplating glory, it's an unusual sensation, not unpleasant and extremely powerful. This is it, my time to triumph, I've glimpsed the gold and now I want to touch it. The second half starts well and we're dominating possession, it's virtually a masterclass, but with scant reward for our efforts. I'm playing with an abundance of confidence, showing real poise and purpose, timing my tackles perfectly, every pass hit with freakish accuracy. *This must be what it feels like to be Frosty, invincible, the lucky bugger!* Finally, an opportunity presents itself, Frosty's guile and endeavour has earned us a free kick on the edge of the Germans box and the main man himself stands over the ball, primed to take it. What can our midfield maestro conjure up from his legendary box of tricks? The Germans assemble a fearsome wall, of God knows how many men, tall, wide, practically impenetrable. Frosty takes a few paces back and puffs out his cheeks, England expects… and by jove, does he deliver. It's the sweetest strike I've ever witnessed, over the wall and past the motionless keeper in a heartbeat. Frosty's brilliance momentarily stuns the crowd into silence before bedlam ensues. Everybody piles on the scorer, Lionheart included, as raucous joy spills over. With only fifteen minutes to go the next goal will surely prove decisive.

The initiative has shifted, we now have something to lose and subsequently we're playing with fear. The confidence and swagger I previously revelled in has deserted me, and so it seems has our luck. A speculative German shot takes a nasty deflection, leaving Lionheart stranded. It's cruel, but that's sport and there's precious little time to bemoan our bad fortune. There is still a handful of minutes to salvage a well deserved draw and we're on the attack with yours truly! In my far from illustrious football career, daring forays into the oppositions half have been as rare as Easter snow, but this is no time for shrinking violets, England's pride is at stake. Spurred on by breaking a few sliding tackles, I'm making good progress down the right wing, I look up, Frosty is galloping into the area. This is it, my defining moment, a chance to create something memorable and etch my name in wartime folklore. I'm close to the byline and running at a fair lick, a split second to find the perfect cross. I manage to hook my foot around the revolving ball, sending it floating across the German area. Boots or no boots, I've never hit a ball so well and the defenders are scrambling. As it flies through the thick winter air I realise my job is over, I've done all that I can do and all that you can do is enough. The ball is hanging for what feels like an eternity and Frosty is surrounded by a gauntlet of German players, but this is no ordinary man, this is Davy Frost, a silver tonged, silky skilled lovable rouge with a penchant for winning. Emerging from a glut of defenders, he rises magnificently, to head the ball powerfully in to the gaping goal. He immediately swivels, points to me and claps in recognition of my efforts, it's all the glory I'll ever need. The roars ring out for England, but before I can celebrate with my mate they're replaced by gasps of exasperation. Instinctively, I turn to the linesman and bugger, he's ruled it out, bloody offside! In the face of staunch complaints, Sergeant Bevan blows the final whistle and Germany win a hard fought contest. Consigned to history, that will always be the goal that never was and I'm sure people will pontificate long in to the night, but goal or no goal, I lived my moment.

"I timed that run perfectly mate, I swear."

I smile and shrug my shoulders. "Relax mate, we played a great game out there."

"Didn't we, that cross Jacko, it was a thing of beauty."

"I'll never stroke another one that sweetly as long as I live."

"Isn't that the truth, bloody German officials!"

We both break out in fits of laughter.

Barring the odd gripe, the result is quickly forgotten with the Germans proving themselves magnanimous victors and ourselves dignified in defeat. I'm sure in time the record books will be filled with tales of many more technically skilful matches, but few will be more significant than the kick about we enjoyed on the day Christmas came to Flanders Fields. Losing to this fine bunch of men on the football field is better than beating them on the battlefield.

Darkness has descended with an air of inevitability. Amidst a flurry of fond farewells, the crowd is thinning out quite visibly. With a foreboding sense of sadness, there are hugs, handshakes and more than the odd tear being shed. Some give a final wave, while others can't bear to look back as they troop off to enjoy Christmas dinner. With the Boxing day blues looming large, it's a tasty treat tinged with sadness. I've been back to the trench to fetch my special cognac and a couple of glasses, now I need to find Wilhelm so I can bid him farewell and good luck. I'm getting worried, I haven't seen him since the game finished. My eyes are squinting in the darkness as I scan the area, I should have bought a torch back too. *Where the bloody hell are you Wilhelm Becker?* Suddenly, behind me, a familiar voice breaks out of the shadows.

"Hey, Jack, I do hope one of those glasses is for me."

I swing round to Wilhelm standing there, sporting one of his signature grins. I'm sure going to miss those.

"Good evening, Wilhelm, well yes, of course."

I place the glasses on the ground, crouch down and pour out two generous measures.

"It's cognac, I do hope that's ok," I say, passing him a glass.

"Perfect, thank you."

"To your continued good health and happiness, Wilhelm"

"To yours too, Jack, and friendship."

"Yes, friendship, I'll drink to that."

We clink glasses before both indulging in a healthy swig. I can feel the warmth spreading a cross my chest, it feels good.

"Apologies, for the rash tackle, Wilhelm, you were too darn quick for me."

"No worries, Jack, is was quite a match and harsh on you chaps at the end."

"Maybe, but you're worthy winners."

"I suppose," he replies graciously, "but you played an outstanding game. Has Frosty got over it yet? He's quite the character and one heck of a footballer. The way he struck that free kick was something else."

"Wasn't it just. He's slowly coming to terms with the result, I don't think he's use to losing. No doubt we'll dissect things over supper."

"Take care of him, Jack, he's a special guy."

"I know, I will, with all my muster. I'm fortunate to count him as a friend, my best friend." Wilhelm nods, appreciating the sentiment more than most.

"Well, Wilhelm, it's been the most terrific day and a real pleasure to meet you. I mean that most sincerely, you're a fine young man."

"It has, it really has, an extraordinary day and I've enjoyed meeting you too, Jack." He sighs deeply and takes another large gulp, now appearing a touch downcast. "Tomorrow, Jack."

"Tomorrow?"

"What do we do tomorrow? Wake up and start firing rounds off as if none of this even happened, as if today never existed? Just act like the events of today no longer matter, it's not right Jack, today matters, it bloody well matters. I don't want to fight anymore, I won't do it. Things have changed, it's so very different now."

The poor bloke is becoming increasingly agitated with every sip, but sadly I can't offer any crumbs of comfort.

"I know, Wilhelm, I understand, but I fear we will have no choice. The Generals will not allow this situation to continue."

"What can they do if we all refuse to fight?"

"They'll start shooting us, new recruits arrive every week. The truth is we're replaceable, our very lives are expendable."

"So, they'll shoot all of us if we down tools en mass."

"They won't have to my friend, a handful of shootings will be enough for the rest to fall back in line. Those executed will be labelled as cowards and buried dishonourably in mass graves, unmarked I expect. With reputations soiled, remembered for nothing more than bringing shame on their families, their country. Be it in life or death, the bastards have got us."

Wilhelm looks mortified, bowing his shaking head in sombre acceptance. "Cowards," he murmurs, "they'll call us cowards?"

"I'm afraid so, old boy."

"I can't do it Jack, there's no fight left in me, I've nothing left to give."

"Now, listen here," I say abruptly, my harsher tone startles a sobbing Wilhelm.

"You must pick up a weapon again, stand a post and carry on. For Freya, for baby Anna, it's your only hope of making it back to them. You'll have to sacrifice your soul, endure a living hell, we all will, but what matters is getting home and piecing your life back together. The life you love so dearly."

I feel bad for dishing out a portion of tough love, but he needs to hear it.

"I'm sorry, for raising my voice, Wilhelm, but I need to know that you will continue and give yourself a fighting chance. The thought of even picking up a rifle tomorrow makes me feel sick to my stomach, let alone squeezing the trigger. To treat special friends like my coldest enemies, well it goes against every moral fibre woven in to the heart of a decent human being. The most heinous of actions, but it is the desperate reality that engulfs us, in part, created by today. Nothing can ever be the same, we made it personal."

"You're right, Jack, of course you are. I'll continue, somehow through the numbness I'll continue."

I reach over and pat him firmly on the back. "Good man."

I pour out another scrumptious serving of cognac for Wilhelm. I planned to keep some for supper, but his need seems greater than mine, the scars run deeper. To watch his twisted and tortured mind unravel, it's heartbreaking, if I could bear some of the pain for him, I would, gladly, but suffering doesn't work that way. Thank God for alcohol, at least I can offer that and a kind ear. Under a growing realisation that this really is it, our final exchange, the conversation is drying up, overtaken by the sheer magnitude of the moment. We're left with long periods of silence punctuated by the odd word while the bitter night air bears its teeth.

"So, when this is all over?"

"Yes Wilhelm."

"You will bring your family to Lubeck?"

"Of course I will my friend, we'll have a grand old time," I say firmly, and I really mean it.

It's a crazy dream with precious little chance of coming to fruition, but its our dream and I'll be dammed to relinquish it while there's breath in my body.

He smiles, it's the first one in a while. "We will indeed."

I smile back and nod purposely. Maybe this is the perfect time to depart, on a positive note, but neither of us appear willing to pull the curtain down on a friendship that blossomed and lived, but for a day. We're both shivering though, the cognac has ran dry and my stomach rumbles for roast turkey!

"This is it, isn't it?" Asks Wilhelm.

"I'm afraid so." I confirm regretfully.

We both stare at each other, how do you condense the events of today, the time we've shared, in to a closing sentence? We can't just start blubbing like a pair of girls blouses, time to wheel out the famous British stiff upper lip. I'm one hug from crumbling so opt to reach out and shake his hand firmly.

"Wilhelm, old friend, you're a fine young man and by the grace of God I wish you safe passage, back to the arms of Freya and your beautiful daughter, Anna."

Wilhelms eyes moisten.

"May God speed you, my dear pal, Jack Crosby. You have a big heart and you're going to be a wonderful father. Go and live out your dreams with the lovely Rose and your new baby. Can I ask one thing of you Jack?"

"Anything, my good friend."

"If it's a boy, will you call it Wilhelm?"

We both burst in to fits of laughter, what a guy.

"I will consider it, for sure."

"Farewell, my friend."

"Goodbye, old boy."

With a nod of recognition, we both turn and head for our respective trenches. I can hear his footsteps growing ever fainter, but I daren't look back, I'm not strong enough. Under the weight of an avalanche of emotion, tears stream down my face. I wipe them away, but the salty little buggers keep coming. Maybe it would have been easier if today had never happened at all, easier to carry on waging war against a faceless enemy, but I can never wish this wondrous day out of existence. In the cold hard face of brutal adversity, it has been a triumph for the human spirit and everything mankind holds dear. Tomorrow, with the deepest sense of regret, I'll discharge my rifle and pray to God Wilhelm isn't the unlucky recipient. The thought of him dying at my hands, it's more than my fragile heart can take. *When will these blasted tears stop, oh Jack Crosby, pull yourself together, you big girls blouse!*

The Show Must Go On

'It is terrible to think that on one day we can be at such peace, with such good feeling, and on the others we must occupy our minds inventing diabolical methods of destroying one another.'

Officer, Highland Regiment.

Boxing day at Rose's parents is always a lively occasion with an open house policy being adopted. Friends, neighbours and family descend from far and wide to enjoy the ample hospitality on offer. Rose's mother puts on the most incredible spread complete with homemade trifle, the only one I've eaten containing sliced bananas indulgently sat on a thick bed of custard, *simply delicious*, and my own personal favourite, roast turkey sandwiches. These Christmas leftovers are a real treat, combining sliced turkey with sage and onion stuffing and cranberry sauce. One bite takes me right back to my childhood, I'm quite literally nibbling on nostalgia.

My fiancée looks beautiful in a figure hugging sparkly black dress. My fiancée, I still can't believe that she is betrothed to me. She's busy playing the perfect party host, as she welcomes guests, hanging up coats and topping up drinks, always with a smile and kind word. Music is playing, people are dancing, the house is alive with happiness. I grab Rose for a quick cuddle and to snag a piece of cheese from her serving plate. *Oh my days, that tastes divine, I'd quite literally sell my soul for a mouthful of mature cheddar!* Later I'll get to lay my lips on hers and lose myself once more, the mere thought is irresistible. Until the beautiful manifestation of that exquisite moment, I'll fill the surmountable void with turkey and trifle! *Goodness gracious, these sandwiches are running a little low...*

I open my heavy eyes to find Boxing day morning bathed in a glorious shower of silence, other than the larks chirping merrily in the winter sunshine. It was gone 6 this morning when I finally nodded off, with the remarkable events of yesterday still churning over in my mind. It scarcely seems believable, the most decadent of dreams. I'd ask Frosty to pinch me if he wasn't snoring his head off. In a few short hours we'll commence our first shift of sentry duty, just like any other day in the trenches. But it isn't, the thought of it alone is making me wretch. Yesterday seems half the world away, we traded jokes, well wishes and addresses, the currency of human kindness. Today, like savages, we'll deal only in bombs and bullets. May God bestow mercy and peace upon us, or at the very least forgive our transgressions. Suddenly, the silence is rudely disturbed by the screeching of car tyres. There's only one person that arrives at the trenches by that mode of transport and only on very rare occasions, General Arthur Hughes. For our special truce and far-flung hopes, it signals the beginning of the end.

A visit, from a 4 star General, to the front line is never a good thing, only a Field Marshall ranks higher. They mostly concern themselves with strategic planning, covert suicide missions being a particular speciality. Word of the infamous truce have probably permeated through the entire Western Front, before reaching the golden gates of his swanky chateau. I can picture the hierarchy last night enduring silver service with steam pouring out of their ears, I do hope news of our impromptu, yet considered despicable actions, swapping killing for kindness, didn't spoil their Christmas feast. I wouldn't imagine he's cutting short his celebrations to deliver Christmas cards. We've had our festivities, now comes the fury.

I spot an imposing figure marching briskly through the trench, flanked by his two trusted Lieutenants, no doubt on route to Sergeant Bevan's dugout. Unfortunately, my instincts are correct, it is the aforementioned General Hughes, he has a face like thunder. Tough men cower as he passes for fear of incurring his wrath. I wouldn't wish to be in Sergeant Bevan's soon-to-be quaking boots right now, the poor sod. Judging by his stony demeanour, General Hughes possesses a lust for vengeance.

"Good morning, Sergeant Bevan," he screams at the top of his lungs, his echoing voice sends a flurry of fear reverberating through the trench. The startled officer leaps to attention, heart in mouth.

"Good morning, General Hughes," he says, stuttering with fright. "How are you today, Sir?"

"Sit down, Sergeant," he shouts in a menacing tone that conveys he's in no mood to exchange pleasantries.

"Yes, Sir."

"Call me General, God damn it" he barks, "you insolent man!"

"Of course, my sincere apologies, General Hughes, how can I help today?" Ashen faced, his voice now trembles, much to the perverse delight of his superior officer. His lieutenants stand either side, bolt upright, expressionless with eyes staring forward. One man holds court in this theatre of screams, gleefully seizing the opportunity to exude his authority and remind the little man who calls the shots. Sergeant Bevan knows exactly what this performance is about, but to his great credit, however scared, he's determined not to wilt and give the irate bastard the satisfaction.

"There have been rumours, Sergeant Bevan."

"Rumours General?"

General Hughes's contorted face reddens, he thrusts it to within inches of Sergeant Bevans, but remarkably, under fire, he maintains an air of calm defiance, shredded nerves made of steel. Expecting capitulation, General Hughes pauses, not breaking eye contact for a beat. If he wasn't so pissed off, he'd probably admire this cool display of indignance, but the tightly coiled tyrant is seething.

"Do I stutter, Sergeant?" His voice softens, adding an additional layer of menace.

"No, General."

"Rumours, Sergeant, dark ugly rumours."

"What are the nature of these rumours, General?" Sergeant Bevan retorts.

"Don't play dumb with me, Sergeant, and I'll thank you to be mindful of your tone when addressing a superior officer."

"My deepest apologies, General Hughes."

"These rumours pertain to actions committed under your watch, actions of the most repugnant nature. "Sergeant Bevan stays silent, not a solitary flicker, his resolve steadfast. Caught in a spiral of impending doom, he must be terrified, but outwardly, there's ice in his veins.

"I am referring to acts of cowardice," he slams his fist down on Sergeant Bevan's desk, even the Lieutenants flinch! "Acts of treason committed against King and country," he slams his fist down once more with increased vigour.

"Cowardice, Sir, treason? I can assure me that my men are…"

"Don't insult my intelligence, Sergeant Bevan," he interrupts. "How dare you possess the gall and arrogance to lie to my face. I have it on good authority that you and your men were wilfully engaged in the act of fraternisation. What do you have to say for yourself, Sergeant Bevan?"

Painfully aware the game is up, the harassed officer ponders his reply carefully. He is an intelligent man, possessing cunning and guile in abundance, but even with his impressive arsenal of attributes, this is one hole too deep and dark to dig himself out of. Unequivocal denial will only serve to add more fuel to the General's raging fire, almost certainly earning himself an immediate bullet between the eyes. On the flip side he can hold his hands up, fall to his knees and beg for clemency, but this is a proud man, and a courageous one at that.

"Well, Sergeant? I demand an answer this instant."

"How was your Christmas day General? The commanding officer looks bemused. "Comfortable, one imagines."

"I beg your pardon, Sergeant."

"A roaring fire crackling away no doubt, and one would expect, a bounty of luxurious food and drink." General Hughes's face turns crimson, he's seething, but Sergeant Bevan, showcasing some big potatoes, continues unabated.

"Hearty portions of fine fayre washed down with chilled champagne. Who knew the trappings of war could be coated with such splendour?" He steps closer to the General and looks him squarely in the eye, there is no retort. Embarrassed by the curt depiction of his overindulgence, he momentarily gazes at the floor. Sensing an unexpected chink in his armour, Sergeant Bevan bravely presses on.

"My men and I woke up on Christmas day to the ungodly stench of dead friends and comrades rotting in the deathly bowels of no-mans-land. Freezing cold, miserable and miles away from loved ones, that is the Christmas we faced. Is it any wonder we…" Suddenly aware of the implications of his actions, he pauses.

"Any wonder what? Please continue, Sergeant."

"Is it any wonder that we lacked the necessary desire to fight?"

"So you admit it Sergeant, you were unwilling to fight? This was a clear refusal to fight for King and country."

"No, General," he replies firmly, "absolutely not. None of my men refused to fight yesterday, nor would they ever."

"I see, so no instruction or direction to engage in combat was forthcoming from yourself, is that what you are telling me?"

"It wasn't like that, the occasion overtook proceedings. The appetite to fight diminished on both sides through Christmas Eve, and as a result, the guns fell silent. It wasn't planned, I can assure you, it's how things transpired."

"So Christmas is to blame, is that what you're telling me?"

"It's difficult to explain, but yes, I suppose so."

"I've never heard anything so ridiculous, Sergeant."

"With the greatest respect, General Hughes, you weren't there. It all happened spontaneously, the German's started singing and we responded in kind."

"Singing! Sergeant, this is a bloody war for Christ sake, not a carol service!"

"Oh yes, I'm well aware of that, General, little things do remind me. "

"I won't warn you again, exercise caution with your tone, Sergeant. Now tell me, which side initiated the fraternisation? Who arranged the party in the middle of no-man's-land that you and your men wilfully participated in?"

"Well, General, a formal truce was arranged on Christmas morning."

"Now we're getting to it, between who?"

"Myself and General Muller met in the middle and agreed a short truce in order to afford us the opportunity to give our men a proper burial. You know, the rotting corpses strewn across no-mans-land. I'm sure you must understand how important that is to the men."

"I see, casualties are an unfortunate tragedy, but inevitable in war. This does not give you an excuse to have cosy chats with the enemy. I have it on the highest authority that mass gatherings occurred, going on long into the night. The instigators must be brought to justice."

Sergeant Bevan laughs. "Justice, war affords no justice, Sir, only injustice," he scoffs, "decent young men brimming with potential, shipped into the depths of hell, and for what, General? Enduring the most frightful misery in squalid conditions day upon day, all to spend their last desperate moments dying alone in agony. What has all this bloodshed achieved, neither side has advanced more than a square meter in months. Honour, duty, however you dress it up, it's the most despicable and shameless business."

General Muller bows his head.

"So yes, I'm guilty of arranging a truce to allow our men and theirs to be buried with a semblance of dignity, and I'm not sorry, General Muller, nor will I apologise."

"I understand Sergeant, but this was not the end of it. Burying our men is one thing, but engaging in conversation with the enemy, playing football together, taking photos, these traitorous actions cannot be tolerated under any circumstances. The main perpetrators must be severely punished to serve as a lesson to the other men. This isn't how wars are conducted, Sergeant Bevan, not under my watch."

Sergeant Bevan stares coldly at the General, his rage calmy teetering on a treacherous precipice. "I don't believe we received the guidebook, General."

"Don't get smart, Sergeant, I'm in no mood for your cocky insolence."

"You have the sheer audacity to breeze in here after spending Christmas in the lap of luxury and call us traitors, you bastard!"

Enraged, General Hughes leaps to his feet, only to be forcefully pushed back on to his chair.

"I haven't finished speaking, General Hughes," he says firmly.

The lieutenant's, who have remained stoney faced up until this point exchange shocked glances, as the General looks on, dumbfounded.

"You talk of treason and dishonour, but have no clue as to what it is really like to fight a bloody war from the trenches, but those poor German chaps across the way, they know only too well."

"They are the enemy!" Shouts the General.

"Maybe, but they shed the same red blood, cry the same salty tears and suffer the same broken hearts. They're just like our chaps, innocent young men for Christ's sake, fresh faced and naive. Then, is it any wonder our desperate souls crave the same state of serenity, on Christmas of all days, when the spectre of sacrifice looms ever so menacingly within our disturbed minds? Our only crime is in fulfilling a desire to experience, but for a day, how it feels to be human and decent. Yes General, we chatted with the German fellows, asked them about their families, hopes and dreams, their very lives. We laughed, we joked and yes, even played football together, and you know what?"

"What, Sergeant?"

"It felt bloody marvellous, to exist in a fleeting fragment of time unscathed by the imminent threat of death, thoroughly liberating. For the briefest of golden moments, yesterday I forgot I was at war, that I was standing in a blood soaked field, far from those I love so dear. Amongst so called enemies, vast swathes of human kindness softened hardened hearts, who are you to deny us that, to label us as despicable traitors? My fretful mind is plagued with regrets General," he says sternly. "I give orders that send young men to premature deaths, but yesterday, I'll never feel or display a shred of remorse over the events that transpired. If that makes me a traitor, General, then so be it, do your worse, but for my life, there's precious little left to take."

"And your men?"

"What of them?"

"They are of this opinion too, proud of their actions?"

"Now, listen hear, General Hughes, their participation was solely down to me, I'm the instigator and I'll take what ever punishment you deem fit to dish out. I waved them on to the battlefield, all they're guilty of is following my command. They should not pay for my misguidance and abuse of power."

"Your loyalty to the battalion is commendable, but they freely engaged in the act of fraternisation." Sergeant Bevan looks crestfallen, impassioned pleas to absolve his men of blame are falling on deaf ears. "I gave them no choice, General, and take full responsibility for my actions. Make an example of me, if you must, but please I beg of you, leave my men alone, they've suffered enough."

Deriving pleasure from Sergeant Bevans desperation, General Hughes smiles, he really is a sadistic bastard. It's the final straw for the exasperated

Sergeant, something snaps. He moves close to the General and thrusts his scarlet face forward, their noses are almost touching, neither man flinches.

"Step back, Sergeant," screams the General. He draws his regulation revolver and thrusts it under Sergeant Bevans chin, the tension is palpable.

"Go ahead, you'll be doing me a favour, go on, put me out of my misery. Come on, you coward, what are you waiting for? Squeeze the trigger and be done with it."

The General's hand is trembling as he stares in to the whites of Sergeant Bevan's eyes, they're cold, filled with intensity and devoid of fear.

"Kill me, General, I deserve it, kill me now."

"Don't tempt me, Sergeant, I'll do it."

"Come on then," he goads, "set me free from this Godforsaken war."

"Do you really want to die, Sergeant, is that what you really want, a bullet through the brain?"

Sergeant Bevan nods his head defiantly, all respect for authority and lust for life has ebbed away leaving a new found willingness to die, diminishing the General's once considerable power. A reluctance to shoot ensues the continuation of this fraught standoff, with neither man willing to tear themselves away.

"Shoot me, please, General Hughes and exhibit my lifeless corpse in front of the men, this will restore order and give you back the control you desire," pleads the Sergeant.

"I'm not sure you deserve the luxury of such an easy way out."

"Please, General, discharge your weapon and set me free. You have to do it, I'm a traitor. I've dishonoured the King. Take my life and lay me to rest in the fields of Flanders, with my brave men, those who have fallen."

"Enough, Sergeant," screams the General, returning his revolver to its holster, "there will be no further punishment, let that be an end to it."

Sergeant Bevan slumps back in to his chair, broken, his head cradled face down in his hands. He begins to sob, in a rare display of compassion General Hughes pats him on the back, pours out a few brandies and grants him a moment. He may enjoy ample more finery than the frontline has to offer, but he's not immune to the heat from above, more of a bishop or rook, but still embroiled in the same barbarous game.

"There you go, Sergeant, get that down your neck."

He looks up to see the glass glinting ever so invitingly and regains modicum of composure.

"Thank you, General Hughes, and I'm, erm I'm…"

"There is really no need, Mike," he says, his tone now considerably softer. "I can only imagine the strain you chaps are under and the misery you've all endured, witnessing death on a daily basis, it's no way to live, so I do understand, but.." He pauses to facilitate careful contemplation. "Look, this is strictly off the record and I'll deny these words till my dying breath."

"Yes, General."

"I do understand your actions, how can you not crave respite from the torment of war? Particularly at Christmas, but officially I can not be seen to condone those very actions."

"I understand, Sir."

"I know how it must look, we seem an eternity away from the blood and bullets, living a privileged existence. Your indignation is warranted and wholly understandable, but let me assure you, Sergeant, insomnia plagues me incessantly. To oversee the tragic demise of so many brave young men, it's a burden that's impossible to bear."

Sergeant Bevan nods.

"The tragic loss of life is horrific, and like you, I want a swift and conclusive end to all this bloodshed, but I do believe the cause is noble. If we allow the Germans to sweep through Belgium and then France, the very shores and country we love will be under attack. We must offer staunch defence, until in time a peace treaty can be agreed."

"Let's hope it's sooner rather than later, General."

"I'll drink to that, Sergeant, and the continued good health of you and your men."

"Thank you, General, and to you, too." Smiles are exchanged to conclude an unexpectedly cordial exchange, humanity knows no hierarchy. After a few minutes of quiet sipping, the General places is empty glass on the table and lets out a sigh.

"Sergeant Bevan."

"Yes, General."

"Christmas has now passed, and regrettably the chilling winds of reality loom menacingly in the shadows. The German offensive will not relent, and neither can we. However ugly and unwelcome, war will have it's way and we must be ready for it. Do you understand, Sergeant Bevan?"

"Yes, General Hughes, I understand, it's business as usual."

"I need to know that you're up to the task, Sergeant, and stand ready to lead the men. Any friendships forged must be forgotten, it's back to basics, kill or be killed."

"Yes, Sir, I'm ready. You can count on me."

"Good man, good man."

"Upon your departure I'll gather the men together and restore some focus in readiness for battle."

"Excellent, Sergeant, I'll inform the Field Marshall that operations will commence forthwith."

Sergeant Bevan nods with more than a hint of resignation.

The sound, once more, of screeching tyres informs us that the General has delivered his message, leaving behind a wave of overriding dejection that quickly washes through the camp. Forlorn hopes of a peaceful passage into the New Year have almost certainly been scuppered, leaving poor old Sergeant Bevan to deliver a prophecy of doom.

"Good morning, men. I've just had a meeting with General Hughes where the events of yesterday were discussed at considerable length. It's safe to say that top brass are not best pleased with reports emanating from the front, that we wilfully engaged in fraternisation, but thankfully nobody will face punishment. God only knows we've been punished enough. However, General Hughes has reiterated that the war must recommence today."

There are audible groans and sighs while others just simply bow their heads, but the feeling of utter despair and disappointment is felt by all. After a magnificent day feasting on freedom, we must once more sample the twisted taste of battle against the same people we gleefully mingled with hours earlier. One imagines they're now stood in muddy trenches being fed the same gruesome instruction.

"Yesterday, men, well, it's something we'll carry in our hearts forever and I wouldn't dare stand in front of you today and demean it in any shape or form. By all means, cherish the memories, I know I will, but please understand that a memory is all it can ever be now, however beautiful. We met some bloody nice blokes yesterday, salt of the earth characters, but those friendships must be forgotten if we're going to successfully carry out our mission. In the absence of peace, we must persevere and be relentless in our quest for victory. Men, I understand the gravity of the task we must undertake, especially with yesterday's events still fresh in our minds, but make no mistake, there will be no let up from our German counterparts or mercy shown. At precisely twelve hundred hours battle will recommence, please take care of each other and may God be with us all."

We start to disperse, just over an hour to slip back in to the mind frame of a monster.

"One final thing, gentleman, before you go. I was mightily proud of each and everyone of you yesterday, the way you all conducted yourself was first rate. You're a credit to yourselves, your families, the regiment and the country you serve so tirelessly. Thank you, gentleman. Private Crosby, can you please come with me."

One final leisurely stroll into the beating heart of no-mans-land to relay the grim, but inevitable news that hostilities must recommence. My legs feel so terribly heavy, but that's nothing compared to the weight of my sorrowful heart. It's the same four figures who stop in the middle and share a round of customary handshakes. Wilhelm greets me with a friendly nod, but the trademark grin is conspicuous by its absence. *The poor bloke is even struggling to make eye contact, I do hope he's alright.*

"Good morning, General Muller."

"Good morning, Sergeant Bevan."

There is an uneasy silence enveloping the growing acceptance that this will be the last time we'll ever talk together. It's only a day since our first meeting, but so much history has been etched into the crumbling walls of my mind, it feels like a lifetime ago. Friendships forged in adversity leave an indelible imprint, whether it lasts a day, a year, it doesn't matter, they're eternal. I'll find a way to carry on, but not forget.

"Well, Sergeant Bevan, I believe this is the last waltz."

"I fear so, General Muller, my bosses are very pissed off."

The General laughs. "I can imagine, I've had a few stern words to contend with myself."

"Quite. I assume, General, that your superiors are as keen as ours for hostilities to recommence."

"Keen as mustard, as you Englanders might say."

Sergeant Bevan allows himself a chuckle. "Yes, very good, does twelve o clock suit you, General?"

"It's as good a time as any, I suppose."

"Ok, my men will fire three shots in the air at midday to signify, regrettably that we are once more at war."

"Thank you, Sergeant, we will return three air shots to confirm our understanding."

"Splendid, General Muller, and thank you."

"What for?"

"Yesterday, thank you for yesterday. The participation of you and your men made for a fine day all round, it really was something to behold."

General Muller smiles. "It was quite the party, wasn't it, your men too should be commended for their behaviour."

"It certainly was my friend, a splendid time indeed."

"Whatever happens, Sergeant Bevan, we will always have yesterday. The bastards can force us to fight each other, but they'll never take that from us."

Sergeant Bevan nods and smiles. "Not in this lifetime. We'll begrudgingly fight on, but in the absence of hate."

"Until we meet again, Sergeant Bevan."

"It has been my great pleasure, General Muller."

A final round of handshakes are exchanged, accompanied by nods that reek of realism. The last remnants of our glorious Christmas truce taste only of deep sorrow and lingering regret. A joyous interlude set within a barrage of brutality, but painfully, all so fleeting. Sergeant Bevan and myself trudge back to the coalface of grim reality in silence, both besieged by a glut of dark emotions. Neither of us need to acknowledge the agonising feeling of emptiness that rumbles through our churning stomachs. Yesterday, this barren land I now tread so wearily was brimming with laughter and conversation as kindness breathed new life into its decaying roots. Now, it's no-mans-land once more, dark and discoloured with young blood, where the brave souls rest. A sharp, violent pain throbs in my chest, I swear that I can feel my heart breaking.

Boom, boom, boom!

The Midnight Hour Approaches

'Tonight is Hogmanay, and many of the bright lads who might have been singing 'Auld Lang Syne' round the Steeple are singing just as lustily round the camp fire. We were stationed in buildings close behind the firing line, and to these quarters our first-foot was the Pipe Major playing a lively air. To take the place of the clock chimes a Sergeant fired a shot in the air, after which there was much handshaking and interchange of good wishes.'

Private W.M. Soutar, 5th Bn, Black Watch.

New Years Eve 1913, I've never experienced a time so enriched with excitement, a plethora of plans bounce around my bloated brain, like bubbles dancing on a boiling saucepan. So juiced up on love, I can only picture a golden road ahead, littered with limitless possibilities. Incredibly, the woman who occupies my dreams, inhabits my life and we have a wedding to arrange, a life to design. It's fair to say there's an abundance of blessings to celebrate, prior to the dawning of a new year.

With the factory doors primed to open in less than 36 hours, my festive marathon of overindulgence is almost at an end. I've always found this week rather peculiar, given all the build up and anticipation. After the crescendo Christmas creates, normality suddenly feels so normal, but then, after all the chaos there's New Year. Hot on the heels of a season giving thanks for all I hold dear, it's the perfect opportunity to refocus and cast ones hopes upon life's unruly waters to the backdrop of a fresh sunrise. You get to start all over again, it's a chance to dream, and who doesn't love a bit of dreaming?

I've forgone the annual bash with Frosty down the Dirty Duck in favour of sharing a cosy fireplace with the woman I love. It's a rather grand event with live music, warm beer and their infamous pickled eggs, but tonight all I want to do is close the door, leave the world outside and lose myself in Rose's adorable gaze. Kneeling together on the fireside rug, the flames shimmer seductively within her dark smouldering eyes. It would take a lifetime to fully appreciate the magnitude of their unparalleled beauty, fortunately I have that. I'm merrily sinking in to an abyss of admiration

"In nineteen fourteen, I'm going to become Mrs Jack Crosby," declares Rose excitedly.

"I know, my darling," I gush, "I can hardly believe it, we're going to be married."

"It's going to be perfect Jack, a year to cherish." She leans forward, the anticipation sets my heart racing.

I close my eyes and savour a long lingering kiss imparted impeccably from her soft lips. It feels divine, just like the first. "I love you, Rose."

"You better bloody had, Jacky boy" she says with a grin, "because this is it for me, I'm all in, you Jack Crosby, are my forever and I'm crazy about you."

"Good," I reply, "because you're never getting rid of me Rose Elizabeth Thornton. I'm going to love you so hard and never stop, nothing on this earth can deny us our happy ever after…"

There is a little known paradise that lies a mere mile beyond the frontline, a sanctuary from the mud and mayhem, and for me a place to call home until eighteen hundred hours on New Years Day. Billets provide sweet refuge from the elements and a comfortable bed to rest one's ravaged mind and body. The farmhouse is neatly tucked away, well off the beaten track, in a cosy corner of rural Belgium that's managed to stay relatively unspoiled by war. Our job, whilst inhabiting this charming building, is to remain as inconspicuous as possible. Noise, light and any comings and goings must be kept to an absolute minimum. If the German's get a whiff of enemy life within these walls, we'll be bombed to kingdom come.

I'm bunking with Frosty, Lionheart, Joker, Sergeant Bevan and a rather studious young chap called Barry Roscoe, or Bookworm as we've affectionally dubbed him. Barry is a student of life, a thinker, devouring information through incessant reading. While the Frosty's of this world labour effortlessly in life's limelight, Barry prefers to blend in to the background. This often proves difficult when he is called up on to settle copious arguments. Nobody questions the Bookworm, he's the font of all knowledge and his word garnishes respect. With his head usually buried in something deep or meaningful, you'd hardly know he's here, but I have a lot of the time for the Bookworm. When he does speak, its always interesting and often insightful. With so much bull and bravado flying around, our camp needs a brain to keep us grounded, a wise head resting on young shoulders that acts as a calming influence amidst the chaos that threatens to envelop us.

Despite the considerably plusher trappings, I've awoken early, niggled with pain my stiff body needs time to adjust to comfort and recover. The battlefield contained within the corners of ones mind offers precious respite, but the physical toll trench warfare inflicts on the body is equally inexhaustible. I now have aches in places I didn't even know I had places. I contemplate moving, in search of nourishment, but think better of it. My inability to sleep is only due in part to my creaking joints, I'm also duelling with an ever wandering mind. The last few days endured in the trenches were of the ilk I've sadly become accustomed to, but this fresh bevy of bullets has done nothing to dull the memory of Christmas Day.

I don't know if Wilhelm is still alive, I'll probably never learn of his fate, but the conversations we shared will happily haunt me forever. The path of life is long and meandering, whilst merrily strolling down it I'll no doubt encounter a whole host of people, each a unique soul and in the main, jolly decent. In the ensuing years, I fear the vast majority will all but fade from memory, but a special few, the ones who touch my heart, will resonate deeply, they're lifers, coveted and impenetrable by father time. My dear friend, Wilhelm Becker, belongs to the latter. The nature and briefness of our rendezvous no doubt adds a layer of mystique, doing little to dampen the memory, but it's so much more than that, something historic, a moment shared that will gloriously endure. I allow myself a smile, cherished moments, they are the true essence of living.

Suddenly, with the events of Christmas still raw in my mind, I feel a compulsion to commit my thoughts to paper and compose a letter to Rose. I reach over to the bedside draw, straining, I rummage through its contents in search of the required creative tools.

My dearest darling, Rose,

I am penning this from the comfort, and relative safety, of a quaint Belgian farmhouse, having experienced the most scarcely believable Christmas Day. Even to me this will feel like writing the most nonsensical piece of fiction, but my darling, as God is my witness, I swear these humble words depict an accurate account of the remarkable events that unfolded this Christmas time upon the battlefields of Flanders.

In my last correspondence, I described a scene of much merriment on Christmas Eve, with singing and cheering evident across both sides of no-man's-land. I assumed that was that and expected customary hostilities to resume on the morn of Christmas. So, you can imagine my sheer delight and relief when a truce was arranged, initially to lay the dead to rest, but thankfully extended to celebrate the remainder of the day. The burial service was both moving and respectful, with soldiers from both sides working together to complete the darkest of tasks.

Then, in the afternoon, we all met in the middle of no-mans-land, yes, both British and Germans stood together joking and laughing like the best of friends. Lots of their chaps spoke the Kings English fluently and I have to admit, you couldn't hope to meet a more decent bunch of fellows. Just like our boys, they're sick and tired of this wretched war and pray for its swift demise. I even joined in a hastily arranged game of footie against them which proved to be terrific fun. To be able to chat, laugh and walk freely around was utterly joyous, I've never felt anything like it, such a beautiful day. Only a day earlier we were blowing chunks out of each other, it's absolute madness! Even while writing these words, the absurdity is not lost on me. I'm still struggling to believe this really happened, thank God I was fortunate enough to partake.

There was one particular German chap I got rather chummy with, his name was Wilhelm Becker. A real larger than life character who had a grin as big as his heart. Having just become a father, the poor fellow is really struggling with being so far from his loved ones, something I can wholly relate to! Wilhelm spent a few years in London, while training to be a solicitor and as a result we were able to communicate quite smoothly, we talked until well past dusk, he really is the most aimable young man and I only wish good things for him. I hope you get to meet him one day.

Once more we are now waging war, but with friends, it's so difficult to comprehend. I do hope Wilhelm will be ok and a permanent resolution is forthcoming. With heavy hearts so devoid of hate, we will of course fight on, but I fear it has become the most laborious task.

My deepest apologises, Rose, I have selfishly prattled on about myself for the best part of a page, how was your Christmas, darling? I do hope you had the most splendid time with our families and feel well rested. I talked of you constantly on Christmas Day and thought about you even more. This has to be our last Christmas apart, my hapless heart aches so relentlessly for your fire.

I've had a few days now to digest the special news delivered in your last letter. I'm still more than a touch nervous, but ever so excited. Lasting a lifetime, parenthood will be our greatest adventure. Please, take great care of yourself and our precious baby. Tonight I will think of you from the luxury of a warm bed, drifting away to gorgeous dreams of the next time I can hold you close and how wonderful it will feel…

Oh, I nearly forgot to mention, the cognac was delicious, my darling. Wilhelm and I polished it off in quick time while marking the dying embers of our fleeting friendship. I'm still to break the news to Frosty that it's all gone!

Talking of Frosty, I think he's keen to see in the New Year in one of the local watering holes, but I'm not so sure. It's going to be a bittersweet moment when the clock strikes, all sat around pondering what a fresh year has in store for us. There is so much to dread here, but I will try my darndest to remain hopeful and not dwell too much on the painful truth that I should be kissing you at midnight. To be in your arms as the New Year breaks, my heart craves nothing more.

Happy New Year my beautiful Rose, I love you so dearly.

My undying love, now and always,

Your Jack

After soaking my old bones in a warm bath, I'm starting to feel human again. Following a spell in the trenches, the basic necessities don't suddenly feel so basic. If it wasn't for knowing I'll shortly be back there, this scenario would be teetering on the shores of happiness. Dry clothes, a roaring fire and good company to wile away the precious hours in relative contentment. I walk into the amply spaced rustic living room to find my muckers all sitting together around the forementioned fire, cosily cracking away. Unsurprisingly, Frosty is holding court and he appears somewhat animated.

"Come on lads," he cries, "it's the biggest night of the year, and our last before, well you know."

Poor old Frosty, his impassioned plea isn't whipping up much enthusiasm among his battle weary brothers, but he's never been one for taking no for an answer, or abject silence for that matter. The picture of persistence, he pushes on with undiminished vigour.

"I know we're all tired, it's been a bloody tough winter, but that's why we need this, hell, we deserve this." The comment evokes a few soft mutterings of agreement, it's like a red rag to a bull. "That's the spirit chaps, lets go out for a few beers and see in the New Year properly."

Surprisingly, Bookworm raises his head from some heavy reading matter. "It might not be the worst idea," he says, "to mark the occasion with a social gathering."

Frosty is flabbergasted, but grinning inanely as encouragement arrives from the most unlikely of quarters, Bookworm is hardly renowned for his party lifestyle. "Nice one Bazza. See lads, that's coming from the cleverest man in the room, it must be a good idea!"

"I suppose a couple of beers won't hurt," adds Joker, "might even be a bit of a laugh."

"Precisely," says Frosty, "what about you Jacko, fancy heading in to town to sink a few pints?"

I quickly mull over the suggestion, not really feeling it, but don't want to appear a misery guts. "Maybe, are you up for it Lionheart?" I ask, cunningly deflecting the attention, or is that cowardly?

He shrugs his broad shoulders, hardly a glowing endorsement, but I don't expect his reaction will incite too much criticism from Frosty. Sergeant Bevan listens intently, remaining tight lipped throughout the exchange. Frosty knows that if he can curry his favour, then the others will surely fall in to line, here goes nothing.

"Sergeant Bevan."

"Yes, David."

"What do you think of the idea, us all going out for a few drinks on New Year's Eve?"

"A few," he says raising his eyebrows.

"Well," replies Frosty with a grin, "just a little tipple to celebrate."

Sergeant Bevan sits back and slowly strokes his chin, leaving Frosty on tenterhooks. "Well, David, as it goes I think it's a rather splendid idea."

"Oh, really" replies a shocked Frosty, "well, I mean thank you, Sir."

"Yes, just what the doctor ordered. I think we can all do with a tonic, count me in, young Sir."

"My pleasure, Sergeant Bevan," he says looking brazenly smug.

"David is spot on, we have indeed endured the most challenging of times, thankfully with hearts still beating. Lest we forget our fallen friends, never to see the dawning of a New Year. It will be my honour and privilege to see in nineteen fifteen with a distinguished band of brave young fellows such as yourselves."

Wow, as invitations go, that's a bloody hard one to decline.

Owing in part to a distinct lack of clean clothing, we donned full dress uniform for the short walk along the banks of the Yser Canal on route to the Red Hart Estaminet. It's a small, but popular, café style bar offering coffee, beer, wines and by all accounts a mean egg and chips too. I've previously enjoyed the odd jaunt into the village with Frosty, and a few of the others for some light refreshment, but never Sergeant Bevan, he tends to keep his distance from a social standpoint.

The night, cold and crisp in nature, crackles with mystery and I'm excited to see what it brings. Bathed in candlelight and teeming with cheer, the quaint bar oozes character, feeling warm and inviting on entry. Through patches of thick smoke I spy clusters of jolly folks merrily drinking their wartime woes away. There is a mix of soldiers and locals, with the latter welcoming us by the doffing of caps. It gives me a warm fuzzy feeling, perhaps our efforts aren't in vain. Fortunately, owing to Sergeant Bevan's foresight and vast network of contacts, we have secured a decent sized oak table, reserved in a cosy corner. With six beers promptly ordered, we retire to our nook and bed in for the evening. A pretty amiable blonde lass appears with a tray full of frothy memory blotting juice, momentarily pricking Frosty's interest, and then…silence. It appears the round of drinks has arrived with an unwelcome dose of sobering reality. I take a sip of beer and look around the table, heroes stare back at me through fearful eyes. I wonder how many of the fine gentlemen seated here at the birth of a New Year, myself included, will live to see its conclusion.

"Come on lads," says Frosty, "this is like a bloody funeral for the living." The observation raises a few smiles and the odd chuckle. "I tell you what," he continues, "this isn't half a bad drop of ale."

"Yes," replies Sergeant Bevan, "very agreeable, this continental stuff."

"Works for me," chirps Joker.

"Aye," adds Lionheart, "I can't complain, a few more of these should get us in the mood."

Bookworm nods meekly in agreement, the poor chap looks so socially awkward, like a fish out of water without some reading matter in front of him, but fair play to the nervy lad for making the effort. He may even learn something from us reprobates for a change!

"Right," shouts Sergeant Bevan, firstly clapping, then rubbing his hands together. "For starters men, I'm not Sergeant Bevan tonight, ok?

Collectively, we look bemused, prompting clarification.

"This evening, I'm one of the lads, holding no greater rank than any man seated at this table. Please gentleman, call me Mike."

I've never looked at Sergeant Bevan as one of the boys, let alone addressed him as Mike. The polite request feels alien to me, others however are quick to adapt.

"Whatever you say Mikey, me old pal," says Frosty.

"Mike will be more than sufficient, David."

"Right you are, Sir, apologies, I mean Sergeant Mike, whatever you say."

Oh boy, this is going to take some getting used to.

Already deep into a third jug each, initial pleasantries have long been dispensed with. Tongues loosened with lubrication, have given way to a whole host of revelations and admissions. Bookworm, for instance, has confirmed under playful duress that despite being just shy of thirty, he's yet to sample the fruits of love. There apparently was a moment with a cute librarian called Nancy, but the finer details of this brief encounter as far as we're concerned, remain a closed book. Lionheart on the other hand, has let slip that during his childhood he spent many a pleasant hour playing with dolls, only to entertain his little sister, of course. Besides the odd smirk, and in spite of consuming copious amounts of Dutch courage, no one feels brave enough to start ribbing him, not yet, but the night is young.

"Stick with me, young Bazza, I'll get you some action," says Frosty confidently, "no bother."

A night on the pull, the poor lad looks terrified, turning a whiter shade of pale at the daunting prospect, but smiles meekly.

"Thanks Frosty, but if it's all the same to you I'll wait."

"Wait, for what like?"

"Well…for love."

"Love," laughs Frosty, "for an educated lad you have an awful lot to learn. No disrespect intended, but you'll be waiting a hell of a long time. That drivel may exist among the pages of some mushy novel, but this is real life. Get in, get out, and don't look back, that's my advice son."

"Last of the great romantics," I say sarcastically. "Good on you Bookworm, hold out for love."

"Easy for you to say," Frosty scoffs, "not everyone gets what you've got, you lucky bugger."

With no legitimate grounds to disagree, I smile, trying to not appear too smug. When all's said and done, I am a jammy sod!

"What about you Joker?" Continues Frosty, "have you ever been in love?"

"I've had my moments," he grins, "but I guess nothing resembling love has breached my horizon. It's out there though, I'm sure of it."

"Well, I'm in love" booms Lionheart.

"Really?" I reply, that's wonderful."

"Absolutely." He stands up and flexes his legendary biceps. "Every time I look in the mirror!"

The whole table roars with laughter, to be fair, they are mightily impressive.

"What about you Mike?" Asks Frosty, "any pearls of wisdom to share on the thorny subject of love?"

"Well, David," answers the rather flustered looking Sergeant, "now you're asking. I know what it isn't, and that's running hand in hand through fields of buttercups, there's much more realism to it than that. I'm not quite sure I can define it in a handful of words, but I've shared almost all of my adult life with a truly exceptional woman."

"Better hope your missus doesn't find out," quips Joker.

Sergeant Bevan chuckles, "quite Daniel, now where was I, yes, love, that's it. I guess, the point I'm making is that love can manifest itself in all manner of ways, sometimes it's as simple as caring about someone, worrying about them, their happiness. It doesn't sound grand, but its real, that's love I suppose, isn't it?"

"Yes, Sir, I mean Mike, that's love alright."

"I think that calls for the first toast of the evening," announces Sergeant Bevan, getting to his feet. He may be sporting the guise of an ordinary bloke tonight, but he'll always have our respect, instinctively we all rise. "To the sweethearts we've left behind, and those yet to be discovered."

"To the sweethearts, God bless them."

"Well men, I think that's quite enough sloppy stuff for now, what do you say to another round of beers with six whisky chasers?"

"Now you're talking, Michael," roars Frosty.

A chorus of slurred cheers ring out, with a musical accompaniment of loud banging on the table. The atmosphere has turned on a sixpence, from subdued to decidedly raucous, even Bookworm is slamming away with all his muster. This could get messy.

The bar is now bursting at the seams, in readiness for the midnight melee, but a few of our boys appear to be flagging somewhat. No such problems for Davy Frost, he returns to the table affectionately clutching a bottle of dark rum, when it comes to drinking, he's a thoroughbred.

"Right boys," he says while pouring some shots, "last hour of nineteen fourteen, let's see the old girl out in style."

"It's been a bloody tough one," adds Lionheart, "but lets hope there's something better waiting on the other side of midnight."

"Here, here," cries Sergeant Bevan, "to better times men."

"Better times."

"As we look forward with hope," he continues, "lest not forget our brave chaps, the ones who have paid the ultimate price."

I bow my head and remember them, the perished souls who wilfully shared our endeavour. Marching cheerily, shoulder to shoulder to the frontline, chests bulging with pride, honoured to be serving our King and country. Few could have envisaged the devastation that lay menacingly in wait. We sit here tonight making merry, but by the grace of God.

"To our dearly departed friends, may they live on in our hearts for evermore."

"To dearly departed friends," we reply wistfully.

We sit back down, understandably the mood now strikes a slightly more sombre beat, the mere mention of death will do that, but one of Sergeant Bevans greatest strengths is his ability to raise lowly spirits.

"Ok men, I have an idea. Let's just, for one beautiful moment, imagine that at the stroke of midnight peace is declared. Given that we'll soon be returning to Blighty, why don't we go around the table and each name the one thing we're looking forward to the most, something sorely missed, loved ones apart, they're a given. Something else that represents home to you."

"Roast potatoes," blurts out Frosty immediately.

"Sorry, David, did you say roast potatoes?"

"I did indeed, Micheal, roast potatoes!"

"Really," I ask in astonishment, "roast potatoes, is that it?"

"Oh my dear friend," he says grinning and shaking his head, "these aren't just simple roast potatoes, I'm talking about my dear old Ma's roast spuds, the beating heart of my beloved Sunday's. Now boys, try and picture this."

Instinctively, we all lean forward.

"I enjoy a leisurely lie in, sleeping off the Saturday excess, drag myself out of bed for about eleven and settle in to a lovely warm bath. By midday, I'm propping up the bar in the Dirty Duck, beer for breakfast. With a big old log fire crackling away, the mood is decidedly mellow. I chat with mates, usually boasting about the previous evening's exploits or talking football. In the looming shadow of the working week, it's a wonderful way to while away those sacred Sunday hours. Come mid-afternoon, last orders finds me suitably oiled and craving a crafty kip on the couch, but first I have to navigate the short walk home."

"Erm…and roast potatoes," asks Joker.

"Hold your horses, pal, I'm getting to it. Anyway, I'm merrily plodding along, pretty much oblivious to the outside world and it starts." Beaming with delight, he pauses, there's an array of puzzled faces staring back.

"What does?"

"This feeling of excitement, its brewing in the pit of my stomach. I know it sounds ridiculous, but it's all I can think of."

"Roast potatoes," asks Lionheart, "is it roast potatoes?"

"In part," laughs Frosty, "but not exactly, it's home. Even though I've only been away a few hours, I'm suddenly experiencing sharp pangs of nostalgia. The sensation intensifies with every passing step as I inch ever closer, by the front door it has reached fever pitch. Then I open it and…oh my word."

Frosty pauses leaving us all hopelessly intrigued, he's overcome with emotion. A momentary lowering of his cheeky chappie façade, it's the rarest of occurrences, but he manages to regain his composure.

"It's the most divine smell wafting through the air, the scent of Sunday. The meat is roasting away, usually beef or chicken, and then I see my dear old Ma standing there, chequered apron on, smiling warmly. No matter what state I rock up in, the old girl, she always has the most adorable smile for me, bless her little heart. I must have caused her no end of grief over the years, but the love, her love, it just keeps coming in spades. She's devoted herself to me, given everything, I hope to God she realises how much I love her."

He breaks down, quietly sobbing his heart out, around the table there's not a dry eye to be found. Sergeant Beven reaches in his pocket for a handkerchief .

"I'm sure she does, there you go David."

"Thank you, Sir, I'm sorry, don't know what's come over me."

"That's quite alright David, there's nothing to apologise for old boy."

Wiping his final tear away, Frosty nods and smiles.

"Anyway," he continues, "me Ma, after greeting me with open arms, she takes my coat and suggests I get my head down. 'Dinner won't be long,' she'd say, 'get some rest.' An hour or so later, she'd wake me with a nice strong cup of tea and I'd lay the table for us, the special cutlery, not that she ever sits down for long, she's far too busy fussing over me. I offer to help dish up the dinner, but Ma won't hear a word of it, 'it's ok pet,' she'd reply, 'sit yourself down and relax.' Ma can't abide cold food, so the dinner plate is warmed to within an inch of it's life. She lovingly loads it up with goodies and with the aid of a tea towel, carefully carries it to the table. After setting it down, she always places her hand on my head and ruffles my hair, I guess I've always been the apple of her eye. That's probably one of the reasons my old man scarpered, he didn't feel needed once I came along. Never really knew him to be honest, but I'm lucky, me Ma has more than enough love to go around. Anyway, where was I, ah yes, the plate of food, it smells so good and looks even better. I gaze down and there they are, circling the meat and doused in thick gravy, the jewel in Ma's culinary crown."

"Roast potatoes," we cry out in unison.

"Yes, yes, yes" screams Frosty, "roast bloody potatoes, slow cooked to the point of perfection, no word of a lie."

"What makes them so special, David?"

"Well Mike, imagine this for a moment, a slightly charred exterior that crunches so delightfully in one's mouth, revealing the softest of fluffy centres."

"My word, they do sound rather splendid."

"You don't know the half of it, words alone can not do them justice, they're irresistible, my taste of home," he says proudly, "little pieces of paradise.

Never mind being on a plate, those potatoes belong in a gallery! It's a hefty portion, but I always polish off the lot prompting Ma to ask if I'd like a bit more, go on then I say, but just a little. 'Alright David,' she'll say with a smile, but back comes three quarters of a plate full. I puff out my cheeks prompting a disapproving glance, 'now come on David, you're a growing lad!' I start munching through it and she'd shout from the kitchen, 'make sure you leave some room for pudding, it's apple pie and custard today!'

"Is that good?" Asks Bookworm, I've always been partial to a slice of warm apple pie."

"Oh, don't get me started Bazza, that's a whole new chapter!"

"Thank you, for sharing David, that was truly heartwarming. Your mother sounds absolutely lovely."

"Thanks, Sir, she is, an absolute trooper."

Now I know why I never get invited to Sunday lunch at Frosty's house, it's their special time together, either that or the greedy sod wants all those delicious roasties for himself!

"Ok Barry, how about you, what are you most looking forward to upon returning home?"

Bookworm carefully mulls things over, Frosty's roast potatoes are going to be a tough act to follow. As he continues to ponder, impatience invariably rears its ugly head.

"Come on Bazza," Frosty implodes, "there must be something."

"Ok, David, settle down, please, take your time Barry."

"Ok, I'd have to say the thing I'm most looking forward to is visiting my local library."

Collectively our heads drop amidst audible groans, what else! The irony is too much to bear and Lionheart roars with laughter. We're all trying desperately to hold it in, shaking violently, but it's hopeless, my sides are splitting, even Bookworm sees the funny side.

"Oh my word," says Frosty, "you are priceless me old China, and consistent, I'll give you that."

Predictably, Sergeant Bevan is quick to restore a sense of decorum to the boisterous proceedings. "Is there anything particularly special about this library, Barry?"

"Of course, Sir. It's got a cracking philosophy section, first class."

"It's enough to make a young blokes heart sing one imagines," says Frosty.

"I'll say," replies Bookworm, failing to detect the sarcasm in his tone.

"Can I be so bold as to ask, Barry, what the fascination is for you, with books?"

"Well, Sir, I wasn't a particularly popular child at school, constantly bullied and as a result the library become my sanctuary. I'd hide out there during meal and play times, it felt warm and safe, comforting I suppose. It's there that I discovered my love for literature. At first I was drawn to fiction, the stories became my world and the characters, well, it sounds silly but they started to feel like friends, foolish really." The admission leaves the poor chap looking thoroughly embarrassed.

"Not at all, Barry, there's no shame in that."

"Thank you, Sir. Anyway, as I got older my allegiances switched to works of non-fiction. I've always possessed a curious mind and hungry for knowledge, I guess books feed that addiction. I've realized that there is no limit to how far one can expand their mind, that excites me. I've bought books with me and acquired a few, but's it's not enough to scratch the itch. If I make it home, I can get back to doing what I love."

Sergeant Bevan nods and smiles. “Well Barry, I’m sorry for what you’ve endured, I can’t abide bullies, and your quest for knowledge is admirable. I certainly need to make more time for reading, just like the body our minds need nourishment, and what’s good for the mind is also good for the soul. You’re an impressive young man, thank you for sharing, Barry.”

“Well done, Bazza,” says Frosty, “I didn’t mean to take the rise mate, you’re alright.”

High praise indeed from the infamous Mr Frost, those two are polar opposites which makes it all the more special.

“Quite, David, well said, old boy. Right chaps, who’s next?”

Lionheart clears his throat, the anticipation mounts, what does the big man have in store for us?

“Butterflies,” he announces proudly.

Frosty almost chokes on his beer, spraying poor old Danny Hirst who’s sitting opposite. Ironically, Joker fails to see the funny side on this occasion. “Bloody butterflies,” he exclaims.

“Yes, butterflies,” booms Lionheart with a scowl. “Why, do you have a problem with that Frosty? Because if so, we can always go outside and discuss it further.”

“Now, now,” interjects Sergeant Bevan, “I’m sure David means no offence, it’s just took us all by surprise, somewhat. So butterflies, Reginald, I have to admit to being more than a little intrigued, please feel free to continue.”

“Thank you Sir. I grew up in a very dirty industrialised city, don’t get me wrong, I loved those smog filled streets, littered with all manner of colourful characters, they crackled with life. In stark contrast, visiting my Grandparents in the heart of rural Shropshire, now that was a rare treat. My Grandma, now sadly departed, was the most selfless woman, so kind and gentle. In fact, Frosty, the touching way you described your Ma, it bought back fond memories of her. As a nipper I always had my birthday parties there and my Grandma put on a magnificent spread, red salmon in soft buns, cocktail sausages on sticks and plates of mince pies too, as it was almost Christmas. My Grandad on the other hand was slightly sterner, but just as loving in his own way. It's down to him that I developed my great love for the countryside, he used to take me on the most incredible walks that spanned for hours. We'd wander happily through wooded areas, over bridges and alongside river banks. You couldn't help but be seduced by the abundance of natural beauty surrounding you. Roaming England's gloriously green rolling hills with waves of wholesome fresh air blasting my face, it felt fantastic. I've spent my adult years trying to recreate that feeling, not of the air specifically, but the sense of freedom it instils, being at one with the earths charms. Finally I found it.

"Through collecting butterflies" I ask.

"No, Jacko, I don't collect butterflies. It's fishing, that's when I'm at my happiest."

To be honest, I was having trouble picturing Reggie 'Lionheart' Lewis galloping gaily along the grassy plains, butterfly net in hand.

"Just like your library, young Barry, the lush river banks became my sanctuary, a world unspoiled by the rigour of everyday life. Whenever it felt like things were getting on top of me, I'd restock my trusty tackle box, pack up some butties, a flask of coffee, and off I'd trot for a few golden hours of much needed quiet contemplation."

"That does sound just the ticket, Reginald, but where do the butterflies come in to it?"

"Well, Sir, it all transpired on this one autumnal day a few years back. I was employed in farming at the time, but I injured my hand and was unable to work, money got tight and as a consequence things weren't going to well with the missus. My hand needed time to heal properly, but sinking in a whole lot of debt, it's the one thing I didn't have. To numb the pain, both from my hand and a deepening sense of failure, I drank. Feeling as low as a snakes belly, I'd reached the end of my tether and couldn't see a way forward. I'd always been the strong one, the person people depend on, reliable, but beset by weakness, I felt a disgusting sense of shame. It's my job to support my wife, but if I'm not providing then what good am I to her, what's my purpose in life? Useless, bloody useless, that's how I felt, desperate, hopeless and unworthy of her love."

Wow, Lionheart is brutally exhibiting his vulnerabilities, its compelling and perhaps the bravest thing he's ever done.

"It was particularly cold, but with an unforgiving icy breeze, came the gift of a brilliant blue sky, tailor made for gazing. The world was weighing heavy on my shoulders, intuitively I reached for the rod and headed for my favourite fishing spot. It had never let me down before, but on this particular day I unwittingly made the mistake of taking my troubles along for the ride. I sat there, quietly munching on my cheese and pickle, but all it tasted of was despair. I stared for hours at the calm water and envied it's state of unparallel tranquillity. My troubled mind, growing ever darker, refused to rest and let me be. The unrelenting bastard had invaded my grassy patch of heaven, infiltrating the inner sanctum of my soul. It had me beat, on my knees, I was done with this world."

Amidst shocked gasps Lionheart takes a moment.

"If it's too painful, Reginald, then we can leave it there."

"No, Sir, I need to get this of my chest, I want to."

"Ok, lad, if you're sure, but take your time."

"Thank you, Sir."

Lionheart inhales deeply, determined to shed his demons.

"While dwelling within the dark crevice's of my disturbed mind, something appeared upon the water, a vision if you like. It should have horrified me, but instead offered up a sick sense of comfort."

Fuelled by a cackle of conversations, the bar bristles with energy, but around our table we're entangled in a torrent of tension that almost feels tangible, you could hear a pin drop.

"Crikey," yells out Joker, unable to contain himself a moment longer, "what the hell was it that you saw?"

"It was me, mate, my lifeless body, face down, floating serenely on the water. I was at peace, set free from the worry, no longer at its mercy. In that instant, I felt happy, unburdened if you like, I'd found the answer and weirdly it didn't scare me. For a brief moment I wanted to be that person, I yearned to be free, totally free, of the pain, shame and stress, of the very world I'd learned to love. I looked around the river bank, there wasn't a soul to be seen. If I'm doing this, then I'm doing it properly, last thing I need or want is saving. This is my ticket to tranquillity and absolutely not a cry for help. I calmly finished my sandwich, it tasted delicious, took a big gulp of coffee and stood up. In a slow, but deliberate fashion I inched towards the edge of the river bank, this felt right, my time to die."

"Goodness gracious, Reginald," bellows Sergeant Bevan, "well thankfully you're still with us, so what changed your mind at such a late juncture?"

"Well, Sir, it's the most peculiar thing. I was just about to throw myself in when out of the corner of my eye I glimpse this thick bush of vibrant purple heather, sculpted by the elements, unruly in appearance. As I watch it swaying softly in the breeze, this butterfly descends ever so elegantly and nestles right on top. Suddenly, I'm transfixed with wonder, unable to tear my eyes away. The butterfly gracefully flutters his wings, revealing the most gorgeous shade of turquoise, punctuated with orange spots and a black trim. Mesmerised by its sheer majesty, something clicked in my head and I began to weep uncontrollably. I started to recall fragments of beauty held within life's rich tapestry, roses that blossom vividly from thorny stems. Initially, my thoughts were consumed by the immediate surroundings, the stunning landscape and cheese and pickle butties! Then feelings of love permeated through the mental mire, my darling Jean, the captor of my heart, the future we often talked about, kids, dogs, a nice cottage close to a running stream, somewhere pretty to live out our days. Excitement fluttered delicately, I wanted it all, every last plan we dared to dream, I wanted to live! I returned home with renewed hope and relayed the whole story to Jean. We spent a lot of that night crying into each other's arms, but the load was lightened and things started to get better. I'll never forget that day on the river bank, coming perilously close to ending it all, I've been in love with butterflies ever since."

"Bravo," cries Sergeant Bevan, "bravo indeed."

"Bugger me, Lionheart," says Frosty, "it takes some bloody guts to share a story like that. Thank God for that butterfly, I don't think I'll ever look at one quite the same again."

"Thanks, mate, that makes two of us. I owe that little gem my life." The gentle giant looks tearful, but his eyes are smiley, he's danced with his demons and lived to tell the tale.

"That's splendid gents, absolutely first rate and I heartily echo David's sentiments. I think this calls for another round of drinks."

Three down and I'm still unsure what to speak about, my two great loves are Rose and Frosty! In the meantime, it appears Joker is readying himself, buying me a few more precious minutes. He's an extremely likeable lad, but I don't recall us sharing too many serious conversations, it's not his style. Danny Hirst revels in keeping it light, king of the one liners and the perfect tonic to war. There are only a few things that keep our band of brothers sane, prayer, fags, booze and Danny 'Joker' Hurst, an absolute godsend.

"Well, Daniel, all joking aside, what part of returning home excites you the most?"

"Oh, that's easy, Sir," he says with a trademark grin.

"Really?" Replies Sergeant Bevan, "please, do tell."

"The movie theatre, Sir, I can't wait to go back, its my favourite place. There's a large one on our high street I love frequenting."

"So, you're a bit of a film buff, Daniel."

"I am indeed, Sir, there's nothing quite like visiting a picture house, it's exhilarating."

"It's certainly a pleasant way to spend an evening, I must agree. What is it that specifically appeals to you?"

"Well, Sir, It's the whole experience, I guess. I was a wee child when my mum and dad first took me as a treat, to celebrate my tenth birthday. The thrill I felt walking in, wow, just overwhelming, thankfully it's never left me. Everything about the place excited me, thick smoky air enriched with the heavenly aroma of salty nuts, row upon row of plush red seats, and the sheer size of the place. Bathed in darkness, it offered an element of mystery, a sense something magical was about to happen. Tingling with anticipation, I sat gazing at the curtains, a hush descended, they opened to a backdrop of loud applause, revealing a huge screen, the like of which I've never seen before. Suddenly it came to life, moving images began filling my mind with a flurry of fascination, I was hooked, hopelessly floating in a fantasy blessed with boundless possibilities. I'd found my sanctuary, a whole new world of escapism I'd never stop longing to inhabit. Can you imagine it, Sir?"

"I'm sorry, Daniel, imagine what?"

"Being up on that screen, a star no less, skilfully delivering a performance for people to enjoy, something that allows them to forget their troubles for a while. To possess the gift of being able to entertain, the sense of self-worth and accomplishment one must feel, it blows my mind."

"I see what you mean, one imagines creativity brings its own reward."

"Absolutely, Sir, it's my dream, to sparkle on that silver screen, to be somebody. Somebody memorable."

"Memorable?"

"Yes, Sir, whether loved or loathed, I want to be remembered, you know, leave a legacy."

"Oh Danny boy, you'll be remembered alright," quips Frosty, "fondly remembered."

"Cheers mate." Danny smiles, before continuing.

"Five days a week I go to work, it's a steady job with good prospects that pays well, but I find it a little drab. I look over at my boss, Mr Edwards, a thoroughly decent chap on the wrong side of fifty and wonder, I wonder when the dreams died, when he stopped chasing the rainbow. Then I think…"

"Yes, Daniel."

"Sorry, Sir, I think that's going to be me in twenty odd years. A weary accounts manager, dead behind the eyes, the thought makes me shudder. Walking in with the masses, another face in the crowd, each day as rigid as the last, surely there has to be something more out there, more than just clocking on and counting down the hours."

"There is a lot to be said, Daniel, for putting in an honest day's graft."

"I know Sir, and I don't want to seem ungrateful, but my heart isn't in it. My parents are proud of me and I feel this pressure to please them through hard work and I do work hard, but its not enough. It feels like my whole future is already mapped out, a life less ordinary, but then there's this creative passion raging inside, it remains caged for forty odd hours a week, niggling away at me, aching to break free."

"Then you must unleash it Daniel, go hunt that rainbow down, if you firmly believe acting is your true calling."

"I do, Sir, wholeheartedly. I want to start with a bit of local theatre and study drama in my spare time, then who knows? Life's sky is decorated with an abundance of stars, surely there's room for at least one more, Sir."

"Leave off Joker, you can't be a film star."

"Why ever not, Frosty?"

"Don't get me wrong Joker, you're a funny guy, but the films are all silent."

"I don't follow, mate."

"You can't keep your gob shut for five minutes!"

Joker cracks up, along with everybody else.

"It's funny, though."

"What is?" I ask.

"My dreary job, it's probably more responsible than anything else for sculpting my personality. I use humour to help get through the day and add a splash of colour. Without a smile, I don't know how the day will ever end. Even now, in these desperate times, I have to allow myself the odd smile. It might make me look like an idiot, but I know of no other way to survive this. The scenario has changed markedly, but humour remains my trusty crutch."

"Well, Daniel," says Sergeant Bevan, "I, for one, will forever be eternally grateful for the humour you bring to our camp, a welcome chink of light amongst a mass of misery, and you're no idiot."

"Here, here," cries Frosty, "go out into the world and make it laugh kid."

Amid chants of encouragement the oak receives another round of ardent hammering.
The table falls silent once more and Sergeant Bevan turns his head, five pairs of eyes suddenly burn in to me. The heat of expectation grows ever hotter, I start to sweat.

"This is going to be a bit of an usual answer, well, it feels unusual to me because it isn't something that forms a big part of my home life, not yet, but here goes…" I pause and breathe deeply, despite my semi inebriated state, I feel incredibly nervous. "Writing, outside of impending fatherhood and Rose, I'd have to say writing."

Frosty looks puzzled. "What are you talking about, soft lad? You can write out here, in fact you do, all the time, you're like bloody Shakespeare when you get going!"

"Yes, I do write letters to Rose, but that isn't the kind of writing I'm talking about. There is another world that's existed, well, for as long as I can remember, it's between my ears."

Lionheart chuckles. "I think you may have had one too many, old boy."

I smile politely and press on.

"It's steeped in fantasy, this world inside my head, a fertile land rich with seeds that represent a concoction of crazy ideas. Often without rhyme or reason, some fester and eventually die, but others germinate, growing wings."

"What do you do with these ideas, Jack?"

"Nothing, Sir."

"What, you've never committed any of them to paper?"

"Not a single word."

"Can I ask, why?"

I look sheepishly around the table, feeling hesitant.

"It's ok, Jack, you're amongst friends here."

"Yeah, come on, Jacko, let's be having it."

"Well, I suppose its fear, becoming a celebrated author of sorts. Spending my days scribing the most colourful stories, it's a romantic notion, an ideal I can cling to and cherish. While plots and characters remain prisoners of my imagination, the dream lives, it breathes inside me. The moment I commit my ideas to paper, I'm at the mercy of others, judged and open to failure. I'm petrified of discovering I'm not good enough, hear my craft described as weak, then the dream dies, it dies inside me. It's pathetic really, a burning compulsion paralysed by cowardice."

"It's not pathetic at all, Jack, fear of rejection, the risk of ridicule, its understandable, but not insurmountable."

"Really, Sir?"

"Of course not, my dear boy. Every person throughout history who's ever created anything, be it a concept, product, piece of music or work of literature for that matter, goes through the exact same struggle, but without the struggle there can be no worthwhile victory. We all regret things we've done, this amount of consumption for one when I wake in the morning, but better to do that than live to regret the things we didn't do. The act of giving it a go, realising the fruits of your creative endeavour, that alone is deserving of mans admiration. This fear doesn't make you a coward, Jack, it just proves you're human, flesh and bones. To succeed at anything, one must first learn to fail, many times over in some cases."

God love him, the old boy has come through, just like he always does! A humble man, yet blessed with the most insightful perspective.

"Thank you," I mumble, the reply is wholly inadequate, but in this poignant moment, all I can muster.

"So, Jack, is that a promise then?"

"Sorry, Sir?"

"Can I assume that you are going to start writing in earnest, give this thing a jolly good go?"

"Yes, Sir, that is a promise, once civilian life resumes."

"Why wait, Jacko," adds Frosty, "make use of all the dead time away from the trenches."

"I don't think I can mate, I'm not making excuses, but it's the ideas, they've stopped popping inside my head, well ever since… I fear this blasted war has dried up my creative juices, robbed my mind of clarity."

Lionheart nods. "Aye, this wretched war," he sighs, "it's got a lot to answer for, but don't worry lad, they'll come back."

"Can I ask a question?" Says Bookworm politely.

"Of course, mate."

"These ideas, the stories you wish to write, what are they about?"

"Well, they're the most brutally honest audience, but I want to write for children. The ideas are a bit of a mishmash, one day it can be the wild west, furry aliens on another. I guess, it's the creative licence that writing for children offers that appeals to me, their imaginations spiral so beautifully beyond the banal confines of reality and crave content. I want to be able to do that, feed their imaginations and keep them merrily dreaming, wouldn't that be something to behold?"

"Indeed it would young man," adds Sergeant Bevan, "something rather special."

"It's exactly what my father did for me, telling the most fantastical tales, all of his own creation. A skilled raconteur capable of transforming any bedtime in to a world of wonder, his words preserved the precious magic burning within me. A feeling lost all too quickly for most, I really ought to thank him for that sometime, hopefully one day."

Suddenly, my thoughts are blotted with a dabbing of darkness, *will I get to thank him or has the opportunity passed? He's not getting any younger and wasn't enjoying the best of health when I last saw him, my God, what if he's deteriorating and Rose doesn't wish to burden me with such worrying news.*

"Jack, Jack, are you ok old boy?" Asks Sergeant Bevan, his firm tone breaks my troublesome train of thought. I'm grateful, it's a habit that promises nothing, but untold misery.

"Yes, Sir, I am, thank you."

"No, thank you, Jack, your father sounds quite the fellow and don't worry, you'll get an opportunity to thank him personally one day soon. As for cowboys or furry aliens, whatever the subject matter may be, I look forward to reading your first story."

"Thank you, Sir."

"Well, gentleman, I want to thank you wholeheartedly for your participation and the candour displayed by each and everyone of you, I couldn't be prouder. I'll just get us some more drinks, we'll need to toast the New Year." Sergeant Bevan jumps to his feet like a scolded cat.

"Hold your horses, Mike," says Frosty, "where do you think you're going?"

"Well, to the bar, David, we need more drinks."

"Not so fast."

"I beg your pardon, David?"

Shocked by his bolshy tone, all eyes gravitate to Frosty.

"This whole sharing exercise was your idea, Sir, we all did our bit, so…"

"So?"

"So, now it's your turn, Sir."

"Oh, I see, but it's almost midnight now and I'm sure everybody's heard enough of me for one evening." He laughs nervously.

"Nice try, Sir," replies Lionheart, "but I, for one, would love to hear about the one thing about home you're looking forward to the most."

"Me, too," chimes in Frosty, his reply is accompanied by a few mutterings of agreement.

Poor old Sergeant Bevan, unable to pull rank after the whole 'I'm one of the boys tonight' speech, looks an awfully pale shade as he slides back into his seat.

"Ok, gentlemen, if you insist, I suppose I can give it a go."

"That's the spirit, Sir," says Frosty encouragingly.

A hush falls, given the mans exceptional vocal skills, I'm anticipating something to savour. The pressure growing from the combined weight of expectation around the table might account for his distressed demeanour, when it comes to Sergeant Bevan, we've grown accustom to greatness.

"Oh dear, Lord," he mouths softly before pausing, If only my speech had taken us to the hullabaloo of New Year, he'd have been spared this ordeal.

"Well chaps, its erm, ballroom dancing," he whispers.

"Sorry, Mike," asks Frosty, "did you say ballroom dancing, by any chance?"

There are a few sniggers, much to the dismay of our embarrassed Sergeant, he looks mortified.

"No, David, I didn't."

"That's funny, Sir," replies a grinning Frosty, "because I could have sworn that's what you said."

"No, not at all, it was boxing, that's what it was. Oh yes, jabs, hooks, uppercuts and all that good boxing stuff, I can't get enough of it."

"Really, Sir," replies Lionheart, "so you're a boxer then?"

Sergeant Bevan slumps his shoulders, looking resigned and sighs, the pretence appears more painful than the truth. "No, not really, I can't abide any form of violence. Ballroom dancing, that's what I miss, ok, there you have it, please feel free to scoff to your hearts content."

"Ok, twinkle toes, calm down."

The table erupts with laughter, sharp and quick witted, the retort is vintage Frosty. Sergeant Bevan can only smile and doff his hat in begrudging admiration.

"You bloody bastards," he replies with a grin, "sod the lot of you." He sits back, tight lipped, with his arms folded as the laughter slowly subsides.

“All joking aside, we’d all like to here more about your love of dance, Mike,” replies a smirking Frosty in the most serious tone he can muster.

“Really, are you absolutely sure?”

We all nod sincerely.

“With no more taking the rise, David?”

“Cross my heart, Sir.”

“Ok then, well, I guess it all started at the seaside. My dear wife, Jean, and myself along with another couple, Bob and Mary, have long since enjoyed summer trips to Blackpool. There is a tower there that was erected towards the end of the last century, it houses a rather grand ballroom. So, one summer not so many years ago, we were enjoying a leisurely afternoon in the hotel bar, rain was tipping down as it often does, and Jean suggested going dancing. I glanced at Bob and gave him a wink, we both assumed this was an opportunity to slip out to the pub, leaving the ladies to it, but much to our dismay it soon became apparent that we were expected to accompany them and dance! It all started there, somewhat unexpectedly, my love affair with ballroom dancing. The ladies hot footed it down there with two grumpy buggers in tow, to their credit our miserable mugs did little to dampen their enthusiasm, they both looked so beautiful. With Jean on my arm, walking in there, I should have felt nothing, but pride, stubborn old sod.” He shakes his head regretfully, but then starts to smile.

“Thankfully, my bad mood, proving no match for the opulent surroundings, faded in a heartbeat. The ballroom was breathtaking, a den of decadence showcasing the most splendid crystal chandeliers and a stunning balcony. A gentleman was on a stage playing the organ and couples were floating across the ample dancefloor, they looked happy, smiling and chatting away. The weirdest sensation enveloped me, an urge to dance, but cowardly, after catching a glimpse of Bob, I suppressed it. It was evident he didn't share my new found desire, so we headed for the bar, finding a nearby table. Jean and Mary sat impatiently as Bob sulked and I gazed on admiringly. The movement was so graceful, like watching art, I was mesmerised and itching to give it a go, but where would that leave Mary? Arms folded and sporting a face like thunder, Bob wasn't going anywhere too soon and I somehow had to coax him out of his comfort zone, this mission was going to require all my skills of persuasion and more. I rattled through my first drink and invited an unsuspecting Bob to accompany me to the bar, this was my opportunity."

"*How beautiful do Jean and Mary look, old pal,*" I said, "*they've gone to great effort for tonight, I think a quick dance is the least we can offer . Just look at them, keen as mustard to trip the light fantastic.*"

"*Don't I know it,*" he replied, the poor bloke looked petrified.

"*Look, old boy, I don't want to do this anymore than you,*" I said lying through my teeth, "*but we must think of the ladies. Come on, one little dance, how hard can it be? It's either that or the dreaded cold shoulder for God knows how long.*"

He nodded in resignation and headed back to the table, like a lamb to the slaughter. I walked up to Jean and outstretched my arm.

"*My darling, Jean,*" I said, "*would you afford me the great honour of this next dance?*"

I'll never forget her face, dripping with affection, like the first flourish of love, I went weak at the knees. This time, laden with swelling pride, I took her hand and walked her to the dancefloor, we stopped and turned towards each other, then I looked at her, really looked at her. She was magically back in all her glory, the sweet girl who made time stand still all those years ago at the local Lyceum. In that wondrous moment, I fell in love with her all over again, then the music started."

Sergeant Bevan appears a complicated creature, a dignified man, well respected, whose grown weary whilst toiling under the burden of leadership in the face of death. Masterful at burying his feelings, he displays a rigid public façade, ensuring few will ever witness the full gambit of his emotions, but today we're seeing the man behind the uniform, he's every bit as impressive.

"We began to move, almost instinctively, swept away on the coattails of a mosaic of music, it felt both joyous and effortless. I'd danced my way out of the doldrums, which was more than can be said for poor old Bob, he looked clumsy and awkward, like a fish out of water. We danced on until the music died, like teenage sweethearts in the chaotic throes of early courtship. The evening began with trepidation, but ended with a sweet kiss under the grandeur of light. It's a night that will live long in the memory, similar to this one gentleman."

It's a speech delivered with the upmost sincerity, earning a well-deserved round of applause.

"Well," says Frosty, "this night won't be ending with a sloppy kiss, Sir."

Sergeant Bevan laughs loudly "Thank heavens for small mercies David."

"So, Mike, did you continue dancing?" I ask.

"Oh yes, all over the country, the music is in my blood now."

"All over the country?"

"Yes, I've visited festivals and performed in competitions," he says proudly. "My tango caused quite the commotion in the Croydon divisional finals, I can tell you."

"Wow," says Frosty, "you and the missis must be semi-professional by now."

Sergeant Bevan grimaces, appearing awkward. "Well, David, erm, its Mary, she's my competition partner."

"Oh, you sly old fox, Sir. I'm beginning to see the attraction of all this dancing," he sneers.

"I beg your pardon, David," he thunders, shooting Frosty a look capable of freezing fire. "Jean's my darling wife, and Bob is my oldest friend, furthermore he was best man at our wedding."

"Sorry, Sir, I didn't mean anything by it, just pulling your leg."

Sergeant Bevan nods and takes a deep intake of breath before continuing. "Jean still enjoys to dance socially, and we often do, but it became apparent quite early on that Mary and myself possessed similar levels of talent and passion for ballroom dancing, Bob and Jean were the ones who encouraged us to take it further. We always travel as a foursome, make a trip of it, they're are our biggest fans. We've claimed a few runners up spots, but the big prizes have so far eluded us. Hopefully we can pick things up, you know, when its over. My dear friend Bob is over here to, though I haven't heard from him for a while." His expression becomes pained. "I really must write to him. Tomorrow, I'll do it tomorrow…God willing."

In a matter of minutes, we'll witness the birth of a New Year, and all the hope it encompasses. The night has surpassed all expectations, laughs, tears, good liqueur and a raft of revelations, but it has still menacingly bought us back to where we started, heroes staring back at me through fearful eyes. We've drank ourselves sober and with sobriety comes the dawn of stark reality. The New Year offers up more questions than answers, more dread than hope, more death than desire.

What will become of my friends, the brave souls seated around this table? Will Lionheart get to spend another leisurely afternoon sitting on a river bank ogling butterflies, or Barry browsing to his hearts content at his beloved library? Will 'Danny Joker' Hurst ever grace the silver screen or Sergeant Bevan quickstep his way to glory? Then there's me, still living in my head, too scared to unleash my imagination for fear of ridicule. That leaves my best mate, the incomparable Davy Frost, I hope and pray he gets to sample those delicious roast potatoes again.

So many dreams lie dormant, unfulfilled, may God bless the bloody lot of us. Tonight has shown we are more than just frightened young men hell bent on drinking our worries away. We are unique vessels, each carrying our own precious cargo, but bonded by one common goal, the aching desire to be free. Who amongst us will see out the year we're about to toast.

One final round of whiskies arrives at the table, they're doubles, it feels appropriate. As the countdown reverberates out around the pub, Sergeant Bevan stands to his feet and we quickly join him.

"Right chaps, this is it, we're about to welcome in nineteen fifteen, a New Year and with it, renewed hope. You're a fine body of young men and I'm proud to be your Sergeant, but even prouder to count you among my friends, even you Frosty! May this New Year bring each and every one of you and your loved ones the peace and joy you covet and richly deserve."

"Here, here, God bless you, Sir."

Midnight strikes, we raise our glasses and toast to the unknown of all our tomorrows. Instinctively, my mind shifts to Rose and the child destined to change our lives. My God, I'm so desperate to live, but later today I'll be back in the trenches. People all around are making merry, but in reality other than the date, nothing has really changed. Frosty throws his arm round me.

"Happy New Year, mate, and here's to many more of them."

"Cheers, you too, pal."

"Frosty."

"Yes, Jacko."

"It's going to be alright, isn't it?"

"Of course, its you and me forever, kid."

"You and me forever…"

My Darkest Day

'They have to stay there while shell after huge shell descends with a shriek close beside them. Each one an acute mental torture; each shrieking tearing crash bringing a promise to each man, instantaneous, I will tear you into ghastly wounds, I will rend your flesh and pulp your arm or a leg, fling you, half a gaping, quivering man and like these that you see smashed around you one by one to lie there rotting and blackening.'

Charles Bean, Australian war correspondent.

Proudly exhibiting a prize conker on my first day at a new school wasn't the brightest idea, I quickly realised this when confronted by three envious boys of burly stature in the cloakroom at playtime. I guess a severe beating is just a rite of passage for the new kid and I shouldn't take it personally, but that won't make it any less painful! Cornered and cowering, I waited to feel the pounding of cold fist upon my unblemished face, but instead hear a voice authoritatively articulate these immortal words.

"Hey, you bunch of daft lugs, scarper, before I do something you'll regret."

There was three of them, all bigger than this slim cocky young lad, but they exited sharply, with not an utterance of complaint. That was the first time I met David Frost, in that moment he became my hero, its been that way ever since. There was something about him, an alluring quality, not necessarily his looks, but the way he conducted himself, boys wanted to be him and the girls, lots of girls, wanted to be with him. Whether it be the bullies or boffins, Frosty garnished admiration and respect from all quarters, even the bloody teachers loved him, the jammy sod got away with murder! The mere fact we became firm friends meant swift elevation to the higher echelons of school society rendering me untouchable and under his wing life was comfy and always entertaining.

Some might say I've lived my whole life in Frosty's shadow, after all, he's been my guardian angel, there through every step of my journey into adulthood, but with my cool head and his confidence, we complemented each other. I became his rock, the voice of reason, a close and trusted confidant, regardless of what people think, it's been a journey well lived. I owe a lot to David Frost, so much more than being spared that initial beating, it's a debt I'll never come close to repaying. All I can do is fight until my dying breath to protect him and pray it's enough, I won't leave him to decay in the fields of Flanders, that simply can't happen.

On first glance, one can be forgiven for taking a disliking to Frosty, he's brash and full of himself, but with charisma aplenty, a master of seduction. After five minutes in his company, you'll love the bugger forever. Ironically, for a man so lavishly adored, the one thing that still eludes him is true love, the everlasting kind. Maybe love doesn't fit the image, and then there's the roving eye condition he suffers badly from, but amongst the girls he's courted, more than I can remember, there's one who stood out. We tell each other all manner of things, from our darkest fears to wildest fantasies, but he never speaks of Ruby Stevens, the girl who broke his heart.

Ruby worked briefly at our ironworks, in the offices, a few years back. She was slender in build, with flowing locks of wild auburn hair, long smooth legs and a mischievous glint in her eye. Driven and ambitious, Ruby knew exactly where she was heading and what she wanted out of life, adventure. The clerical job was just a summer stopgap to allow her to amass some spends before traveling the globe. When she walked, ever so elegantly, around the factory the productivity dipped as a mass of tongues scraped across the dusty floor. She was naturally flirtatious, with a bubbly personality, spraying winks and smiles like confetti upon an army of admirers. It felt like the whole world was in love with Ruby Stevens. Men started coming to work with their hair neatly combed, reeking of aftershave, desperate to grab her attention and snaffle her heart, but predictably, the much coveted Miss Stevens only had eyes for one guy.

With Ruby on his arm, my best mate became the envy of the workforce, I'd never seen him happier or more smitten. Frosty has never been one to shy away from discussing his romantic conquests, but with Ruby, despite colleagues begging for details, he never exercised the opportunity to kiss and tell. They were strawberries and cream, clicking from the outset and loved up to the eyeballs, but this all-encompassing love balanced delicately on precarious foundations.

Ruby came with a foreboding fragility-here today, gone tomorrow, never hiding her desire for far flung adventure. She'd failed to account for falling in love, but I had a feeling that even experiencing life's greatest emotion was incapable of derailing her dream. Ruby had plans, one autumn day she'll board a boat from Southampton, the ticket had already been purchased, the first enactment of her destiny, but now there's Frosty, a seasonal fling with that forever feeling.

For Frosty and Ruby their beautiful summer breezed by, a Mardi Gras of memorable moments lived out under a blossoming blanket of love, but neither could fully shake the ebbing flow of time that silhouetted against an ever diming sky. I barely saw my mate, other than at work, he was in love, but time began moulding elation in to exasperation. Caught between desire and duty, the poor lad began discovering that love isn't all rainbows, hearts exist in a land diseased with unflinching realities.

"She wants me to go with her mate, to America."

"Wow, you mean, permanently?"

"Yes, I think so."

"Are you considering it?"

"Well, yes, I think I can scrape enough together for a ticket."

"Beyond that though, how will you both survive?"

"I guess we'll live on love." He laughs nervously, it's a beautifully romantic notion, but utterly ridiculous. Even wondrous love has to exist within a vacuum of cold rigid practicalities.

"Ruby has some savings and we'll pick up jobs as we travel, it will be fun," he says unconvincingly. "To be honest, Jacko, my heads all over the show, should I go lad?"

"Sorry, mate, I really don't know. This is huge, it has to be your call."

He looks deeply troubled and understandably so, he's always been a homebird, loves his creature comforts, the Dirty Duck, his mates and his dear old Ma's cooking. In this manor, he's the man, a big fish in a small pond, but this was a ticket to the unknown, albeit it, laden with love and a generous sprinkling of surprise. I genuinely didn't feel comfortable advising him either way, both paths lay riddled with regret, but the regret of not seeing what could be, never knowing how far love can take you, that will surely prove the least palatable.

"It's me Ma, I'm all she's got, the old girl, it'll break her dear old heart. Then there's Ruby, she's bloody everything."

"Do you love her mate? It's only been a few months."

He laughs and nods his head ruefully. "Months? I was there in minutes. It'll never happen to me, you know, all that sloppy stuff, that's what I thought, but it bloody well has! If only she'd stay, then we can start to build a life together, I don't need adventure, just her."

"Have you asked her to stay?"

"No, her blessed heart is set on travelling, I can't be the one to stifle her dreams, kill that gorgeous free spirit she possesses, also I don't think I'd like the answer. I've always loved my life, you know, really enjoyed it, but now."

"What is it, mate?"

"If I go back to exactly how it was, before Ruby, it may feel tainted and ordinary, a little too ordinary to bear."

I quickly realized that Frosty was seriously contemplating an exciting new life, one that didn't include me. Selfish thoughts began to flood my scattered mind, I could lose him, forever, dread consumed me. I've never been without him for as long as I can remember. The scenario terrifies me, but this was my greatest friend, he deserves impartiality.

"I can check in on your Ma, bring her groceries, and the like, you know, look after her."

"You'd do that mate, for me?"

"Of course I will, you're my best friend."

"Thank you, Jacko, but how do I tell her? It's just been the two of us since the old man bolted, she dotes on me."

"I know, but she'll want you to be happy, we both do, and if that happiness lies with Ruby, then…"

"Are you telling me to go, pal?"

I spot a chink of hope glistening through his tired eyes, bleary circles embellished with worry.

"If you're sure, that this is what you really want, then yes, you must follow your heart and trust in wherever it takes you."

"I'll miss you mate."

He grimaces and pats me firmly on the shoulder, I nod, recognising the pain that lies in wait.

"Me, too." More than you'll ever know.

In spite of my guidance and support, he still cuts a forlorn figure, internally duelling with his demons. After deciding to sleep on it, he departs, leaving me to ponder a Frosty free existence, somewhat drab and empty I fear. A noon summit at the Dirty Duck beckons with all the appeal of an execution, the fate of four people hangs precariously in the balance. I retire to bed shivering with terror, Frosty's new found love could turn in to my greatest loss.

Frosty bounds into the pub looking surprisingly fresh faced and chipper, he clearly hasn't experienced the type of sleepless night I've endured. If anything, he looks totally at peace with the world, what a difference a day makes!

"Morning, mate, you seem a lot brighter today."

"I'm just fine and dandy, me old mucker, isn't it the most beautiful day?"

"So, I take it things went well with your Ma?"

"Erm, I decided not to tell her."

"Why, Ruby leaves in less than a fortnight."

"Yes, but I've decided to stay." He grins, like a man in possession of a juicy secret, something isn't adding up.

“I don’t understand mate, what about love, you know, Ruby and following your heart?”

“Never mind all that, Jacko, I thought about it, leaving me Ma behind, rattling around in that big old house, all alone, it will destroy us both. I can’t live with that, so I’m going to ask Ruby to stay.”

“Are you sure that will work? She doesn’t seem the type for turning and as you said, she’s a free spirit.”

“With my powers of persuasion, oh please, I’m Davy Frost for goodness sake, I can charm the birds from the trees and provide all the excitement she’ll ever need.”

He winks, appearing confident, but behind the bravado I sense an underbelly of fragility infected with fear. Understandably so, given its his first time in love, I’m worried for my friend and unable to disguise it.

“Relax, Jacko, I’ll assure her that they’ll be plenty of time for travel, but for now, let’s just be in love. That’s what I’m going to say to her, let’s just be in love and savour it.”

“Do you think that will work, it’s a beautiful sentiment, but is it enough?”

“Hopefully, but if not, I’ve got an even bigger reason tucked up my sleeve.”

“What’s that?”

“I’m going to propose marriage!”

“Bloody hell, mate, that’s some gesture, it’s for keeps, you need to be really sure.”

“I’ve never been surer of anything in my whole life. White picket fences, kiddies running around, tea on the lawn, I never thought I needed those things, never mind wanting them, but with Ruby I do. I really do, it all makes sense with her.”

“If that’s how you feel, then there’s only one choice, go get her mate, lay your love on the line. From the bottom of my heart Frosty, I hope it works out for you."

"I guess I'll find out on Sunday afternoon, we're going for a picnic down by the river."

Armed with a heart full of hope, marriage on his mind and the sun on his back, Frosty set out on his merry way, trotting down the crooked path of destiny. A man so accustomed to succeeding, forced into contemplating failure due to the gravity of what he might lose, the nerves must be shredded…

The day has felt brutally long, I'm hungry, but struggling to eat and tired, but unable to sleep. Frosty's masterplan must have long been instigated, well at least the weather stayed fine, although the rain's now hammering down. I take to my bed in a state of restless wondering, is it congratulations or commiserations, the wait is torture. I picture an unsuspecting Ruby sat by the river, looking forward to luncheon and a carefree afternoon, she's still so young. I've no doubt she loves him too, you only have to see them together, but I fear this will all come too soon for her, she's asked for a travel companion.

It's getting late, my thoughts momentarily drift to work, another week of grind! They're disturbed by a thudding bang on wood, it startles me. I race downstairs and reach for the door, my hearts pounding. A saturated figure stands in the doorway, it's Frosty, his drained features, stripped of charm, languish lifelessly. It's chilling, lacking focus he looks forward, motionless and silent, I'm staring into an abyss of pain. There's a strong stench of alcohol, but he appears sober, all too sober. Frozen in a state of subdued sadness, he crumbles, tears escape from his hollow eyes , slowly at first, but it soon intensifies into all out weeping. I fling open my arms and his head sinks into my chest. No words are exchanged, this isn't the time, I just need to hold tight and allow the hurt to drain freely from his broken heart.

I never asked him what transpired between them on the river bank that fateful Sunday afternoon, I still don't know. Ruby didn't return to work, not even for her pay and Frosty has never uttered her name once in the ensuing years. The following Wednesday he rocked up at work, brazenly displaying his full coat of arms. The old Frosty in all his glory, quite an accomplishment given how deep his raw scars of lost love must run. He'll never admit as much, but I know he still thinks of her, the girl who swept through town like a tornado, before scarpering forever with his heart in tow. Time is God's greatest healer, one day he'll feel strong enough to discuss Ruby Stevens and then, perhaps give himself permission to fall in love again…

The morning after the night before, as a marching band plays inside my head, I can barely contemplate opening my eyes. God knows what time we left that watering hole or how on earth we found our way back to billets. Sergeant Bevan's whisky chasers have a lot to answer for! Given how deathly silent the house sounds, I'm probably not the only one suffering at the altar of overindulgence. It's the last morning in billets, from civilisation to desperation, a well-trodden journey I'm all too familiar with. This blasted throbbing shows no sign of abating, but it's a penance worth enduring to experience a night so steeped in magnificence and enriched with emotional splendour. I walked away from that table, or rather staggered, with a wonderful sense of belonging burning warmly inside me. We're all incarcerated in this living hell, but there's something remarkable keeping our souls afloat, it was evident last night, a tight bond forged through shared struggles that nestles on a bed of endless empathy. I shake my head in wonder at the enigma of war, *how can one feel so incredibly fortunate and desperately unlucky at the same time?*

"Left, right, left, right," barks out Sergeant Bevan as we march briskly back to bedlam, albeit with shoulders slumped slightly lower than when we journeyed in the opposite direction.

A light, but persistent drizzle adds to the subdued mood as we advance, each wrestling silently with their own disturbing thoughts. It's still afternoon, but appropriately darkness has descended and a chilly breeze is making its ugly presence felt.

Without the luxury of a Christmas impasse, four of the most fearful days imaginable lie menacingly in wait. The bombs and bullets are getting louder, ever closer and more alarming, *why won't they stop, please make them stop?* All I can do is suppress the fear by wishing another segment of my life away. Shells whistle through the air, illuminating the grey slated sky and shaking the very ground we walk on, it's a tightrope of terror that stretches for miles. Like poison, anxiety flows richly through my veins causing a violent churning of the stomach, a familiar feeling, but still deeply unpleasant. My worn boots infiltrate the sodden fields of Flanders and the feeling intensifies, burning like acid. No matter how many times I arrive here to inhabit this hell with nothing but a prayer and scant hope, my soul sorrowfully succumbs to its deathly stench. Internally, my mind rages at the injustice, but the deep rooted trepidation is as inevitable as night following day. Our destination is reached without incident, it's raining a little harder now, how fitting.

The residing battalion are thankful to see us and the handover is swift, their struggle is paused, but the pain of leaving more behind is scorched across their haggard features. The briefest of briefings is followed by handshakes and the customary well wishes. I recognise one of their chaps appears to be missing, but dare not speak of his fate, labouring on loss will serve no purpose for either party. Seemingly, the advent of a New Year bought no repeat of the relaxed frivolity we'd enjoyed a week earlier, but by all accounts it had been commemorated with sustained period of respectful inactivity and the consumption of beer and wine. A small, but hollow, win for the hierarchy, they must be so proud. Mercifully, we have Sergeant Bevan in our ranks, a master in the art of resurrecting sunken spirits.

"Good evening men, and a very Happy New Year to each and every one of you."

"Happy New Year Sir."

He pauses and shakes his head. "Exchanging well wishes, a new year breaking, it all feels a trifle peculiar. This is normally a time of great celebration, a moment for optimism and making plans, and yet men," he sighs deeply, "here we are once more, donning our battle worn boots and standing shoulder to shoulder, ready to protect King, country and the people we love."

"Here, here," a lone voice cries.

"Quite, young Sir, thank you. There's no sugar coating this, it's a thankless task and I want to commend you, not just for your bravery, but also the unwavering sense of duty you display on a daily basis in the face of great atrocities. I'm both humble and proud to lead you into conflict and beg the Lord for our safe passage."

As words go, they don't get much more heartfelt than that, it's so much more than hollow platitudes calculatedly delivered to gee us up for war, Sergeant Bevan appears close to tears. His cumbersome load contains the combined fears and desperate hopes of a battle bruised battalion, one growing ever more weary and depleted.

"The struggle is exhausting, but worthwhile, we mustn't loose heart men or focus, not for a solitary moment. We will fight on stoutly, with continued vigour to honour the fallen and ensure their dying wasn't in vain. Gentlemen, please allow me to begin the year with a moment of prayer."

Sergeant Bevan has never struck me as the religious type, but the sustainment of war adds a coating of hope to all manner of practices forged in the devils shadow. Heads reverently bow in anticipation of his biblical address.

"Our gracious Lord, grant us the depth of courage and strength of conviction to rise above the daily challenges we encounter and keep safe the cherished loved ones we strive to protect. Through the prevailing of eternal peace, hasten our safe passage from this enduring deprivation, and almighty God, please bless the decent fellows we begrudgingly treat as foes and the spirts of the dearly departed fallen. Amen."

"Amen," rings out in reply, before we disperse, treading the wooden boards, our sole protection from a watery grave in this chamber of mud.

A rat emerges from the soggy foundations, scurrying for his life across a raft of boot laces. We could really do with drafting a new cat into our ranks, since the untimely passing of Mr. Whiskers, hygiene standards have slipped even further. Whenever a dead body is discovered, they'll be at least three of the furry critters gnawing at the corpse, unceremoniously targeting the eyes first, before burrowing through the flesh. Four days loitering on the doorstep of death feels insurmountable, a mental monster, all I can focus on is the next few hours and what's for supper!

"What a difference a day makes, eh mate?" Says a shivering Frosty, "from a cosy warm bar to this miserable pit."

"You're not wrong, lad, it feels worse than ever, but what a night."

"Not arf, top draw, who'd have thought it, Lionheart a butterfly lover, it has got me thinking though."

"About butterflies?"

"No, you daft sod, about life, you know in general like?"

"What of it?"

"Well, it was listening to all those stories that did it, made me take a long hard look at my own life."

"Oh, all since last night," I say with surprise, "so what are you thinking?"

"Well, I know some folk believe in heaven and all that, but for me, I think this might be it, our one ride on the merry-go-round."

"Possibly, but I agree, you have to make the most of it."

"Precisely my point, Jacko, one thing this bloody war does give a man is perspective. Life's too precious to waste and I'm keen, you know, keen to start living mine, to the full like."

"You do have a good life waiting for you, you're Davy Frost, for God's sake, everybody loves you, is that not enough?"

"I don't know, I'm blessed, well, not withstanding our current situation," he says playfully slapping the trench wall. "I just think there's more out there to experience, maybe it's time to settle down, have a stab at finding my forever." He flashes a huge grin. "I can't keep breaking hearts all my life, a man needs to sow his seed and lay down roots."

"Wow, the infamous Davy Frost going steady," I joke.

"Hey, less of the steady lad, I'll never lose it, but there comes a time in a man's life when his priorities change. Look at yourself and Rose for instance, you're settled, happily married and expecting a little kiddie. That's an impressive piece of pie my friend, I've got to grab me a slice of that action, what's your secret, Jacko?"

"My goodness, you almost sound jealous" I say laughing, "there really is a first time for everything."

"Alright, alright, not so much of it."

"Sorry, mate, there's no secret, you just need to find the right girl, for me that's always been Rose, she's the whole pie."

"Easier said than done."

"I don't know, mate, you've had your moments."

He rolls his eyes, but doesn't reply, the silence is awkward, this feels like the time.

"Do you ever think of her mate."

"Who?" Replies Frosty with a nervous laugh, "there's been so many."

"You know who, Ruby."

"Ah, Ruby, yeah, she's crossed my mind once or twice," he replies with a distant look in his glazed eyes.

"I know how much you loved her, but there will be someone else out there, I promise you. It can feel elusive at times, but when you're ready, love will be waiting."

Frosty smiles ruefully. "Hark at us, Jacko, babbling on like a soppy pair of girls blouses, what will people think!"

I smile, Frosty's emotional drawbridge is raised, my signal to stop probing.

"It's funny though, mate, that you should mention her, Ruby, a coincidence like."

"How do you mean?"

"Well, there was a letter waiting for me when I arrived tonight. It's been years, but the instant I recognised the scent that had been doused all over the lilac note paper, my hands started shaking. It's the part of my life I've buried and grieved for, spending every day battling royally to expunge it from my mind. But the persistent little bugger endures and now, out of the blue, there's this letter."

"Wow, that must have come as quite a shock."

"You're telling me, mate, my heads in a jam jar, but even before I allowed myself to read a word, there were pangs of excitement. One little piece of paper has got me dreaming like a fool. It sounds pathetic, but I was scared to read it, just wanted to prolong the feeling of hope before digesting the words. How can one person hold such power over another, make such a deep an imprint on their life, their heart?"

"It's love, Frosty, an uncontrollable force as ferocious as the oceans that surround us, capable of bringing the strongest man to his knees, but also of transporting the lowliest soul to the highest peak of elation."

"Aye, that's love alright, you just can't get rid when you're done." Poor Frosty looks perplexed, but we both laugh at the sheer complexity of the conundrum.

"So…have you read the letter yet?"

"I have, mate, over and over." He pauses, his face gives precious little away. I want to respect his privacy, but I'm itching to know what the infamous Ruby Stevens has written. I sit quietly, but who am I kidding? Curiosity always wins out in the end. The situation screams out for some sensitivity, I adopt the softly, softly approach.

"So, how's she doing, Ruby?"

"Ok, I think, by the sound of it."

"Oh, that's good news."

Another frustrating interlude of silence follows, Frosty's not renowned for being a tight-lipped Terry, her words must have given him some serious food for thought.

"Been up to much, you know, since you last saw her?"

"You know Ruby, mate, wherever she lays her hat."

"Great, that's really great, I suppose."

This is like running in treacle, sod it, this sensitivity lark isn't cutting the mustard. "Look, mate, you can tell me to mind my own business, but."

"Jacko," interrupts Frosty.

"Yes?"

"Mind your own bloody business."

"Understood, mate, say no more, it's just you seem troubled and I think getting it off your chest might help."

Frosty grins. "And you're dying to know, aren't you?"

"Well, there is that," I concede, "but a trouble shared and all that."

Frosty sighs. "I guess it can't hurt, my mind seems to have reached an emotional impasse, incessantly churning."

"Ok, good, let me help."

"Ok, mate, but this goes no further mind, I've got a reputation to uphold!"

"Of course, goes without saying, so, why has she written?"

"Well, firstly she contacted me Ma, that's how she got my contact details."

I nod.

"Apparently, she's been worried about me, you know, with the outbreak of war and all that. She wants to know if I'm alright and how I'm doing."

"That's really nice, mate, so is it just the shock of hearing from her? It doesn't sound like bad news."

"Don't get me wrong, I'm absolutely thrilled to receive her letter, especially after what happened by the river. To tell you the truth, I'd given up on hearing from her ever again, but the letter, it contained a bit more than mere pleasantries."

"How do you mean?"

"In the letter she told me that she's still in love with me, in fact, she's never stopped loving me. It's everything I've longed to hear, I should be jumping for joy, but I feel frightened." He smiles sheepishly. "Ridiculous isn't it? I've got bullets whistling past my lugholes, yet it's this harmless piece of paper that terrifies me."

"Listen, mate, it's not stupid at all, this woman broke your heart, it's understandable to feel a bit scared."

"Cheers, pal, thought for a minute I was turning into a big sissy. It's just that day by the river, when I asked her to marry me, the way she answered."

"What about it?"

"She just said no. Without so much as a pause, dismissed my heartfelt proposal out of hand, it cut me in half. She wouldn't discuss it any further, the reply felt cold and final. There I was, down on one knee like a prized pratt, offering her the world and all I got back was a no, nothing more, just no. I swear, some part of me, deep inside, it died that day. It's still too painful to think about, and now she's back, with her beautifully formed semi colons and perfect spelling, offering me the world!"

"Crickey, you mean."

"Yes, everything I once promised her, all the years ago, she now wants more than ever. It doesn't even matter where we are apparently, as long as she's with me. She referred to that day by the river as the biggest regret of her life, she claims it's haunted her ever since and it's only shame and pride that's stopped her getting in touch sooner, my God, I so want to believe her."

"Ruby was incredibly young back then, Frosty, she's grown up, maybe this is what she wants, a life with you."

"It's plausible, I've no doubt her words and motive are genuine"

"So, what's the problem? This is everything you've ever wanted, she's everything."

"I know, the whole thing has knocked me for six. She wields such power over my emotions, that's what frightens me to death. To have your happiness, your very heart residing in the palm of somebody else's hand, to concede all that control. I don't know if I'm strong enough to surrender my misgivings and fully commit."

"I know exactly how you feel, mate, to have so much hope and happiness rolled up in another person, Rose is my world, the reason I get up every morning and carry on, but the alternative is even scarier. Love can be terrifying, Frosty. It's a risk that comes without guarantees, but if you want to taste that sweet honey, there's always a possibility you'll get stung."

"That's quite poetic, mate, I can see why you want to be a writer!"

"Thanks, it was rather good," I say proudly while basking in the glow of my creative effort. "So what are you going to do now, maybe write back? I assume she's enclosed an address for correspondence."

He nods. "She has indeed, somewhere down south, just shy of London. She'll be expecting a prompt reply, I suspect, Ruby's not the kind of girl who's used to waiting. Of course, I'll write back, it's the polite and proper thing to do. But I'm unsure if I can find the right words, perhaps I should keep it light, duck the pertinent questions and buy myself some time?"

"Is more time really going to make a difference?"

"I don't know mate, probably not, inaction only serves to build more fear, but at this moment procrastination feels the most attractive option." He shakes his head in dismay. "Just hearing myself say the words out loud, I sound so feeble, a sorrowful excuse of a man."

"Hey, mate, it's a perfectly natural reaction, don't beat yourself up about it. Ruby hurt you, she really hurt you, there's no shame in admitting it, nobody wants to expose their old wounds and feel vulnerable. You're human mate, just like the rest of us, fumbling around in the shadows, searching for a piece of everlasting happiness." I smile to offer added reassurance. "With an absence of nervous fear, one can only imagine how dull life would be, it's excitements evil twin!"

He laughs, shaking his head once more, but this time more in wonder.

"I suppose, this is a good problem to have, mate. Yesterday I sat at a table poignantly discussing roast potatoes, and today, through written word, Ruby has re-entered my life. In my dreams she's never left, coming alive every night. In that world we're so deliriously in love, floating around serenely in this big beautiful bubble, impenetrable from the wrath of reality. But ultimately, dreams end and life takes over. Sometimes, I wish I could sleep forever, existing only in dreams."

"Oh, I see, well therein lies the issue with Ruby."

"Sorry, I don't follow."

"She is the merging of your emotional equilibrium, two worlds, delectable dreams skirting with real life, the only person capable of blurring your reality."

Frosty looks bemused.

"These dreams though, Frosty?"

"What of them?" He says protectively, "they're not mucky if that's what you're getting at, well most aren't."

"No, it's not that, but they might be telling you something."

"Do you think?"

"Yes, I do, this woman consumes your thoughts, think about it, in a way this invitation is a manifestation of your dreams."

"Eh, speak English, lad."

"Sorry, got a bit carried away, what I mean is this is that the moment you've dreamed of for so long, this letter is an opportunity, your gateway to paradise. Try taking fear out of the equation for a moment, there's nothing else holding you back, is there?"

"No, I guess not, it's all fear."

"Ok then, good, we're getting somewhere."

"Are we?"

"Yes indeed, listen, Frosty, this is my advice to you."

He leans forward, eyes widening.

"Don't let fear steal your dream, it's a rocky road paved with nothing, but regret. You love this woman and you want to be with her, that much is true?"

"Yes, more than anything."

"Then, my friend, there's only one choice, give yourself to her wholeheartedly and don't look back. You owe it to each other to find out where this crazy kind of love can take you. Ruby makes you happy, so cherish her and the days you spend together, no matter what eventually will be, it's far better than harbouring a heavy heart laden with regret for the rest of your life."

Frosty smiles and throws his arms round me.

"Bugger me, Jacko, they broke the bloody mould after you were created, where would I be without you?"

"Don't be daft, mate, I'm the lucky one."

Frosty loosens his grasp, he's close to tears, but appears extremely happy. I've lightened the load, granting him permission to get excited about his future, it feels so good. Life can be a complicated jigsaw, but in Ruby, I feel confident Frosty has found the missing piece.

"So, you're going to write back, soon?"

"I am indeed, as soon as I calm down enough to think straight. I'll write something meaningful, probably not in your league, Shakespeare, but it will be from the heart."

"Brilliant, well done, mate."

"Thank you, Jack, sincerely, thank you for everything. I know that I can come across as a right cocky so and so, but inside I'm as frightened as the next bloke. You make the difference, my dear friend, you're the glue that holds it all together. I'm no good at all this emotional stuff, but you need to know this, how much I…erm, I love you."

"Pardon?" I say with a beaming grin.

"Don't bloody come it, you heard, and I won't be repeating it this side of heaven."

"Thank you, David, I."

"Don't you bleeding well dare, there's been more than enough soppiness for one day!"

I smile, safe in the knowledge he knows only too well, so much in life goes unspoken, but he knows.

"There's just one more obstacle," adds Frosty.

"Ok, mate, let's be having it."

"How the heck do we get out of this ghastly hovel and start living our lives again?"

I shrug my shoulders, we both laugh, gunfire continues crackling all around, but Frosty possesses the happy knack of decorating our muddy cell walls with humour. We sit, both clinging desperately to the last knockings of supper time, but as meal breaks go, this one has been highly rewarding. Perched on the edge of inevitability, Frosty lets out a deep sigh.

"I suppose we better get our backsides out there, Jacko."

"Aye, I'm afraid so, my friend, once more into the unforgiving night."

"It's weird, but I suddenly feel like I've got so much more to lose," he shakes his head, "daft old sod. It will be ok, won't it?"

His expression reeks of deep concern, I place my hand on his shoulder. "Don't worry, we're going to get through this, I've got you mate."

He smiles. "Sweet, because I'm too young and good looking to die," he says partly in jest, but shakes his head demonstrably. "It's not right, fit young men having to contend with thoughts of death, nobody would wish this life on their worst enemy. They dressed it up as some heroic crusade decked in glory, but it's a bloody suicide mission, the lying bastards."

I grab his head with both hands and hold it firmly. "Listen, mate, we're all hurting out here, but this isn't the time for anger, it will only serve to cloud your judgement. We both have long golden futures ahead of us, sweethearts to kiss, babies to cuddle, but we have to go out there and fight for that future, fight to survive, do you understand?"

He nods intently.

"Good, mate, good because it's not our time, this bloody sewer isn't going to be our destiny, ok?"

"Yes, mate, got it, let's stay alert and keep ourselves alive."

"Good man, that's the spirit, remember, all this shit's temporary. Common sense will prevail, but until then it's head down and one day at a time, Private Frost, nothing more, just keep counting those sunrises."

"Aye, aye, Sir" he says standing to attention and saluting. "Do you know something, Jacko?"

"What's that, mate?"

"You can be quite scary when you want to be, but thanks, Jack, I needed that."

"Cheers, Frosty, shall we hug?"

"In your dreams, soft lad."

The days and nights that follow are brutal, a veritable shower of shell and shot, with blood aplenty spilt on both sides. Following a brief taste of freedom, there seems a shared determination to break the stalemate and triumph at the earliest opportunity, but sadly, renewed intensity brings chaos and carnage in sorrowful abundance.

The night air is filled with the desperate groans of dying men, blasted from the confines of the trenches, be it friends or foes, the sounds are no less harrowing and only death, wars one true freedom, will silence them. There's barely a wink of sleep to be had, I cover my ears in a futile attempt to blot out their cries, but it doesn't, nothing will. They're accompanied by the all-too-familiar revolting stench of decaying death. It's impossible, as I lay staring into the darkness, to prevent a ghoulish gallery of images infiltrating my morbid ridden mind. Young men with limbs blown off, their concluding minutes on God's green earth spent slowly bleeding out, one can't start to comprehend the untold suffering endured in their final agonising moments. Some scream out for help, their calls growing ever fainter, while others manage to summon up the names of sweethearts, declaring their eternal love or deepest regrets, a final plea for absolution. Then there are the brave souls who silently bear the pain, taking what comfort they can from the finality of the situation. To hide my perceived weakness I sob ever so quietly, shedding tears for comrades and strangers alike. I scrunch my eyes tight to stem the flow, offering up a humble prayer for the dying, God knows who's listening, I've never felt more forsaken.

A third day in the mire, my mental horizon brightens a touch as thoughts inevitably drift to the hallowed handover, it's the faintest of shifts, but enough to raise my spirits. The passing of time gradually alters perception, ninety six hours felt unsurmountable, even impossible, but less than forty and I'm ticking them off in earnest. It's a mental exercise that must be conducted without the loss of focus, lapses tend to result in a bullet through the brain, scant reward indeed!

Thankfully, throughout this frenetic period the unofficial breakfast truces are still being rigidly adhered to by both warring parties. I spot Frosty sauntering through the trench brazenly flaunting his cheerfulness, much to the surprise and annoyance of a glut of weary warriors, but he whistles away regardless. There's no need to ask what's put a spring in his step, I'm finding it infectious, in a minefield of misery, it's wonderful to witness his joyous state, made all the sweeter by the fact he's my best friend.

"There you go, mate, grubs up," he declares, tossing me a bacon sandwich.

"Oh, cheers, Frosty," I reply gratefully, "this is just the ticket old boy, my stomachs been groaning since dawn."

"No problem, get stuck in, lad."

I don't need a second invitation, gorging gleefully on its crispy contents.

"Steady on, Jacko, you'll give yourself a belly ache."

I nod and begin chewing slower, *my goodness, it tastes even better.*

"Right, mate," he says rubbing his hands together, "what do you fancy doing today?"

"How about staying alive, that'll do for starters."

"Grand idea, I concur wholeheartedly, my learned friend."

"My, you're full of beans this morning."

"Why not? I have my plentiful good looks, roguish charm, and best of all mate, the love of a beautiful woman waiting in the wings. It appears the world is dancing to my tune."

He winks and I nod my approval.

"I'm pleased for you, mate."

"Thanks, it's a weird sensation given our predicament, to feel happiness in the most hopeless place. His expression turns sour. "I hear them, you know, out there and inside my head, the despairing cries, eventually giving way to stricken last breaths, it leaves me cold and broken. I don't mean to disrespect the chaps who are tragically dying around us, but this happiness, it's unexpected and difficult to control, it comes in snatches and I feel guilty for deriving enjoyment from it."

"Don't feel guilty, mate, the heartbreak, that chilling sense of helplessness, we're all afflicted by sorrow. There isn't a man here who won't take those cries to his grave. So, if you spot a chink of happiness glinting through this veil of suffering, vigorously extract all the joy you can. Don't banish the light, for goodness sake, keep it burning, these days are dark enough."

He smiles and nods. "God bless you, Jacko."

"Hey, lads," screams Lionheart from across the trench, "the Sarg needs a word."

"When?"

"Now, come on, look lively chaps."

We exchange uneasy glances, in affairs of war urgency tends not to bode well.

We arrive at the double, to find three freshly poured whiskies lined up across a table, now I really am worried. Sergeant Bevan is standing, he looks agitated, greeting us with an uneasy smile.

"Ah, good morning chaps, please help yourself."

"Bit early isn't it, Sergeant?" asks Frosty.

He shakes his head. "Believe me David, in this place it's never too early."

"Oh, in that case, cheers boys."

"Good man."

Clearly wrestling on the horns of a dilemma, Sergeant Bevan begins to pace while we sip and wonder.

"Look chaps, yesterday I had the dubious pleasure of a late night visit from General Hughes."

I can hear the collective sound of our hearts sinking.

"Oh," I reply, "how did it go?"

"Well, let's just say we enjoyed a heated exchange, he didn't mince his words when it came to conveying the sense of disappointment currently felt by top brass."

"Oh dear, have they ran out of clean towels again?" Frosty retorts with utter distain.

"Quite," replies Sergeant Bevan, appreciating his embittered sentiment. "Apparently the distinct lack of progress will not be tolerated a second longer."

Lionheart leans forward. "Is this it, Sergeant Bevan, the big one, are we going over the top?"

Internally, I gasp, suddenly contemplating the unthinkable, the three words guaranteed to send a chill down any soldiers spine have been given licence to breathe. *How can one prepare themselves for such a mission, to charge headlong in to enemy fire with such reckless abandonment?* Fatalities are the only certainty afforded in the ultimate do or die scenario, it's just a question of how many before the enemy trenches can be breached, if at all. In a civilised society, why is this senseless course of action preferable to conducting peace talks in? Governments appear content to sacrifice fledging souls rather than getting around a table and thrashing out a resolution. Man has been blessed with a host of God-given talents, but here we stand, tragically concentrating all of our efforts on destroying each other. How the divine powers stationed above must weep for a world once created, that bleeds so needlessly.

"No, Reginald, not this time I'm happy to report, but in order to appease General Hughes I have agreed to carry out a small reconnaissance mission."

"Reconnaissance mission" I ask, "what does that entail?"

Sergeant Bevan sighs heavily.

"Look chaps, I'm not going to sugarcoat this, officially it's a factfinding expedition, but that doesn't make it any less hazardous. Our job will be to observe the enemy and report back, but I must warn you, this involves treading perilously close to the German trenches."

"Bugger me," says Frosty, "it sounds risky, what do we stand to gain from this?"

"Good question, David. This exercise is potentially a prelude to a full on attack, therefore we're being tasked with gathering as much intelligence as possible. This means observing their night time operations, where their snipers are deployed, spotting weak spots in the trench wall and so forth.

Needless to say this operation is strictly on a need-to-know basis and I require my very best chaps on this one, it will be just us four."

"When?" I ask.

"It's zero three hundred hours, tomorrow morning."

"Blimey," shouts Frosty, "that's less than a day."

Sergeant Bevan nods, causing an exchange of anxious glances coupled with a distinct lack of enthusiasm.

"So, you'll be coming with us, Sergeant Bevan?"

"That is correct Private, I would not ask you to do anything I'm not willing to do myself. General Hughes isn't keen on my participation, but I was adamant. If I die, out there in the field, leading my men, then so be it, that's preferable than nervously waiting to learn of another's fate."

His loyalty is commendable, most mere mortals would plump for the sanctuary of the sidelines.

"Listen men, I realise this is a big ask, huge in fact, I'm asking you put your very lives on the line, it's not a plea I make lightly, but I will understand if you'd rather not do it, this is a request gentlemen, not a command."

"So, this is our choice?"

"Yes, and whatever you choose, there will be no recourse, of that, I promise you."

Immediately, Lionheart stands to his feet. "Count me in, Sergeant Bevan," he bellows.

"Thank you, Reginald, I really appreciate it."

"I'm in, too, Sir," I add, albeit with a touch less conviction, "whatever you need."

"Thank you, Jack, splendid." It's not a prospect I'm relishing, but its an easy choice, all eyes now drift to one Private, David Frost.

"Well, if you're all going, who am I to spoil the party?"

Classic Frosty, he was never going to let me go alone.

"Thank you, David, top man."

A few moments of quiet contemplation follow as the gravity of the situation begins to sink in, only the vigorous slurping of whisky can be heard.

"Ok, chaps, I wish to reiterate my deep appreciation for your brave compliance, words simply aren't enough to convey my upmost gratitude. You'll all be excused from sentry duty this evening, so please get some rest, we'll reconvene at zero two hundred hours for a briefing prior to the commencement of the mission."

"Thank you, Sir."

We each receive a firm handshake and a personal thank you upon leaving, Sergeant Bevan looks relieved, for him I'm sure the task of asking us felt a more daunting prospect than the mission itself. Our short walk back to post is conducted in deathly silence, we're fully aware it's a suicide mission, pure and simple, when faced with one's mortality, there's much to mull over.

Another chilly day succumbs to eerie blackness , I try to rest, but it's an impossible task with the spectre of death casting it's unsightly and ever darkening shadow. I'm still a young man with lots to learn and experience, *heck, I've barely lived, gazing at too few sunsets and enjoying nowhere near enough kisses.* Surely, God has a grander plan for me than this, to lay down and relinquish my last breath under a disturbed sky, amidst a decaying dirt filled bog of broken dreams, there has to be more. I've found a crazy, beautiful love in the warm inviting arms of Rose and there's the magical pitter-patter of small footsteps to look forward to, my futures never felt so enticing. *I've had a taste of life's golden honey, surely He wouldn't be so cruel as to snatch the whole pot from my despairing grasp?* I shake my head in fury, damn this blasted war and what it's reduced me to. Bemoaning its injustice will not alter the moment that mentally incarcerates me, a fate fraught with fear. My mind, in dire need of escape, painfully bulges whilst continuing to play out torturous scenarios in slow motion. Mercifully, a welcome reprieve arrives in the form of a strong urge to craft some correspondence, to Rose.

My dearest, darling Rose,

Happy New Year, my sweetheart!

Here we are, 1915, the birth of a new year, granted, the circumstances could be better, but I firmly believe this will be our year. We're going to be parents, welcoming the gift of new life into our perfect little world, there can be nothing more precious.

How were your New Year celebrations? I hope you had a swell old time. Myself and some of the lads, Sergeant Bevan included, enjoyed some drinks in a local watering hole. It turned out to be a very special evening indeed, the kind that'll stay with me. We drank to loved ones, our health and heartily toasted the golden notion of peace imminently breaking out. Well, the whiskies were flowing and one can still dream, try as they may, at least they can't take that from us! Then there were Frosty's beloved roast potatoes, but that's a story for another day!

I do love you, Rose, with every beat of my aching heart. I realise that I write these words as a matter of course, but please don't think for a single moment that the frequency of my expression diminishes its meaning. My love, for you is limitless, greater than the number of stars inhabiting Gods majestic sky and being apart is unbearable. Come what may, my love for you will endure a lifetime and beyond, if I must haunt you then so be it! I live to be a good husband and in time a good father too, my greatest fear is in ever letting you down, because you, my angel, deserve every wonder this world has to offer.

I don't mean to worry you, but if the worst were to happen, my darling, you must bravely carry on and in time, love again. That is my wish Rose, in the absence of guilt, please find the strength to love again. Excuse my act of allowing this painful realism to spill on to the page, but I beg of you, please heed my words if that fateful day comes.

Needless to say, I will fight to my last breath to make my way back to you and the gorgeous life we share, let's not forget that I have Frosty beside me, my guardian angel, he sends his love, by the way.

This time tomorrow, I'll be back in billets and happily dreaming of the next time I'll get to kiss you. My leave has been pushed back to coincide with the birth at my request. It feels like an eternity, but every passing day brings me a step closer to you.

I love you, my Rose, now, forever and always.

Your Jack

I sit back and allow the moment to settle, composing a letter to Rose is always an emotional experience, particularly today. I dab my eyes with a handkerchief before returning to peruse the sum total of my literary efforts. I feel I've pushed things as far as I can, choosing to omit all mention of the dreaded mission. In war, one must be mindful of how much misery a single word can inflict, even the tone of the letter can speak volumes. I know from experience that every sentence will be dissected through the course of multiple readings, these simple letters are the only link we share, all we have to cling on to. This piece of paper could serve as my last ever contact, *bugger, there's always so much more to say! Well, that's that I guess, job done.* I'll pop it into the postmaster on route to our early morning rendezvous.

It feels darker than death, but the night is still and dry when us three brave, but worried souls arrive at Sergeant Bevans den. Once again, we are greeted with the welcome sight of fresh whiskies, only there are four poured this time and thankfully they're more generous.

"Good morning, men."

"Good morning, Sergeant Bevan."

Our gracious host looks dog tired, eyes sporting lead lined lids which are adorned with dark circles, the great toll of war has never appeared more evident, poor bugger, but the trooper still musters a smile.

"As you were, and please, help yourself to some refreshments, it will help stave off the cold."

"Aye," says Frosty, "and give us some Dutch courage."

Sergeant Bevan smiles. "Quite, David, we can all use a dose of that."

Good old Frosty, regardless of its severity, he's still capable of lightening any mood.

"Ok chaps, let's get down to business, our aim is to get as close as possible, preferably undetected, observe their set up and movements, then get the hell out of there."

"Here, here, I'll drink to that," adds Frosty.

"What happens if we're detected?" Asks Lionheart.

"Well," interrupts Frosty, "we're brown bread, aren't we?"

"Not on my watch, David," counters Sergeant Bevan, "but at the earliest indication we've been rumbled chaps, run like the bloody blazes!"

"Right you are, Sir," says Lionheart with a nod.

"Ok chaps, if we're to be successful tonight then composure is critical, we have to stay calm and be deliberate in our actions, the only sound permitted must come from our beating hearts." He reaches in to his tunic breast pocket, pulling out a crumpled piece of paper before flattening it on the table. "Please, excuse the crudeness of my diagram, but we will exit the trench here and proceed on foot to the enemy trench, which is situated approximately eighty to ninety meters away. I estimate the sniper points to be situated here and here, those are the ones we know of. It's imperative we're close enough to survey the terrain and condition of their defences, seek out any weak spots, that sort of thing. We all have pocket flashlights, but these must be used sparingly, for obvious reasons."

"How close exactly?" I ask.

"Close enough to hear them breathe, listen to their conversations, I speak a little German, enough that may prove valuable. We need to observe how the enemy operates, understand their mindset."

"Pretty damn close then," shouts Frosty, "blimey!"

"Indeed, but we'll assess things as we go, your safety is my primary concern."

"So, we're going to be approaching on foot then?" Enquires Lionheart.

"Yes, Reginald, initially, but we may revert to crawling the nearer we get, obviously we'll drop to the ground in the event of enemy fire or if we get the slightest inkling of detection."

I'd never dare say it, but internally I'm questioning the merits of the mission, I mean, how much will we see or learn in the dead of night? Courtesy of General Hughes, this frivolous concoction carries the severest risk for minimal reward. This haphazard thinking feels like nothing more than an ill-fated exertion of authority, belated punishment for Christmas. I guess the bastards can always get four more warm bodies.

The Devils hour approaches and the whisky's run dry, predictably the mood is pensive and communication is limited to the odd word or grunt accompanied by numb expressions. I glance at my comrades and wonder, on the precipice of their gravest endeavour, what thoughts flow through their besieged minds? Personally, I can't think past Rose and how my imminent actions could affect all that she's dreaming of, leaving her world in tatters. If I go to my maker tonight, at least I'll die content in the knowledge I've loved and been loved fervently, but I won't be the one who has to soldier on. The thought is bitterly vile, I can't allow it to settle and burn briskly from the inside out. I quickly revert to my memory well, in search of something more wholesome, first kiss, last kiss come to that, whatever staves off these blasted demons. Surprisingly, I'm whisked back to a Rose free moment, it's from my childhood, nothing life affirming, but nice nevertheless.

My six year old self is sat at the dining room table eating tea, right arm patched up following a nasty fall earlier in the day. If only Billy 'bad boy' Jones hadn't dared me to jump off that garden wall on to the concrete! So, I'm feeling a little sorry for myself, hence the quivering bottom lip, but my delicate condition allows my wonderful mother to indulge in her speciality, making a right royal fuss of me! I'm literally being smothered with cuddles and kindness as she lovingly caters to my every need, thank you Billy.

"How is it feeling now pet, is there anything else you need?"

"Another drink, please."

She smiles warmly and kisses my forehead. "Coming right up, my cherub."

Its gloriously relentless, I feel so special and deeply loved, the centre of her universe. The arm is sore and stiff, but the joyous attention is outweighing the pain, hopefully it will heal slowly! There is a divine smell wafting in from the kitchen, the pain pauses as my senses are overpowered, it couldn't be could it? Pudding is normally reserved for Sundays or special occasions, but unless I'm very much mistaken, something sweet and delicious is bubbling away in that kitchen. Oh boy, am I in for a treat, mums puddings are irresistible, a sugar coated slice of paradise.

"Something smells good."

"It's a treat for my brave little soldier, you can have as much as you like."

She brings out a jug of something warm and an empty bowl, it's custard, the anticipation is delectable, my groaning stomach is doing cartwheels. I hear the oven door open, my mother reappears wearing oven gloves and carrying what looks like a steaming hot pie, before placing it carefully in the middle of the table.

"It's cherry pie," she says proudly, "your favourite."

I feel like crying, there's nothing on this earth more delectable than my ma's cherry pie.

"Thanks, Mum," I say trying to check my excitement, I am in a lot of pain let's not forget!

"It just needs to cool for a few minutes."

"Ok."

It's the longest few minutes of my life, desperate to devour it, all I can do is stare longingly at this perfect creation, beneath the golden brown pastry, coated in glistening sugar, lies fresh cherries encased in a thick fruit jam filling. Finally, she cuts a generous slice out of the pie, places it in my bowl and douses the glazed masterpiece in custard.

"Careful, my angel, the filling will still be hot,"

I nod, but tuck in regardless, it's moreish, everything I anticipated and more, as I chew my head floats in a pool of pleasure.

"Right, men," says Sergeant Bevan, placing a small tin on the table, "put some of this burnt cork onto black out your faces. We'll offer the enemy nothing more than the whites of our eyes, so try not to smile too much," he says dryly.

Sergeant Bevans rare stab at humour elicits a ripple of laughter that grows into a wave, smashing through the tension, the release is manna from heaven, but it subsides quickly.

"Ok, men, we will proceed across the terrain in single file, I'll be out in front, so follow my lead at all times, if I stop, drop or run and so forth. Furthermore, I must insist on no talking for the duration of the mission." Our gazes naturally gravitate to Frosty.

"What?" He says in astonishment, before rolling his eyes, "ok, fair enough, message understood Sarg."

"Good, now chaps," he says in a more deliberate deeper tone, "we're going to be confronted with some grisly sights out there, downright deplorable scenes."

We lower our heads, conscious of the heart wrenching debris we must navigate, the ravaged corpses of the brutally sacrificed. In life, we're presented with a beautiful blank canvas, so rich with possibilities, but, then there's war, a brush capable of painting the ugliest of portraits.

"Nothing can prepare us, but we must summon up the strength to remain impassive to its horror, when we're safely back, then we can weep for our brothers."

We nod, it's a harrowing truth unquantifiable by mere words.

"Right then," says Sergeant Bevan standing to his feet, "the hour has found us, but before we depart, please allow me to lead us in a short prayer." We bow our heads once more in readiness, allowing his final words to wash over us.

"Our almighty God, please watch over the brave souls of this magnificent band of men and grant me the strength to lead them through the darkness and safely home. Amen."

"Amen."

It's brief, but delivered with immense poignancy.

"Right, men, the best of British to all of you."

Firm handshakes are exchanged, one last act of defiant solidarity before we offer ourselves to the unforgiving night. I look Frosty squarely in his bloodshot eyes, they're warm, but framed with fear and

I can't imagine mine are faring much better. Inexplicably, he summons up the courage to smile and I reciprocate, God bless him.

"Back for breakfast, eh, Jacko?"

"Bacon sandwiches?"

"Of course, warm and greasy."

"I'll look forward to it mate."

We both nod, comfortable with the understanding we share. Our very existences have, for the main, been entwined, through whatever sweetness and sorrow life casts, that's the way it is and always will be. There can be no separation, even in death, if the journey ends tonight, then we'll die together, two friends forging one river of blood.

A whistling wind would have provided the perfect foil for our covert foray, but alas, the night affords stillness, delivering an eerie quietness. One by one we shuffle out of the trench, our mud lined, rat infested prison cell that now feels like sweet sanctuary. I'm standing on perilous ground, in the graveyard of fallen heroes, an angels paradise for the recovery of lost souls. Thankfully, the distinct crackle of enemy fire remains conspicuous by its absence, inferring our entrance appears to have gone unnoticed. I want to look anywhere, but down at the human carnage, unfortunately though, it's a necessary evil if I'm going to navigate the cluttered bomb ravaged terrain quietly, like the proverbial mouse. Begrudgingly, I briefly lay my tired eyes upon the darkly devastation and shudder, it's like the last days of hell, bare carcasses dominate the landscape, long since stripped of flesh and dignity. Skulls, once home to hopeful eyes, encasing fertile minds capable of concocting a cluster of the most audacious dreams, now nothing more than empty shells, tragic remnants of sacrifice and wasted potential, the most repugnant hallmarks of a bloody war. Man is blessed with an impressive armoury of talents, the ability to create stunning works of art, music that moves the soul and great pieces of literature that fuel imagination, but their greatest gift is a limitless capacity to love. Yet look at this wasteland, shamefully steeped in desolation, a horrific homage to our most hideous trait, the desire to destroy.

I'm moving ever so slightly towards the enemy, walking on egg shells, with every precious step deemed a success. The fear, while unwelcome, is wholly necessary when one is in survival mode, no other emotion is capable of attaining such a high state of alertness. I'm acutely aware of my beating heart, the thud grows ever more deafening as I edge closer to an ill-fated destiny. Lionheart is directly in front and Frosty to the rear, but consumed by the moment, I can barely hear them breathe. A frighteningly large rats scurries across my boot laces, suitably startled, I suppress the urge to swear and keep shuffling forward. Ever so faint voices come into earshot, *bloody hell, we're almost there,* standing on the treacherous shoulders of a chilling reality. Sergeant Bevan stops walking and holds up his hand, I stand, as motionless as my quaking body will allow, the cold night air gently massages my face, *is this the last thing I'll ever feel?*

German voices carried on the breeze appear clearer, I can't help but recall my dear friend Wilhelm, a beautiful but, tortured soul, I pray he still resides amongst the living and I haven't just trodden over his scant remains. Sergeant Bevan squats with the all the serenity of an accomplished ballerina and lays down, I follow suit immediately, but with slightly less grace. Face firmly in the mud, I inch towards a baron land only fools dare to tread. Its coarse, I can taste it, the blood soaked dirt crumbles against my icy lips. Once more, our brave Sergeant comes to a halt and beckons us forward with his right arm, *sweet Jesus, this is frightfully close.*

On one side of the trench wall, two German soldiers continue chatting away, thankfully oblivious to the four foes precariously lying next to each other on the opposite side. I can almost reach out and touch their defences, a cough or sneeze away from an agonising death by firing squad. Clutching a flashlight, I have no desire to engage, but I must show willing and risk the quickest of blasts. To be honest, at this precise moment, I couldn't give a monkeys about how the German defences look, I just want Sergeant Bevan to turn round and lead us cautiously home, back to our own dirt-ridden-rat-infested patch of hell. Unsurprisingly though, from what I can see, their defences are in fine fettle, bloody German efficiency! The talking ends abruptly, leaving our thudding heartbeats exposed. My rigid body lies frozen in fear, too scared to exhale, is this it, I hold my breath and hope forlornly that a second cloak of conversation will be generously gifted, a continued silence will ultimately prove our undoing.

Thank God, voices shatter the tension, we're still ghosts, albeit on the cusp of extinction, but at least we're moving again, initially creeping backwards on our bellies in a gingerly fashion. I've managed to pivot my body round, but snaking across this rugged crater filled terrain is painful and draining, slicing away at my skin. A task made harder by the need to quietly nudge the bones of Braveheart's away with my outstretched arms, a gruesome endeavour indeed. I'm existing purely on an appetite to live, the desire lends fuel to my aching limbs. Sergeant Bevan initiates a pause to our arduous progress, my battered body gratefully devours each precious second of rest, blood oozing from my knees and elbows seeps through my tattered clothing. I can see our trench in the distance and long to be cocooned within the confines of its thick muddy walls, but for now, those walls feel hopelessly out of reach.

Sergeant Bevan slowly rises to his feet, this is it, the final push home. It begins at a snail's pace, but naturally gathers momentum due to the influx of adrenalin. I'm over halfway, *my goodness, maybe everything is going to be ok, we're going to make it back.* I can sense it, precious victory, life, love, the blessed gift of opportunity, all lies within my grasp, but then, catastrophe, Lionheart stumbles…and crunch!

"Der feind, der feind," cries out, followed by "Feuer, Feuer!"

The booming command is accompanied by flares illuminating the night sky, we're stranded, sitting ducks. A soldier will often wonder how he will react if faced with this moment, the one when their very life is in the gravest of danger, but the truth is all one has is instinct and the good grace of God, mine is to run and it's a popular choice shared by my panic stricken comrades. Hot on the heels of an explosion of light come flurries of fire and the screeching sound of shells being launched high into the night, landing menacingly in the mire of no-mans-land, causing huge tremors. All I can do is pray for the Lords clemency and frantically pump out my arms and legs. I can feel the bullets whistling by, they're perilously close, but our hardy chaps are staunchly fighting back, it's a full scale battle!

"Argh," screams Lionheart, collapsing to the ground, fuck, the big man is down.

Closely flanked by Frosty and Sergeant Bevan, I check back and rush to his aid. Clutching his leg, the poor bugger is writhing in all manner of pain.

"It's my right leg, Sir, a blasted ricochet."

"Come on chaps, lets get this good fellow home."

Lionheart shakes his head defiantly. "No, Sir, please, just leave me here to rest and save yourselves. I've enjoyed a decent life, please Sergeant Bevan, I beg of you, walk away and let me go, it's my time."

I've never witnessed an act of such selfless bravery up close before, it's everything this courageous man embodies, but Sergeant Bevan is having none of it.

"I won't hear of it, Reginald, not on my watch, young man, Jack, grab his other arm, and David, his legs, as quick as you can."

"Aye, aye, Sir."

He's a man mountain, but freakish strength can often be summoned from the bodies of weary men pitted against unrelenting adversary.

"One, two, three and lift."

Yes, we've raised Lionheart! Armed with renewed determination, we're running for our lives once more, often sideways when the earth quakes, dodging deep craters, strewn skeletons and a shower of shot and shell, but running and barring death or serious injury, we're not going to stop.

> "Come on," screams Frosty, "we're going to make it."
>
> "Almost there chaps," cries Sergeant Bevan encouragingly.
>
> "That's it lads," a pain stricken Lionheart interjects, "one last push."

I'm just trying to keep my legs moving and stay upright, while wrestling with the knowledge that a bullet could nestle in the back of my skull at any given moment. The threat of impending death is powering my adrenalin fuelled body on at a canter, tired limbs now feel possessed.

"We've bloody made it," cries out an elated Frosty, lunging for all his worth, "we're going to live!"

Outstretched arms drag us back into the trench, to a crescendo of raucous cheers. Lionheart is whisked off to the medic with a suspected flesh wound, he'll be back, stronger than ever. The energy dissipates immediately from my sapped body, exhausted from the monumental endeavour and overcome with relief, I collapse in to Frosty's arms.

"I've got you mate, it's going to be ok, I've got you."

"It's as we first thought, Reginald, has suffered a rather nasty looking wound, but he's going to be as right as rain following a few days rest," a relieved Sergeant Bevan informs us.

"It'll take more than a nick to keep that big bugger down," replies Frosty.

"Quite, David, the man's a hero, willing to die in the field, just to give us a fighting chance. If we'd left him behind, my goodness, I'd never forgive myself, better to die by his side than live out a hollowed existence."

For me, there can be nobody more worthy of admiration than Sergeant Bevan, the man bleeds loyalty by the bucket load. If it had been my decision to make, I'm sure I'd have made the same call but, in that moment, with death on the doorstep, bombs raining down and bullets zipping past your ears, who knows? Life or death scenarios, they're the ultimate test of a man's character, tonight, he passed with flying colours.

"Sergeant Bevan."

"Yes, Jack."

"Well done, Sir, you did brilliantly tonight," I state with great sincerity, in appreciation of my candour, he nods modestly.

"Yes, Sir," adds Frosty, "bloody good job."

“Thanks, but its me who should be thanking the both of you, fine gentlemen, for your unwavering service tonight, duties performed without question or hesitation, for your unstinting loyalty and…and for risking your lives.” Choked with emotion, he pauses. “Gentlemen, I’ll never forget it, what you did at my request, I’m forever in your debt, now get some rest and we’ll debrief tomorrow, midday, back at billets.”

Billets, in all the commotion I’d lost all track of time, hardly surprising, nothing feels real after cheating death. I should be lying out there, amongst the dusty bones, fresh meat for the army of rodents that plunder the deep disturbing crevices of no-mans-land. I’ll never comprehend fate, but at least I’ve landed on the shinny side of it, from this point on its all a bonus.

“It’s gone four you know, almost handover time mate and then, bacon sandwiches back at the ranch.”

I smile, but don’t reply, my eyelids are dropping, he sounds so faint, I can no longer distinguish between what sounds encompass dreaming or reality, but I’ve had quite enough of reality for one night. Before my worn body duly succumbs, I feel a blanket being placed over me, may God bless you, David Frost.

Boom, one final act of brutal retaliation to rudely awake me from my deep slumber reverberates through trench. Thrust unsuspectedly into a chasm of carnage, I find myself face down in boggy dirt saturated with sewage water. My first thought is for Frosty, my best friend, I have to find him. Clawing my fingernails through the dirt, I manage to push myself up through a pile of shaken bodies. The hit was perilously close, but thankfully didn’t explode in my immediate vicinity, I’ve miraculously cheated death once more, surely there's only so much grace one man can be afforded? In the prevailing chaos I start dragging dazed men to their feet, bleary eyed and bewildered, but none of them are Frosty.

"Frosty, Frosty," I scream, "Frosty."

I pray for a sarcastic quip, something along the lines of 'keep your hair on you big girl,' but nothing. I feel severely nauseous, something darks brewing within, swirling through my mangled insides. Stricken with panic, I drop to my knees and continue desperately rummaging through the pandemonium in search of my friend.

"Frosty," I bellow once more.

"Jack" a faint voice groans, it sounds familiar but, it's not him. "Jack, over here."

"Danny, thank God, are you ok?"

He appears woozy, but physically intact.

"I think so, man, that was bloody close."

"Have you seen Frosty, mate? I can't find him."

"Erm Frosty, oh, my aching head."

"Danny," I screech, grabbing him by the lapels roughly, "concentrate, have you seen him, was he here before the blast?"

He shakes his head. "I'm sorry, mate, he may have been, but I can't remember for sure, it's all a blur, I'm so sorry." He starts to cry, I relax my grip and smooth down his crumpled blazer.

"It's ok, mate, I'm sorry, you've done nothing wrong, I just need to know he's ok."

"I saw him" calls out another voice nearby, "before the explosion like."

It's Bookworm, beautiful Barry Bookworm, slightly disorientated, but coherent.

"Oh you did, thank God, he must be round here somewhere then."

He looks sorrowfully, glassy eyed and shakes his head ruefully. A sinking feeling envelops my rigid body, the last remnants of hope dissolving, something inside me is slowly dying.

"I'm afraid not."

"Sorry, what do you mean?"

His mud splattered face contorts with anguish, he's shaking.

"He left, just before."

"Left? To go where Barry? Where the hell is Frosty?"

"The latrines, that way."

He points in the direction of the blast, the horrific realization causes my world to stand still for a moment, a dagger through my sunken heart. In haste, my frazzled brain serves up a surreal state of numbness, temporarily protecting me from the pain. I'm frozen in a nightmare that's playing out in slow motion, a sinister mishmash of make believe. *Perhaps I'm still sleeping, it's been the longest night, that'll be it, just a bad dream, nothing more than nonsense swirling round my head, but it's not.* The moment passes allowing reality to return with vengeance.

I'm tearing through the trench screaming out Frosty's name, charging right through the epicentre of the valley of vanquished hope. Unashamedly hurdling casualties and bouncing of groggy bodies, I rush dementedly in to the epicentre of devastation, straight into the restraining arms of Sergeant Bevan.

"Frosty, Sir, Frosty, I have to get to him, he needs my help."

I try to force my way past, but he pushes back, clutching me tighter.

"You don't understand, he's my best friend. I have to get to him, please, Sir, he's all alone."

"Oh, my dear boy, my dear, dear boy, I'm afraid it's too late."

"No, no, no, it can't be, we've got to save him, please, there's still time, I have to save him." He forcibly grabs my head, tears are streaming down his ashen face.

"It's too late son, David, well, he's with the angels now."

"No, you're mistaken, Sir, not Frosty, he wouldn't allow it. We're going home together, that's the deal, it's always been the deal. Sergeant Bevan, please, I can't go home, not without him."

"I'm sorry, Jack, so terribly sorry, but there's nothing more we can do for David, he's gone."

It's slowly dawning, I'm not going to wake from this tragedy, escape the sorrow that's starting to consume me, I've lost him, my dearest friend, we were meant to grow old together and have bacon sandwiches for breakfast! I sink my head into his damp tunic and close my eyes, too engrossed in shock to cry for my dearly departed best friend. I can't allow the tears to tumble, it's an acknowledgement of loss, acceptance that David Frost has died, his gorgeous soul extinguished. If I don't cry, then maybe, just maybe, this unbearable pain isn't real.

"I need to see him, Sir, please."

"I understand, Jack, but, I simply can't allow that, it's for your own sake."

"But Sir, I need to see him, I'm begging you, let me hold him."

"Jack, please trust me, I can't permit you to see him, not the way he is, it shouldn't be your final memory of David, believe me, it's for the best son."

Now, they come, ferociously, its brutally real.

We buried Private David Frost on a beautiful Tuesday morning, well, what scant remains my comrades recovered, under a sprawling apple tree close to the river. It seemed fitting, he loved a slice of his dear Ma's apple pie and the way water meandered through land laden with scenic beauty. In the presence of the entire battalion, kitted out in full military attire, I had one final task to perform for my beloved friend.

"It's a tremendous honour, to be given the opportunity, to eulogise about a man's life, but nevertheless a thankless task. How can a man's worth, his contribution to a world now evidently poorer for his absence, be justified in a handful of sentences? I can't begin to scratch the surface, but here goes, David Frost, Frosty, he mastered life. Attaining its greatest riches in abundance, to love freely and be loved unconditionally, beyond this, nothing really matters. In simple terms, he touched hearts and broke his fair share too, men envied, but admired him and woman, well they just fell in love with the lucky bugger. He could be a cheeky sod, flashy at times, but he decorated dreary lives with vibrant splashes of colour, lit up rooms with laughter and always offered up a warm smile, regardless of how he was feeling. The guy pedalled happiness relentlessly, an enduring epitaph engraved across our grief-stricken hearts. Fortunately, we, Frosty and myself, got to share our lives together, from little nippers. I happily existed in constant awe of him, he was, sorry, is my hero and a trusted and fiercely loyal friend, the best I'll ever have. Just the other day he received a letter from an old flame, I'd never seen him happier. After years of secretly nursing a broken heart, the love of his life, his eternal sweetheart Ruby awaited his return, all he ever wanted and deserved. I'll never get the pleasure of seeing what could of become, of my dear friend, David, a man capable of stealing the stars from the sky, but he's bestowed onto me a treasure trove of cherished memories, more than most folk will experience in two lifetimes. Conkers in the playground, beers in the Dirty Duck, it didn't matter, he made the mundane bristle with life, eternally golden and leaves a void that can never be filled. Frosty, if you're up there, behave yourself and never stop spreading your unique brand of happiness. Sadly, this is goodnight, my beloved best friend, but, never goodbye."

"Pack your things up, Jack, as quick as you can now."

"I beg your pardon, Sir?"

"You're booked on the train at eighteen hundred hours."

"I'm sorry, Sergeant Bevan, I don't understand, my leave isn't due for months."

"I realise that, Private, but, I'm granting you a week's compassionate leave."

"But, Sir, the men, they need me."

"Yes Jack, they do, but they need you present, my boy."

"I'm here, Sir, standing a post and ready to fight."

"Look, Jack, since David died, you've been lost, a danger to yourself and the other men. This isn't a criticism, it's understandable, David was a shinning light, we all miss him terribly, but he was your best friend, its bound to hit you the hardest."

"I'm so sorry, Sir, I'll do better, I promise."

"Nonsense, Jack, just take a moment to relax, spend time with Rose and begin to heal. Grief is a dark ugly cloud, my dear boy, the stubborn bastard follows you around, hovering menacingly. It never fully clears, but in time you'll find the strength to co-exist. I need you back here, rested and fighting fit." I nod.

"Good man, now look lively."

"Erm, there is one thing."

"Yes, Jack?"

"Frosty's belongings, have they been sent back yet?"
"No, I don't think so, just the notice," he shakes his head, "his poor old mother."
"May I be permitted to deliver them, personally?"
"Are you sure, Jack, you don't need to do this."
"I want to, Sir, if that's ok."
"I understand, old boy, of course, I'll have them sent over immediately."
"Thank you, Sir."

One small metal box, not much to show for the sacrificing of another cherished young life. A doting mother watches her son leave for war, proud, but racked with worry and hoping against hope this isn't the last time she lay eyes on her beloved boy, then months later a letter followed by a metal box, hardly a fair return. Inside there's a few crumpled photos, one of his mother, another of Ruby and us, I've never seen this before, taken the day we signed up, arms flung around each other and grinning like cheshire cats, two boys off to conquer the world. There's also a watch and a St Christopher pendant, I hastily fasten it round my neck, it's what my dearly departed best mate would have wanted. Laying across the rusty base, a single sheet of paper, it's folded over, bearing no more than a handful of words;

My darling Ruby, I've never stopped loving you and.

Broken

' The whole earth is ploughed by the exploding shells and the holes are filled with water, and if you do not get killed by the shells you may drown in the craters. Everybody is rushing, running, trying to escape almost certain death in this hail of enemy shells. Today I have seen the real face of war.'

German Musketier, Hans Otto Schetter.

One last beautiful day together, a final hurrah in the sunshine, it's all this rotten war now grants us. Tomorrow my beautiful, brave Jack will kiss me goodbye, like only he can, before shipping out to God knows where, leaving behind nothing more than flimsy strands of hope to cling to and a fading memory of the life we shared. Hope, first and foremostly that he'll return safely to my outstretched arms and furthermore, still the same man I fell in love with…

I received the tragic news of David's passing yesterday from my parents, the devastation quickly reduced me to a torrent of tears. I pictured his beloved Mum reading that notice, the one politely informing her that her whole world has been shattered. She won't even be granted the opportunity to bury her son, her cherished and beautifully unique boy, cruelly taken so young, with the music still inside. My heartfelt sympathy is clouded by guilt, derived from a selfish thought I can't shake*, thank goodness it wasn't me receiving that* *notice, Jack and David were inseparable, if he'd been with him at that moment, my God, it doesn't bear thinking about.*

I've often thought of our relationship containing three people, it feels ridiculous now, but in the early days, I was more than a touch jealous, fearing Jack could never love me as half as much as his best mate, but I soon realised there's more than enough room in that big old heart for both of us. Like everybody else, I quickly grew to love David, he was quite the character, a charming man who lived every day with a smile on his face, infecting all he met with happiness. For many, myself included, his tragic passing will leave their days a shade darker, but for my Jack, it's an affliction that runs immensely deeper, David was his ballast, a constant in his life. I'm sat on this platform bench shuddering, I can't wait to see Jack, but I'm terrified, a broken man is stepping of that train and I'm unsure how to begin piecing him together again.

It's a bitterly cold winters day, hence an early dusting of snow is surviving quite comfortably, only it's getting trodden down and turned into perilously compact patches of ice. The platform is swarming with a mixture of well-wrapped parents and sweethearts, no doubt silently battling the same sense of foreboding. The train is running a good half hour late, doing little to quell my anxiety, but one assumes the freezing temperatures are proving a hindrance to the schedule. It's been over four months, since I've seen my husband, after exchanging vows I didn't envisage another night being spent apart, it feels like a lifetime. Our enforced reunion doesn't feel real, a temporary interlude from the stress and separation. This inhumane war has so much to answer for and only one thing left to take.

A whistle blows, I can see the train approaching, *my baby's coming home to me,* we can temporarily shut this wretched world outside and melt into each other's arms. I can't take away his wealth of pain, but I'll gladly share it and help soften the edges. The train grinds to a screeching halt, simultaneously, a row of doors fly open to reveal the devastating toll of war. Men, remembered as young and fit when last in the gaze of loved ones eyes, return crippled, confined to wheelchairs, their limbs blasted to kingdom come. Able bodied soldiers, sheepishly contain their joy among the masses of walking wounded that regrettably outnumber them, once sturdy chaps now exhibiting the scars of sacrifice. For some this war may be over, but for others it is only just beginning.

Amidst the mele of tearful reunions I search for Jack, no sign, I hope he didn't miss the train. The crowd is thinning, I impatiently walk along the platform peering in to the carriage windows, it's alarmingly deserted, *where on earth is he?* The last carriage, *thank goodness, he's there, still seated,* motionless and staring ahead. I tap gently on the glass, no reaction, I strike it more firmly eliciting a slow turn of his head. Oh my darling Jack, so pasty-faced, but I disguise my shock behind a smile, he nods and starts to gather his things. Laboriously, he makes his way onto the platform and stops, mournful eyes staring aimlessly through me. I smile once more, but reciprocation isn't forthcoming, the poor lad looks dazed and distant, a hollow shell stripped of spirit. I don't recognise this imposter standing before me, imprisoned in a swell of suffering, it's unclear how much of this moment he's absorbing.

"Hi, Jack, it's wonderful to see you, my darling."

Nothing, but a silent portrayal of emptiness.

"Jack, it's Rose, are you ok, my love? Can you hear me?"

The train departs as lingering passengers shuffle away to apprehensively begin picking up the pieces of their desecrated lives, decent ones starved of normality, the cold platform suddenly feels like the loneliest place on earth. I'm scared to approach my husband, touch him, hold him, he appears so helplessly fragile.

"Jack, darling, please say something, it's Rose."

His eyes open a touch wider, revealing dark wells of desolation, but it's recognition, if only a flicker. I throw my arms wide open and wait, desperate to feel his troubled head nestling in my bosom. *Please Jack, I yearn to cradle you tenderly and dab away at your pain with my kisses.* He bows his head and starts to shuffle forward, slowly succumbing, his face sinks softly into my chest and I wrap my soothing arms snuggly around him. I can feel his breath gently caressing my heart, it's comforting, a gorgeous feeling I've longed for. His emotionally ravaged body begins to lightly shake, quietly sobbing, a broken heart slowly relinquishing a river of pain one drop at a time. I run my fingers through his thick hair and plant a kiss on his forehead.

"Oh, Jack, I'm so sorry my darling, so frightfully sorry, my love, but I'm here now."

His sobs intensify, I clasp him tighter.

"That's it, darling, let it all out."

"He's gone, Rose, just like that, he's gone. I didn't even get to say goodbye"

"Oh Jack, I know my love."

I can't stem his emotional bleeding and my God, it's breaking my heart, I'm powerless against the shards of pain raining down on his mentally dishevelled body. All I have in my arsenal is comfort and love, lashings of it, to drag his depleted soul back from the brink. Coupled with the passing of time, I pray that it's enough, that I'm enough. I have to be, he's my husband, the father to our unborn child, and the beautiful man I've built my dreams around.

"Come on, Jack, you're freezing, let's get you home, sweetheart."

He doesn't answer, but I start slowly easing him to the exit, a task made all the more difficult by the slippery conditions underfoot. All the way home he clings to my coat, cowering like a frightened child, if I can only get him to the other side of that door, cocooned from all earths evils, maybe things will be different.

"Would you like something to eat, Jack? I'm doing stew for dinner, but maybe a sandwich to keep you going?"

"No, thanks, I'm not all that hungry."

"Ok, pet, if you're sure, Ill get you a glass of water."

"Actually, Rose, I could do with a lie down, I'm tired from the journey."

"Ok, would you like me to join you?"

"Erm, no, if you don't mind, I just need some rest."

"Oh, no, I didn't mean, right, ok, I'll see you soon then. I love you, Jack."

No 'I love you too,' just a strained smile before trudging up the stairs. It's like having a stranger in the house, I still haven't felt his soft lips on mine, it's understandable I guess, but that doesn't stop it hurting like hell. He's always been the strong one, shouldering the burden for both of us without complaint, but now it's my turn to carry him over troubled waters, that starts with getting a hearty bowl of Irish stew inside him.

I'm feeling anxious, it's been hours and still not a peep from upstairs, *should I have left him so long, with just his demons for company?* My thoughts are abruptly ransacked by a descending sense of darkness, it frightens the life out of me, suitably panicked, I race upstairs.

"Jack, Jack, darling, dinners almost ready," I call through the door, carefully disguising the fear in my voice.

No response, I put my ear to the bedroom door and listen intently, desperate to hear any sign of life, it's deathly quiet. My heart is palpitating as I ever so slowly nudge open the door and creep in, *thank God, I can see his body contracting.* Lying on his side, he's staring through the net curtain, into the dark abyss of winter. I kick off my shoes and nervously lay down next to him, both facing the same way, but with an uncomfortable chasm between us. Fearing rejection, I bide my time, choosing simply to exist in the moment with him. My thirst to aid his healing is matched with an unquenching desire to feel his love radiating through my quivering body. The temptation to feel his skin pressing on mine is irresistible, surrendering to my cravings, I weaken, nuzzling gently into the base of his neck and kissing it ever so softly. He remains still, absorbing the affection I'm so eager to bestow, encouraged I plant another, it's more lingering and purposeful. As desperately as I wish to kiss his cares away, the actions are as much for my benefit, I need to feel useful in some kind of capacity, however small, be it kisses, cuddles or conversation, he needs to know I'm here for him in his loneliest hour. I fling my arm over his still frame, resting my hand on his chest, he responds, placing his hand on top of mine and pressing it firmly into his heart. It's a small pocket of paradise, an intimacy that only exists in the presence of two deeply entwined souls. David's harrowing death has bought him to his knees, bruised and battered, but thankfully, back in my arms, it feels like the first step on a long arduous journey.

"Rose."

"Yes, darling."

"Please, don't forsake me, I will find a way through this and back to you."

"Oh, Jack, I never could, we're going to find the way together."

"Promise?"

"Yes, darling, for as long as it takes."

He turns round and faces me, it's tentative, but the first real smile I've seen in more than four months. "Do you want to talk about David?"

"No, not at the moment, it's just too raw, but thank you."

"I understand, darling, but I am here for you."

"I know, and I love you for it, Rose."

"I love you too Jack."

He nods and kisses my cheek, its sublime. "I'm still in a state of shock, it doesn't feel real, I don't want it to be real." He shakes his head, "but however much I tell myself something different, I know it is."

In that moment, I witness the pain ruthlessly taking possession, his beautiful face swells, appearing scarred with deep lesions of grief and regret. I want to vanquish the hurt, smoother it with my kisses and hold his beaten body tightly until the sky turns blue again.

"I fell asleep while he was talking to me, the final time we were together, what kind of lasting memory is that?"

"You weren't to know, darling, it's a tragedy that couldn't have been foreseen. Listen, nothing can diminish your memories of David, he knew how much you thought of him, the man idolised you."

He scoffs. "I'm not sure about that."

"Are you kidding me? He loved the bones of you Jack, you're all he ever spoke to me about."

"Really?"

"Yes, darling, really, he was both protective and extremely proud of you, only the fortunate few get to experience a friendship like yours, something real that endures. I can't imagine how much you're hurting and it won't feel like it now, but in time the pain will dull and you'll come to cherish that friendship."

"I hope so, in time," he whispers in dazed disbelief.

"I promise you, darling, those memories you carved out together, will slowly start to overshadow the sorrow. You'll carry them and David in that big old heart of yours, just leave a bit of room for me, me and this little one."

I take his hand and place it on my swollen belly, he smiles and closes his eyes.

"I will," he whispers, "it's yours, all yours."

We lie, huddled under a protective blanket of love, cradling each other in a serene state of silence. It's a euphoric feeling, one I've ached for, our two broken hearts, tantalisingly close, throbbing in tandem. This is the reality that matters, our reality, within these four walls, as long as we have this, then we're indestructible. Everything else will just have to wait, this atrocious war, the bitter night air, even the bloody stew! *On second thoughts, perhaps a late supper.*

I'm only just getting used to having my husband back, but the week is half over, blasted time marching on so bloody remorselessly. I'm busily familiarising him with normal life, but in a few days this won't be his normality, it's all so fleeting and feels hopeless at times. Jack's alluringly deep, brown eyes remain tinged with a thick sadness, it's going to take time, more than I've got, but using a combination of soup, stew and kisses I've began to slowly chip away at his tough veneer of misery. He remains quiet, but a trifle more content and well rested. The thorny subject of David hasn't been broached since that first evening under the covers, but we've talked about impending parenthood, even going as far as discussing names, albeit without agreement being reached. It's impossible to get Jack excited about his future when his best friend's has been so savagely wrestled away, the guilt alone would eat him up, but I'm doing what I can to gently remind him that he still has one.

The tragic events of the last few weeks serve as a stark reminder, highlighting the fragility of the fabric that binds our very lives together. There is no better state to exist in than that of being so hopelessly in love, the feeling of walking on air with a wholesome heart, fit to burst and a nourished soul. I've lived in this richly satisfying place since that fateful night, at the ballroom, when a bumbling Jack Crosby sat at my table and with one glassy eyed look, changed the course of my life. The poor chap looked petrified, but ever so polite and dashing. In that magical moment, my little world exploded and I just knew we'd never be apart, but regrettably even love, the crazy beautiful variety is susceptible to the rigor of reality. Life is a complex carnival of contradictions, often offering up the test before cruelly delivering the lesson.

Despite being a blessedly blissful inhabitancy, one that transcends all logical comprehension, love masks a dark underbelly of vulnerability. Wrapping all your hopes, dreams and desires around the heart of one special being, a gorgeous soul, one you'll quickly come to realise that you can't live without. Opening ones heart to love is the greatest deed a human soul can perform. An act that rewards the recipient with wave upon wave of God's golden goodness, but that very heart, whilst richly fulfilled, is exposed and risks being broken, often beyond repair. It's a pain beyond anything the bearer will have experienced before, just to imagine its wrath and the devastating consequences left in its wake is too painful in itself. I'm learning this quickly, war has given me a glimpse into the abyss, this is the reality I'm battling against, a daily diet of worry and wondering. With every passing hour, good men are dying. It's tragic, an avoidable travesty of youth, but my only crumb of comfort is they're strangers. I'm unable to put faces to their names, making it that little bit less real, but with the death of David, that delusion has been shattered. This is a man I can picture, someone I loved, a devoted friend who stood shoulder to shoulder with my Jack. If the trajectory of that shell had been a degree either way, my God, I could be imagining his mangled torso right now, my wretched fear has never felt so raw. I've always enjoyed a chat with God, before bed, nothing heavy, just airing a few worries and wishes, but now I'm down on my knees three times a day praying with all my muster, praying for Jack's continued safety and an end to this mindless war. All I have is the remains of this week, just three days before I must wave him off to a life rooted in desolation, not long for God to come up with an answer.

The next two days melt away like snow trapped in the sunshine, ebbing time has never felt so precious. We've remained, voluntarily barricaded, in a world of our own with conversation at a premium, although the silences now feel more familiar than uncomfortable. The opportunity to tend to his needs and quietly wile away the hours together has been wonderful. I'm in his arms, at my happiest, it's where I belong. Tonight will bring a sense of dread that will consume me, but before I face that battle we have one day left to share and must brave the outside world. I will be accompanying Jack to Ma Frost's cottage to return David's belongings later this afternoon, he's yet to really open up about the death of \David, *I'm not sure he's ready for this.*

"I can take David's belongings if you like Jack, darling, you can get some rest."

"No," he says firmly, his abruptness startles me. "Sorry, Rose, but this is something I need to do."

"Ok, if you're sure, honey."

"I am, thanks, and sorry again, I didn't mean to snap."

I smile reassuringly, he appears agitated. "Why don't we nip out a bit earlier? It's a lovely crisp morning out there."

He gazes timidly through the net curtains.

"It will do us good," I continue, "get some fresh air into our lungs."

"I don't know, it looks chilly."

"Come on, Jack, we won't be out too long and we can wrap up nice and warm."

Relenting, he smiles and nods.

"Great, I'll grab the coats and scarfs."

Armed with an ulterior motive, I link my arm around Jack's and lead him down our street. It's bitterly cold, but huddling in closer, I dare not utter a word of complaint. Predictably, the streets show precious little sign of civilisation, other than a hardy old chap who doffs his cap as he passes. The route should seem familiar, but Jack offers no comment, dutifully plodding on in silence. I fear his mind may already have drifted somewhere else, to a troubled patch of land situated in the northern area of Belgium, the place where David lies. Tomorrow he must confront the scene of his greatest tragedy and simply carry on, battling gainfully through the thick sorrowful shadow it casts, *the poor chap, how can his thoughts be anywhere else?*

"How are you feeling, Jack, you know, about returning tomorrow?"

He sighs. "Let's not talk about tomorrow, Rose, it's how things are, I'll be ok."

"I wish you didn't have to go, darling."

"I know, love, I don't want to, but I must, the men need me."

For goodness sake Jack, I think to myself, I bloody need you, like a poet needs the pain, now more than ever. I have to go through child birth alone, not knowing if my newborn baby will ever lay eyes on their father, *I'm petrified, scared to death you'll go the same way as David*, but I smile pragmatically, choosing not to verbalise my selfish thoughts. He's journeying back to the gates of hell, it's the last thing he needs.

"Yes, darling, I know you have to go."

"Rose."

"Yes, Jack?"

"I'm scared, David was so young and full of life, one moment he's."

"Ssh, darling, I know, I'm scared too, but you're going to come back to me, Jack Crosby."

"You can't know that, it's nothing more than hope."

I stop, wrap my arms tightly around him and smile. "Listen, you and me, we're in this for life, do you understand?"

Choking up, he nods.

"Remember that porch you promised me, the one with the great grandchildren playing around us?"

"Yes, of course I do."

"That's the future we're having, our time in the sunshine, just like the picture you painted so beautifully in my mind."

"Oh, Rose, I could spend a thousand lives searching and never find soul that comes close to you."

"You're damn right Jack, and don't you ever forget it!"

We both laugh, it's a nice moment that is poignant, but light hearted, just like the ones we used to share before all this ugliness ransacked our carefree existence. We share a lustful kiss that makes my toes tingle, before continuing on our path, Jack stops suddenly, the familiarity has found me out, unmasking my true intentions.

"Hang on a minute, Rose, this is the way to the Dirty Duck."

"Yes, it is."

He goes pale. "But, erm, we're not going in are we, I don't think I'm ready for that."

"Jack, calm down and look at me."

He turns to me, I take hold of his trembling hands.

"You trust me, don't you Jack?"

"Yes, of course."

"Then you know that I love you and I'll never do anything to hurt you."

"I do, but this is our place, mine and Frosty's. I don't know if I can walk through that door knowing he won't be inside, there's too many ghosts lurking, I'm not strong enough to confront them."

"Jack, I realise what this place meant to David and yourself, how many memories reside within those walls, and I know how much he means to you,. I loved him too, but I think this will be good for you, for us. I'm asking you to trust me darling, please, Jack, take my hand and lets go and lay some ghosts to rest, together."

I wait patiently for his reply, this is a big step and I anticipated some reluctance, but I want him to talk about David, even reminisce and begin to gradually come to terms with his death. He looks distressed, but in meting out some tough love, I'm throwing him a lifeline.

"I don't want to do it, Rose, not yet, maybe later?"

"Jack, please, trust me and take my hand." He grabs it tightly.

"We'll pop in for one drink, if it all gets too much, we can leave, ok?"

He nods and I tentatively lead him to the dusty street corner, where so many precious memories lie in wait, he pauses, gently resisting, before I ease him through the wood stained double doors, wholly aware we're treading on hallowed ground.

The saloon bar is quiet, a predictable consequence of so many men being stranded at war, but a familiar face greets us. Margaret, affectionately known as Mags, cuts an imposing figure, a no nonsense landlady who's never without a cigarette hanging from her mouth, although its not always lit. She's a very chatty and cheerful soul, but woe betide any hapless drunk that get's out of hand, I've seen her drag fellows out in pairs on more than the odd occasion, tucked under each burly arm.

"Hello, Jack, and Rose, it's lovely to see you both."

"Good afternoon, Mags," I reply, great to see you too, how are things?"

"Well, it's a difficult time for everyone, but I can't complain, you have to carry on don't you?"

"Yes, indeed you do."

She smiles bravely, no doubt wrestling with her own private turmoil. Not only is her husband Dennis stationed faraway, fighting for his life, but her young son too. Little Billy Jenkins, barely a man, but now forced to grow up all too quickly. Every day, she summons up the strength to open her doors to the masses, stand behind the bar and offer every custodian a warm smile. I'm unstinting in my admiration for her, these cobbled streets are peppered with unsung heroes.

"Jack."

"Yes, Mags?"

"I was so deeply sorry to hear about David, utterly devastated, he was one of a kind and will be sorely missed around these parts."

"Thank you."

Teary eyed, Jack glances around the room, painfully absorbing the cherished history that exudes from every corner, the scene of a multitude of glorious nights lived out in a drunken haze. I've been lucky enough to experience a few myself. Frosty didn't need an excuse to make merry, he celebrated life. Mastering the art of living in the moment, he turned every night in to New Years Eve. How delicious it must be to derive such joy from the simplest pleasures, he really had this life thing figured out. Mags pours us some drinks and starts to laugh.

"Oh, David, he was a cheeky so and so at times," she recalls fondly, "every Friday afternoon after school, he'd be in here, all swagger and short trousers, begging for a beer. I'd have to chase the little scamp out with my broomstick."

"Aye," smiles Jack, "he could be very persistent."

"I'll tell you something else," she continues, "the nights he was in were special, nobody left the bar early, that man could breathe life into the most dreary

Monday evening." She shakes her head admiringly, "men laughed and woman swooned, what a character. They were my favourite nights."

"Mine too," adds Jack, "he certainly knew how to work a crowd."

"Indeed he did, I bet God's up there now, getting royally entertained."

We all look up and smile, each harvesting our own joyful thoughts about a man who only ever offered up rainbows. It feels so good to enjoy a moment thinking about David in purely happy terms, quietly celebrating his uniqueness, the fantastical fire he bought to a world left so bereft. A group of old dears come into the bar, Mags hugs Jack and kisses his forehead before scurrying off to serve them.

"It feels weird, Rose."

"What does, darling?"

"Sitting down, on these stools, we always stood at the bar."

"What, all night?"

"Yes, Frosty was very animated, you know, telling his stories, he liked to move around, drifting in and out of conversations and sprinkling his magic. The way people's faces use to light up, he just loved making them laugh, they couldn't get enough of him. At first, men would get jealous at how quickly he captivated their girlfriend's attention, but by the end of the night they were hugging him like a long lost brother. Frosty was flirty, but he had honour and never stole another man's sweetheart, well, not in front of him at least." He laughs, but his chuckles soon turn in to tears.

"It's alright, Jack, just let it out, darling."

"He's really gone, isn't he, I'm never going to see him stood at this bar again. Never going to share a few beers and put the world to rights, he's not coming back is he?"

I shake my head despondently, crying too.

"Why him, Rose, out of everyone? Why did they have to take him, a man so blessed and full of life?"

"Oh, Jack, I know it hurts, but there is no rhyme or reason to this."

"That shouldn't have been his time, his destiny, he had Ruby, an adoring mother and so much ahead of him, a life of his choosing. He'll never get to be a loving husband or doting father, Frosty deserved so much more than this barbaric ending."

"His passing is a tragedy, my love, he's gone way too soon, but you'll never lose David, he's part of you now and always will be. Every day you'll carry all those wonderful memories you cherish of the life you shared and the man he was in your heart. They'll never die, I promise you that, I won't let them."

He smiles and nods in agreement, accepting that those beloved memories will over the ensuing years prove to be a great source of enduring nostalgia and comfort.

"Rose?"

"Yes, Jack."

"Thanks for bringing me, I've been so consumed by Frosty's shocking demise, but this has been nice. I needed to remember him, the man he was."

"It's my pleasure."

"If we have a boy."

"Yes, Jack?"

"Do you mind if we call the little chap David."

"Oh, Jack, that's perfect."

Ma Frost's cottage is a stones throw from the Dirty Duck, probably another reason why Frosty was in no hurry to move out. We slip away quietly, avoiding any emotionally draining grand goodbyes, and head through the woods, all the while the metal box Jack must soon relinquish remains tightly in his clutches. A few personal belongings, along with our deepest sympathies, that's all we have to offer a grieving mother. To outlive your child, it must be every parents worst nightmare, and in such heinous circumstances too. Ma Frost is a little excentric with a quirky dwelling, decorated with a host of weird and wonderful ornaments, grey haired, frail and extremely welcoming, but one wonders what kind of woman we'll encounter today. I'm nervous, especially for Jack, parting with that box will feel like giving away a precious piece of his life and Ma Frost may have questions, difficult questions that will force him to relive the trauma.

Jack pauses at the garden gate, staring briefly at Ma Frost's prized apple tree.

"Jack, hold on a minute"

"What is it, Rose?"

"Are you absolutely sure that you want to do this?"

He sighs. "Rose, we've been through this."

"I know, darling, but I want you to be sure, I can do this alone and you could return home and rest."

"Rose, it's ok, I need to be here. I owe it to Frosty."

Ma Frost looks surprisingly perky and overcome with joy to see us, after a round of welcome hugs we're invited in. Her homely parlour is warm and filled with the most divine smell. Sporting awkward smiles, we're both sat bolt upright and unsure how to begin the conversation. *What do you say to mother who's just lost the one thing her entire world revolves around?*

"I've just brewed up a fresh pot of tea and there's freshly baked scones cooling in the kitchen."

"You mustn't go to any trouble on our account," says Jack.

"It's no trouble, pet, just make yourselves comfortable and I'll be back in two ticks."

"Thank you, Ma," I reply, everybody calls her Ma, "they smell delicious."

She smiles and heads to the kitchen to fetch the goodies, whistling as she goes. I turn to Jack, my look of confusion is mirrored, *I suppose grief comes in many guises and who am I to question how someone chooses to nurse a broken heart?* Accompanied by dainty pots of jam and clotted cream, the scones look nothing short of sensational, but my knotted stomach feels incapable of enjoying them.

"Please, don't be shy, tuck in the both of you, my David loves these scones."

"I'm deeply sorry, Ma," I reply, "about David."

She smiles. "David's a lovely boy, good as gold my David."

"I know," adds Jack, "the best."

"Always with that mischievous glint in his eye, he can be a right one at times, but as a son, just golden, that's my David."

Jack places the metal box carefully on the table.

"Erm," he mutters softly, his voice quivering, "these are David's possessions, his watch, a few photos and some letters."

"That's nice, pet," she replies, but doesn't give the box a glance, to look will be an acknowledgement of his passing.

"It was extremely quick, Ma, he, sorry David, well, he wouldn't of suffered."

"I'll pour the tea, pet, say when."

"Thank you," replies Jack, looking a little perplexed, his words don't seem to be penetrating Ma's protective barrier.

Death can be a minefield with multiple methods of navigation, but before the tears can flow freely, there has to be acceptance, a painful realization that life as you know it has disappeared.

"It looks very pleasant outside," she comments, gazing up at the window, "but one imagines rather chilly."

"It's a little bit cold," I reply, "how have you been, Ma?"

"Oh fine, dear, you know, pottering about, the days don't change much, but I mustn't complain."

"Good, that's good."

My eyes roam around the decorative room, desperately searching for a talking point, there are so many photos of David, the apple of her eye. My stomach is still swirling, but out of politeness and a pinch of curiosity I sink my teeth into a scone. *Oh my days, that is delectable, a crumbly work of art,* Jack's already polished his off. Ma Frost leans forward and takes his hand.

"How are you doing, my dear boy?"

"I'm ok, Ma."

"Splendid, you're a wonderful friend to my David."

Jack nods and begins to cry, Ma quickly passes him a handkerchief.

"Thank you."

"Yes, my David is always singing your praises, it's Jack this and Jack that all day long, my goodness. Please don't be sad, my dear boy, I'm grateful to you and so happy he has such a fine friend to share his life with."

His tears intensify and Ma puts her arms around him.

"Don't worry, pet, it will be ok, I'll pour you some more tea. Everything seems better after a good cup of tea."

"But, Ma," replies Jack, "David has died."

"I know," she says calmly, "but I prefer to think of him as just leaving the room, well, for a little bit longer anyway."

"I understand. Ma, it sounds nice."

"It is, I imagine he's out in the world living some crazy adventure, you know, with the widest smile spread across his face. Always smiling, that's my David."

"Yes, always smiling, that's Frosty."

We sit, allowing the sentimental silence to exquisitely wash over us, absorbing every drop of happiness we can squeeze from the moment.

"Rose, I hear you're in the family way."

"Yes," I gush, patting my swollen belly.

"It shows, you're glowing, my dear."

"Thanks, Ma, we're both really excited."

"I bet, you're going to make wonderful parents."

Her façade slips momentarily, she appears glum and regretful, discussing the topic of having children appears a step too far. With so much love to give, she'd had been the most delightful Grandmother imaginable. The war's not only taken her only son, but cruelly stole her future to.

"Gorgeous scones, Ma," I hastily interject, "you must give me the recipe."

She smiles. "It will be my pleasure Rose."

"Anyway," says Jack, "its been lovely seeing you, Ma, but we're going to have to make a move."

"So soon, aren't you staying for dinner?"

"That's very kind of you, Ma, but we couldn't possibly impose."

"Nonsense, my dear boy, it's bubbling away in the oven, there's plenty to go around."

Jack glances at me, but I have no retort, Ma has her heart set on it.

"That will be lovely, Ma," he say relentingly, "what are we having?"

"Beef, seasonal vegetables, oh, and roast potatoes."

The meal, while delicious, left precious little time for Jack and myself. The day had gone better than expected, but left us both emotionally drained. Too tired to make love, we slumped into each other's arms and drifted away. In truth, it proved a Godsend, without the exhaustion we'd had spent the majority of the night, Jack's last, worrying. I've had my allotted week with my husband and all my prayers for peace have fallen on deaf ears, from tomorrow he'll roam the fields of Flanders once more.

At four o'clock this morning he reached over and whispered 'I love you,' before kissing me and climbing out of our nice warm bed. I was half asleep, but it felt gorgeous, like fantasy bleeding into reality. If it's to be my final memory, then it isn't half a beautiful one. No long tearjerking goodbyes, that's what we promised each other for both our sakes. I stayed true to my word and let him slip away with just a short utterance, 'I love you, too, Jack Crosby, come back to me soon.' I heard the door bang and lay staring at the ceiling, my heart slowly cracking with the realisation, I'm a war widow once more.

Into The Heart of Hell

'The first shock was an immense surprise... Suddenly the enemy's fire became precise and concentrated. Second by second the hail of bullets and the thunder of shells grew stronger. Those who survived lay flat on the ground, amid the screaming wounded and the humble corpses... Isolated heroes made fantastic leaps, but all to no purpose. In an instant it had become clear that all the courage in the world could not withstand this fire.'

Charles de Gaulle, French officer.

Sat side by side in the baking hot recruitment centre with beaming smiles, we can't wait to sign the papers being thrust in front of us before proudly donning our uniforms and marching off down the golden path to a celebrated and certain victory. The rose tinted ideal of war has been firmly planted in our fertile, but naive minds, blissfully blinkered and bordering on delusion. It feels like we're embarking on a big adventure and the prospect of war seems heroic, even glamorous, but our hedonistic daydreams would soon be laid to rest on the fields of Flanders when inglorious reality hits. Absurdly, with so much life stretching ahead of us, death isn't even a contemplation. Wide eyed young men with everything to lose, enthusiastically choosing bravery over apparent cowardice and subsequently treated as heroes, we gleefully lap up every minute of this propaganda fuelled charade.

"That's it, lad," declares Frosty, "we're fully fledged soldiers now."

"Yes," I grin, "we've done it."

"Yep, nice couple of weeks training, then it's off to beat up the Boche!"

"Should be back for Christmas, I'd expect."

"Without a doubt my old mucker, we've got them licked, it's nothing, but medals and memories from here on in."

"We'll return heroes," I giddily reply, "can you imagine the reception waiting for us?"

"Full on victory parade I'd imagine, ticker tape, the whole shebang."

"You reckon?"

"Absolutely pal, we'll be the pride of the country, the toast of the town, they'll be lining the streets to welcome us home."

"Wow, won't that be a sight to savour."

"Indeed, they'll probably declare a national holiday. We won't be able to buy a drink for weeks, even months."

"I can get use to that."

"Come on Jacko, let's get on that bus," he exclaimed, "the ticket to a better life."

Just four long months later, his legacy fitted neatly inside a tobacco tin…

Every time I march to and from the front line, I pass it, the apple tree that hangs majestically above the riverside, Frosty's final resting place. I afford it a rueful glance, it serves as a harsh reminder of bitter loss and wasted potential. During rest periods I often leave billets and wander down the riverbank, stopping to spend a quiet moment with him. It's an opportunity to clear the clutter from my mind and keep him in the loop on current events. I know he's not really there, his ferocious spirit has long since transcended this modest patch of mother earth, but it provides a much needed focal point for reflection and remembrance. I can wile away entire afternoons sat under the tree, watching the sun glisten as it gently tap dances across the seamlessly flowing tranquil waters. Just yesterday, a formidable rainstorm gave birth to a magnificent rainbow, its reflection briefly kissed the rivers surface, Davy Frost in all his glory.

I've seen off a savage winter of discontent, it's no mean feat, but nevertheless feels a hollow victory, any sense of achievement is marred by a severe lack of justification for the losses suffered. Those left standing among our depleted ranks are drier and a little warmer, but in the last six months we haven't advanced a jot. The river of blood that cuts deeply through the heart of this weathered land, awash with the floating corpses of a thousand young dreamers, has achieved absolutely nothing. It's a stalemate that can no longer be tolerated by our superiors, the fluffy pillow brigade who run the rule over the lives of virtuous men, casually dabbling with their destiny. What gives those yellow bellied stuffed shirts the right to play God? In a just and decent world no man should wield such power over another, regrettably, this habitat is anything but.

Faint hopes of resolution melted away with the winter frost and the prospect of peace remains nothing more than a pipe dream unworthy of credence. Fresh faced lambs arrive by the bucket load, replacements for those once vibrant beating hearts, now leisurely decaying in the watery spring sunshine. Within moments, a cold harsh reality bites and any remaining exuberance drains from their quivering bodies, a brutal welcome to Flander's fields.

Thankfully, my inner sanctum, but for the loss of Frosty, remains intact and continues to drag me through the darkness, they've been brilliant, putting my pain ahead of their own personal torment. My survival, both physical, and mental, is testament to Sergeant Bevan's soothing tutelage, Lionheart's conviction, Bookworm's compassion and Danny's jokes, boy, how I've needed them, like sundried roses need summer showers. All the while, the nervousness within the camp has fresh impetus, tension is building.

"All I'm saying, boys, is that if we don't mount a full scale attack soon, those buggers will charge at us," says Lionheart adamantly.

"Do you reckon?" Replies Danny with eyebrows raised in a rare display of concern.

"I guarantee it lad, probably in the middle of the night knowing those sneaky sods."

"Crikey, better stay on our toes then."

"High state of alert, that's what Sergeant Bevan called it this morning. The bastards are coming for us, mark my words, unless we get in there first."

Bookworm looks pensive, silently taking it all in before crafting an educated response. I agree with Lionheart, the presence of Generals onsite has intensified recently, somethings clearly afoot.

"It's inevitable in the end," says Bookworm, shaking his head, "even more blood spilt, it's tawdry, an utter nonsense."

"You won't get any argument there, boyo, but I fear the order is coming very soon. General Hughes and his cronies don't come down to this beleaguered bunker for no good reason."

We all nod grimly, haphazard plans are almost certainly being hatched in the murky corridors of power, we'll be the last to know and first to die.

"One wonders, what it'll be like?"

"What's that Barry?" I ask.

"You know, to go over the top and charge headlong into the heart of hell?"

I envied Bookworm's turn of phrase, he can even make certain death sound poetic.

"I don't know, but I imagine the adrenalin kicks in and you hope for the best, it's the moments leading up to it that will be most terrifying."

The statement is met with silent acceptance and lowered heads, each haunted by thoughts of mortality.

"It doesn't feel right though, does it? Men in their twenties sat around contemplating death."

"It isn't," adds Joker, "you could die a virgin mate."

"Be serious Daniel, we're talking about bloody dying here, out in that field, like many before us."

"I'm sorry, Barry, I'm not disrespecting those who've succumbed to death, but it's the only way I can deal with it mate. If I think about it too much, you know, dying, it will send me doolally."

"I'm not ready to die yet," chips in Lionheart, "I haven't had kids, seen them grow up and get married. Never mind being a father, I want to experience being a Grandad one day, too!"

"That would be nice," I add, "to be surrounded by a big family and spend your remaining days loving them intently."

"Aye," says a misty eyed Lionheart, "being part of their lives and watching them grow in to happy people."

"Exactly, that's what life's all about-the journey, sharing moments and nurturing their dreams as if they were yours."

I sigh. "Mines just beginning, there's so much more to come, I don't want to die either."

"Well," says Joker, "it's not for everyone." I scowl and he instantly holds his hand up, old habits die hard.

"I'd like to be a father," says Barry, "and yes Daniel, I know that requires having sex beforehand."

"Steady on Bazzer, I do the wisecracks around here."

"Yeah, having someone to love and take care of, I could get used to that."

"How about you, Joker?" I ask, "will a life on the silver screen leave time for a family?"

"I sincerely hope so Jacko, if the opportunity presents itself, I'd need to fall in love first, but if I get the…" He stops suddenly, the thought appears too raw, a realization that he may not be afforded the time to live out his dreams. I've never seen the old boy look this serious, he bows his head solemnly and sobs, eliciting a reassuring pat on the back from Lionheart.

"It's alright lad, the situation is getting to all of us, why only last night I was blubbing like a baby. One family photo, that's all it took."

"I only need a whiff of Rose's scent from an envelope to set me off, we're all here for you mate."

"Thanks lads, I've just never thought about dying before, not properly. When you're young, it feels like you have all this time to burn, an inexhaustible supply, but now, my God, it feels all too precious."

"It's often the way," comments Bookworm, "it's hard to appreciate the value of something spent so casually, that, I'm afraid is the arrogance of youth."

Danny smiles admiringly.

"Oh Bookworm, I'd love to spend an hour in your head."

With a lively smattering of sporadic fire, another intense day of duelling draws to its sorry conclusion, although in reality it never really ends, the crackle's a chilling constant. The rumour mill continues to churn out all manner of death defying scenarios, but for now, although plausible, each lacks the confirmation to make them credible. The fact Sergeant Bevan has been conspicuous by his absence since first light does little to dampen the flames of curiosity. The growing suspicion is he's been summoned to the Generals residence to talk tactics over tea and cucumber sandwiches. His morning address echoed with conviction, calling for calm heads and vigilance, but offered no clue of an imminent attack. In such trying circumstances, one wonders how he musters up the enthusiasm on a daily basis, it's unwavering and highly commendable. The man must barely sleep, smothered by a blanket of worries, we all are, but his weighs heavier than most, yet the guy never projects a bead onto his men. Thank God, for the bourbon as even the most heroic of unsung heroes need an outlet.

I've shot, shelled and cowered, the soldiers all too familiar routine designed to dodge death for another day, but sentry duty is now done for the night, *halleluiah* I think, too tired to celebrate another small victory in the never-ending slog for survival. My war-torn mind, heavy from the vast absorption of worry, will once more forgo the respite it so desperately craves, but at least I can afford my aching limbs a modicum of solace in one of the numerous manmade dugouts. Carved out of the trench walls, these muddy holes offer a degree of escape from the elements, but not the shells that blaze a trail across the night sky. It's the ones growing louder that leave you in a cold sweat, only once the noise has faded can the old ticker return to normal service. In the trenches, when you close your eyes, there are no guarantees. You're waiting to die, it's a recurring thought capable of turning fit young men blessed with agile minds into zombies.

Without the room to kneel, I lie down and slip a photo from my breast pocket, prior to commencing my nightly ritual with a short prayer. It begins with offering thanks for my continued preservation, but quickly morphs into a despairing plea for this wretched world of war to stop turning.

"Oh Lord," I implore audibly, "allow me to disembark this merciless merry-go-round and float serenely home, back into the welcoming arms of a fit and well Rose, the one I love and cherish above all else. If you can see your way to granting me this one wish I'll never ask for anything ever again, I promise." Before leaving God to stew over my request, I express gratitude for the enduring presence of Sergeant Bevan and my brave brothers, "please keep them sane and safe, oh, and one more favour, your Lordship, if I can be so bold? Check in on Frosty when you get a minute and pass on my kindest regards."

I'm lucky tonight, not all of the dugouts afford you the luxury of lying down, they're extremely confined spaces, the earth is no more than a few feet from my face. Often waking to the taste of dirt, it's the nearest one can get to kipping in a grave. With the aid of a pocket torch I gaze lovingly at the crumpled photo, my angelic Rose, if I fall victim to an exploding shell tonight, she'll be the last thought permeating through my scattered mind, the thought feels absurdly comforting. These rare snatches of rest are the only opportunity one has in the trenches to nibble on nostalgias plentiful bounty. The temptation to live in the past is tough to ignore at the best of times, particularly one dotted with glistening clusters of happiness, but when imprisoned in dire straits, the kind only war bestows on one's senses, it's irresistible. A soldier survives on his wits, requiring intense focus, hence this indulgence must be exercised sparingly. I can't expunge Rose from my thoughts, it's impossible, her soul and spirit enjoy permanent residency, infecting every crevice of my consciousness. But, during these sacred moments of rest, I can allow myself to dwell a little and dream of another life, something beautiful, unspoiled by the treachery of a country I love dearly. I'll stare at this picture until my eyelids drop, marvelling, wondering and hoping, it's the nearest I can get to the long kiss goodnight that geography denies me. We're countries apart, it seems like worlds, but in these stolen moments of tender reminiscence, my beloved Rose feels closer than ever.

I'm restless and wired with worry, it's turning into one of those nights, another bloody one! I can't get the elusive Sergeant Bevan out of my mind, so much so, I slide out of my dugout, spit the mud out of my mouth and head for his much roomier base. The trench is littered with animated bodies as battle rages under a dipping moon, some are firing off rounds while others launch shells amidst folk casually chatting and the odd soul managing to bag forty winks while stood up, much to my envy. I've enjoyed some frank conversations with Sergeant Bevan over the course of this sorry conflict, bending his accommodating ear, on more occasions than I care to remember, but this feels like my opportunity to offer counsel and lighten his load for a change. He's granite, as tough as old boots, but underneath the calm unassuming exterior, an inferno of pressure must rage and wreak bloody havoc. I fear his day spent in the General's disapproving glare, has left the poor chap with a mental mountain to mull over.

A glass half full of bourbon, a pack of smokes and a revolver are all laid out neatly. They're the only things on a pensive looking Sergeant Bevan's desk. He beckons me in with a wave of his hand, placing down a second glass and reaching for an open bottle, I nod and he pours me a healthy dose of sweet poison. The barrel of the revolver is open, thankfully the chambers are empty, but in the other hand, between his finger and thumb, there's a golden bullet. Disconcertingly, he keeps taping it on the table in an agitated fashion, *I'm in way over my head here.*

"The sun will soon be up, Sir."

"I'd expect so Private, can't quite fathom if this is a late night drink or an early morning tipple, cheers anyway."

I raise my glass, his speech sounds a touch slurred.

"Maybe some rest is in order, Sir, you know, before our call to arms."

"Ah yes, our call to arms, you'd be drinking heavily too, my dear boy, if you had to deliver todays message."

I gulp, anticipating it's the prophecy of doom we're all dreading, an imminent and ill-fated jaunt into the heart of hell.

"I take it, today's meeting, didn't go too well."

He smiles ruefully and squeezes the bullet tightly, his finger and thumb are turning crimson. "Well, the sandwiches were top notch, but the company was lousy," he sniggers, "that pompous bastard."

"General Hughes?"

"Aye, that's the fella. Well, for dessert he served up an ultimatum, apparently it's the moment we've all been waiting for, our chance to shine. My God, he sat there with a sanctimonious grin plastered across his smug face expecting some outpouring of gratitude. I ought to have put a fucking bullet right between his beady little eyes."

"An ultimatum, I see, Sir."

"I'm afraid so, and those who refuse will be, as he puts it, 'be afforded the indignity of a cowards death.' I've never heard such hypocrisy," he rages, "what gives that bounder the right to cast aspersions on honourable men? My men,' I should have shot him dead on the spot."

"So, erm, this is it then?"

He pauses, allowing the anger to dissipate. "I'll relay everything in a few short hours, but suffice to say, keep your diary open for first light tomorrow."

His response lacked detail, but reeked of calamitous confirmation, though expected, the admission sent a waterfall of worry crashing through my insides. Never mind someone walking over my grave, this felt like a marching band. I slumped my quivering bones down and took a huge gulp of whisky, never has the spectre of death burned brighter. Confronted with a mental exhibition of vivid images too painful to process, my mind escapes to a cherished corner of Blighty, a tranquil land where the real Jack Crosby lives and breathes, it's a friendly place where people love and rely on me, fuck, there's no escaping this flurry of fear.

"I'm so desperately sorry, Jack, I vigorously resisted, meeting his request with utter indignance, but regrettably, he remained adamant. If only I could of brought the dwindling dream of resolution another precious month or two, I feel I've let you all down."

Crestfallen, the poor chap shakes his head, seemingly unwilling to relinquish the golden bullet.

"Nonsense," I say sternly.

"I beg your pardon, Private?"

"I apologise, for my tone Sergeant Bevan, but not the sentiment. You have no reason to reproach yourself, nobody could have done more for us, not just today, but throughout this whole sorry business. You've led us with wisdom and a calm head, exhibiting courage and dignity at every turn."

"I've tried, Lord knows I have, but this is the final straw, it's all too much Jack. How do I waltz out there this morning? Look squarely into their young hopeful eyes and ask them to charge across no-man's-land, trampling over the bones of the brave, to endure a storm of steel?"

"I don't know, Sir, but when the time comes you'll find the words, of that I have no doubt. We've all been praying for peace, but in its sustained absence there's been an air of inevitability building amongst the ranks, the men are fearful, but understand, they're expecting it."

He nods, but his look of sorrowful resignation deepens. No matter what I say, it doesn't alter the fact that we're twenty four short hours from oblivion and he's the one who has to feed the men a shit sandwich. We sit silently for a few minutes, attempting to drink our woes away, the glasses are swiftly replenished.

"Do you know what this is, Jack?" He asks, holding up the bullet. "Yes, Sir, it's a bullet."

Smiling, he shakes his head. "No, it's not, this my good friend is a golden pill, it really is quite brilliant, magical in fact, allow me to demonstrate."

I look on in horror as he loads it into the revolver, closes the chamber and presses the tip firmly into his right temple.

"Yes, as I was saying, it really is magical, just one pill, it's all that's needed to melt away your troubles. One simple click and they vanish, I'll never have to think about anything ever again. If I place my finger here and."

"No!" I scream, "please, Sergeant Bevan, put the gun down, I'm begging you."

"Why delay death a minute longer, my dear boy? The beast is coming for me, this will stop the worry bleeding from my brain and dampen the wretched fear burning within once and for all. As I was saying, pure magic."

"I know, it's coming for all of us, but this isn't the way, Mike. Please, put the gun down."

Not a flicker, I fear his mind has already drifted to a pain free idyllic afterlife, the vision it's skilfully crafted with the aid of copious whiskies. He smiles, his finger hovers menacingly, itching to squeeze his disquiet away, *I can't do this, watch his brain get splattered all over the mud lined walls, he's my friend, I can't lose another one, not like this.*

"Stop!" I bellow with every ounce of strength my distressed body can muster.

"Why, Jack?" He replies calmly, seemingly at peace, "give me one reason why not."

Can I? In truth, this will grant him the tranquillity he aches for, who am I to deny him this escape? On the other hand, who can say with certainty what the morning sun will bring? Any given day has the capacity to bristle with uniqueness. This can't be how his story ends, it's not a fitting last chapter worthy of gracing this great man's eulogy, he deserves the upmost reverence. I get to my feet and stare intently in to his vacant eyes.

"I'll give you a reason, Sergeant," I seethe, "because it's more honourable to die out there, in the field with your fucking men, that's bloody why."

I've shocked myself, I'd never dream of speaking to Sergeant Bevan in such a brazen manner, but it seems to have had the desired effect. He lowers the gun, placing it carefully on the desk and sinks his head into his hands. I'm not sure if I can detect some faint sobbing, but this is the closest I've come to seeing Sergeant Bevan cry. Not one for teary displays of emotion, he quickly rubs his eyes and nods. Thank God, he's back in the present.

"I'm sorry, Sergeant Bevan, I don't know what the blessed came over me, cursing at you in that manner."

"Nonsense, Jack, I needed telling."

I nod.

"Better lay of the bourbon for a while," he adds sheepishly.

"Are you going to be ok, Sir?"

"Of course, a splash of water, some rest and I'll be as right as rain."

"Yes, Sergeant Bevan, understood."

The natural order is restored, we both salute and I turn on my heels.

"Private Crosby."

"Yes, Sir."

"This never happened."

"Of course, Sir."

"Good man, oh, and thank you…"

At the break of dawn, we stand shoulder to shoulder, like many mornings before, in anticipation of another eloquently delivered frank and forthright address. Being privy to its content, I feel a little uncomfortable while standing among my bleary eyed brothers. I often marvel at how some men can exude such cheerfulness when trapped in the descending gloom of life's darkest moments, a fine virtue Frosty exhibited handsomely. There's chatting, smiling, even laughing, thank God for the cheerful souls who make war bearable, their troubles are no less graver than mine. Sergeant Bevan arrives promptly, well attired and fresh faced, barely recognisable from the shell of a man I encountered a few short hours ago.

"Good morning, gentlemen."

"Good morning Sergeant Bevan."

"Gallantry, men, is not a word I band about lightly, it's a term reserved for heroes, courageous souls worthy of an array of accolades, but fittingly it describes the men I walk amongst every day. Through shot and shell, the brutal elements and barbaric atrocities your brave hearts have endured, gentleman, you have my utter respect and unstinting admiration. It has been my upmost privilege and life's greatest honour to lead you, but alas, I must ask even more of you in order to accomplish our greatest undertaking to date."

Sergeant Bevan sighs and gathers himself, this is wearing heavy. "Gentlemen, I have consulted at great length with General Hughes, subsequently at first light tomorrow, with the aid of our friends in the Brigade we will embark on our most daring mission. The finer details will be communicated throughout the day, but sufficive to say gentleman, this is our time. A moment to stand tall and shape history. We have battled resiliently, to deny Jerry free passage through Belgium, now we must force them back to whence they first came. Gentlemen, this is a chance to write our own chapter, to not only be remembered, but revered and celebrated till the end of time. The ask, is a great one I know, you've given so much already, but the opportunity is even greater. Gentlemen, I'm confident we can execute this mission precisely and emerge victorious."

To many listening, the command Sergeant Bevan is delivering with steadfast conviction will prove to be a death sentence. Despite his grave personal reservations, he's managed to keep the address upbeat, framing it as a rallying cry, it's exactly what the men need at this critical juncture. Better to go charging into the unforgiving night with lungs full of noble endeavour than a heart laden with gloom and misery. In the wee hours since his mental wobble, Sergeant Bevan has pulled off nothing short of a miracle, managing in some measure to buy into the ill - fated escapade. Temporarily squaring things off with his conscience is the only way he can function effectively, he also recognises that offering up anything less will do the men a great disservice.

"So men, for the benefit of clarity, this will be a full scale assault carried out in designated waves. At first light tomorrow we will indeed be going over the top and may God be with us all."

Finally, after fretful nights and lengthy debate, stone cold confirmation that in a handful of hours we will walk the precarious line between glory and eternal damnation. A line that burrows right through the heart of hell. As one would expect, the news is met with a ponderous silence as the reality of the situation quickly seeps into minds already bulging with anxiety, but no obvious discord. Inevitability doesn't make the mission any easier or less harrowing, but it will aid acceptance and compliance. I look around, spying a host of rather studious expressions and realize that this time tomorrow, following our desperate charge through a hail of bullets, a fair chunk will have perished, I may be one of them. This is God's waiting room, all any of us can now to get through this is adopt a 'hopefully it's not me 'mentality, our tenuous fate now rests delicately on the wings of angels.

"Are there any questions?"

Joker raises his hand.

"Yes, Daniel."

"Can I go home, please, Sergeant Bevan?"

The whole line erupts with laughter, including our leader. He's done it again, priceless.

"Only if you take me with you, Daniel," he replies with a grin, "now, are there any serious questions?"

Laughter quickly fades, leaving nothing, but stone cold reality to confront.

“Ok, men, I realise that this is a lot to absorb, but in the meantime we mustn’t allow ourselves to lose focus. Today is just as important, even more so, because at this moment it’s all we can take care of. It demands an impeccable state of vigilance at all times. The snipers bullet is an unrelenting fellow that must be respected at all costs, stay on your metal and don’t succumb to it’s evil charms. We arrived on these shores as individuals, but now stand shoulder to shoulder as one, support each other and consistently do the right things, that is our only path to victory and the fruits of a normal life. May God bless us all today, with the fortitude and fortune to witness another sunset. Amen.”

“God bless. Amen.”

We disperse, quietly shuffling away to commence what now passes as a normal working day, be it manning stations, penning prose to loved ones, eating breakfast or snatching forty winks. It all feels a bit before the Lord Mayor’s show, we’re treading water, this is going to be a peculiar morning.

Supper time is something every soldier aspires to on a daily basis, a focal point that recognises the presence of safe passage, another day almost done and dusted, an opportunity to enjoy some rest, food and a spot of social interaction. Over time, it has become less about the food and more about the conversation, as soldiers, we survive on our wits and the most basic rations, filling foods that lack flavour. If it wasn’t for the steady flow of treats that arrive from home and liquor, we’d have blown our brains out months ago. I wonder what delights I’ll feast on for my last supper, although it’s of scant importance, all that matters is who I’ll share it with.

Friendship forged in adversity is a powerful bond, these are the men who'll take a bullet for me. Once strangers thrown together, they're now, outside of Frosty, the greatest friends I'll ever know. Privy to each's darkest fears, we've shared our worries and pain, but also carry the same simple hopes and dreams. When my mashed up mind is crawling the walls, tackling unscalable monsters, it's their arms that I can see in the distance, waiting to pull me over the mental barriers. Lionheart, Bookworm, Joker, Sergeant Bevan and, of course for one incredible day, Wilhelm, their friendship and the quality time I spent with Frosty, it's the one beautiful thing to emerge from this horrific war. I'd like to think I've been there for them too in equal measure, fuck the medals and hollow glory, camaraderie is the only reward conflict serves up.

"What culinary delights are we feasting on tonight, lads?" Asks Lionheart while sarcastically rubbing his hands.

"Bully beef on hardtack biscuits followed by tinned peaches," replies Bookworm dryly.

"Marvellous, a gourmet treat, salty minced beef on dry crackers."

"Don't forget the peaches," adds Joker.

"Oh, I won't Danny."

"We could always forgo the peaches," I suggest.

"Forgo them?" Argues Bookworm, but they're the best bit."

Grinning, I slip out a small tin from under my coat, their eyes light up, burning with anticipation.

"It's not, is it?" Asks Lionheart.

"Oh, tell me it is," adds Joker.

I know exactly what they're alluding to, Rose's homemade chocolate cake has taken on legendary status around these parts. I've been saving it, but now this definitely feels like the right moment. It's hopeless, I can't contain my neutral facade a second longer.

"It is," cries Lionheart, that lovely chocolate cake made by your fair maidens hands."

"What a treat," exclaims Joker.

"Delightful" adds Bookworm.

Given the hour and all that lies beyond the horizon, it's wonderful to see them all smiling one more time, my brothers. At this opportune moment Sergeant Bevan rears his head, when it comes to sniffing out dessert, this man is like a bloodhound.

"What's that about your person, Private Crosby?" He says quizzically.

"It's cake, Sir."

"What, *the* cake?"

Lionheart, Joker and Bookworm nod like a bunch of giddy kids on Christmas morning.

"Sweet mother of God, I've arrived in the nick of time."

Despite their eagerness to tuck in, we munch through the stodgy main course before devouring the cherished pudding, it heightens the anticipation, life's sweetest form of torture. I've eaten my bodyweight in bully beef during these long months of combat, but it fills a hole if nothing else. The cake handsomely lives up to its billing, performing a decadent dance across my tongue. It's a much needed taste of home and greatly appreciated judging by the content looks on their faces. It's a rare worry-free moment, the last we'll enjoy this side of sunrise. There's nothing my Rose can't do with some flour, eggs and a mixing bowl, but even her sweet creations can't taper tomorrows reality.

"So, chaps, how are you all feeling about tomorrow?"

We look at each other, it's not the easiest thing to verbalise.

"I'm asking as a friend now, not your Commanding Officer, you can be frank, they'll be no judgement."

"Well," said Joker, "I'm living in a state of denial at the moment, still hoping against hope that the big knobs can get around the table and thrash something out at the eleventh hour to save our bacon."

Sergeant Bevan nods empathetically. "We're all still praying for that, my dear boy, and there are worse states to live in, trust me."

"Thank you, Sir."

"Barry, how are you doing lad?"

"I'm not relishing the prospect, Sir," he replies in an understated manner, "every time I think about tomorrow, I get this sick feeling in my stomach."

"It's nerves, my boy, totally understandable."

"I'm hoping to, Sir," he adds, "hoping we catch Jerry napping and somehow get through this ordeal unscathed. I've just started this enthralling new book, it's rather bulky and I would like to see how it ends."

"Quite," replies Sergeant Bevan, "the element of surprise will hopefully prove to be the greatest weapon in our armoury."

He looks towards me expectantly. Bravado has it's place, but among friends on the eve of our greatest triumph or tragedy, I feel no need to mask my burning apprehension.

"Well, Sir, I feel totally numb. Numb and hollow, I'm not ready to die and with so much living left to do, I really don't want to."

Sergeant Bevan looks pained, slowly drowning in our ocean of fears. "I know how you feel, son, one only realises its true worth when it's frightfully all too late. Life offers up so many dreams, what on earth gives man the right to destroy something so precious?"

Anguished looks are exchanged, our likely fate is almost too horrendous to contemplate.

"Well," says Lionheart softly, "I'm bloody petrified at the prospect, charging across no-man's-land, it's suicide, hard to imagine us all making it."

It's a sobering statement that captures the mood perfectly, realizing not everybody will make supper tomorrow, we look long and hard into each other's eyes, it's like gazing into a mirror, from where once hope thrived so fervently, nothing but trepidation remains.

"I fear so, Reginald, death for some is a sorrowful inevitability, but we're going to give it our damndest."

"Yes, Sir," he replies emphatically, "we'll give Jerry a run for their money."

"Good man, that's the spirit."

"Sergeant Bevan."

"Yes, Jack."

"How are you feeling about tomorrow?"

He looks genuinely shocked at being asked, seeming reluctant to answer, we wait patiently, anticipating his reply, will it come from a Sergeant's perspective or the lips of our friend?

"Well, eager for the off as one would expect." His unconvincing reply is fooling nobody, he sighs and shakes his head disconcertingly. "Before I came out for a wander tonight, erm, I wrote a letter to Jean, my wife. I won't be sending it obviously, but it will be sent on, you know, in the event of my passing, The poor girl deserves more than an official notice, she is the most adorable woman. I really should have made a bigger fuss of her, told her more often how much I love her. So, I'm terrified too, men, terrified we won't get to spend our golden years together, we often talked about retiring to the coast, a cottage by the sea and long lazy walks on the beach."

"It sounds lovely, Sir."

"Doesn't it just, our own little patch of paradise." He looks solemnly at us through tearful eyes. "I don't want to die either chaps, but it doesn't hurt to be prepared."

Tears began to flow in all quarters, five men in their prime, prematurely mourning the tragedy and injustice of their imminent passing. It's only when you stare directly into its face you realize, death is one ugly bastard.

I needn't concern myself with sleep tonight, even contemplating the prospect is preposterous. In a few hour's our ranks will be swelled with neighbouring battalion's, dragged from the comfort of billets like lambs to the slaughter, but before the big push I need to write a letter, one I desperately hope never sees the light of day.

My dearest Rose,

If you are reading this, my final correspondence, know that I did everything in my power to forge a way back to your arms and the life I love beyond compare.

Although, regrettably short, I have lived the most beautiful life imaginable, experiencing enough love to fill a myriad of lifetimes. The world is full of dreamers, but few get to really live their dreams, I, not only got to live mine, but I got to live them with you, my beautiful English Rose.

When I charged into the unforgiving night, I did so with a heart bursting with love for you, and at the moment I passed, it can only have been you I was picturing. I know this with absolute certainty, you're my first thought in the morning and last thought at night, the beautiful vision that bookends my day. I don't know how you did it, but every time you kissed me, my world stood still. Please know, that I cherished every single one. I love you, Rose, more than I've ever loved anything and that will endure, I'm always going to be in love with you, death isn't powerful enough to rob me of that gift.

You're going to make a fantastic mother, Rose, kiss our baby every day and tell him or her how much their daddy loves them. Don't doubt yourself, you have the strength within to carry on and live a fulfilling life. Please don't reserve all your love for me, you're young and beautiful with so much to give, don't be frightened to love again and find happiness in the arms of another, this is my dying wish.

To my unborn child, know that while still in your beautiful mother's womb, you were already loved ever so deeply. I'm so sorry, to not be there sharing your life and witnessing the unique person you'll grow into. Your mother and myself were so incredibly excited upon learning she was carrying you, being parents was all we ever wanted. As you make your way in the world be strong and bold enough to dream big dreams, you can be anything you chose to be. I won't be around, so please look after your wonderful mother, but I will be watching proudly along with Uncle David from the gates of heaven. I will always love you, my precious baby.

Thanks, Rose, for loving me so beautifully, you got me through my darkest days after Frosty passed, never giving up on me. I really don't know how to end this letter, given the gorgeous life you bestowed upon me, whatever I write will feel incomplete, so I'll simply say goodnight, my beautiful Rose, until we meet again…

All my love, now and always

Your Jack

I'm content, writing is a simple craft when it comes from the heart. I store the letter carefully in my special tin, the one that houses all of my cherished mementos of Rose. Another nervous glance at my pocket watch, one last painful hour at the doors of destiny to spend contemplating my own mortality. I'm reliably informed that I'm forming a part of the second wave of attack, is that a good thing or not? At least, I won't be braving the initial brace of bullets, but those brave chaps will have the element of surprise, whereas by the time it gets to my turn, I'm sure the bloody snipers will have their eye in! If the first two waves prove successful, then surely the remaining two will enjoy less shrapnel around their ears. This worrying is pointless, I'm pretty confident there's no real winners in any given scenario. I've drunk every last drop of booze in my vicinity, but still feel sick to the stomach. Mental images of heroic survival are dwarfed by thoughts of death, *will it be quick? Bullet, shell or blade? I wonder how it will feel? Painless I hope. Oh merciful Lord, grant me that much at the very least.*

The trench is swarming with pasty-faced sleep-deprived soldiers, all teetering on the precipice of damnation. Trays of neat rum are being doled out, courtesy of the General I'm informed, oh he's too kind, and predictably nowhere to be seen. I might have known, the rum is cheap and nasty, but serves a purpose. Sergeant Bevan has kindly placed my crew in the same wave, himself included, the notion we'll charge and probably die together is comforting in a romantically twisted kind of way. It feels absurd, finding a semblance of beauty floating from the burning embers of impending doom, but enslaved in the shadow of death, I'll take any solace I can glean.

The so, called, masterplan is simple, line up, step forward on the command then 1,2,3, the whistle blows, it's over the top and charge. In other words, climb out the trench and run like billy-o, armed only with a revolver in hand, a head full of fear and a hopeful heart. It's so basic, an utter imbecile can follow it, although even they might question the wisdom of running into the full on fury of German artillery. There are a few further instructions, which aren't so easy to follow, as they fly in the face of human compassion, eyes forward at all times, keep pushing forward at all cost and under no circumstances should we stop to tend to the injured and dying. The first wave stand shoulder to shoulder in relative quiet, gently quaking, but primed to etch their names into the history books. Thankfully, for now, in lieu of breakfast, the enemy guns have felt silent, the faintest opportunity exists to catch them on the hop. Sergeant Bevan, Bookworm, Joker, Lionheart and myself stand directly behind them, nervously waiting our turn like obedient, but frightened children standing outside the headmasters office. Once the first wave depart, throwing themselves on God's mercy, it will be a matter of seconds.

I've pondered at great length about what I'd be thinking if this precise moment ever materialises. Going over the top is the ultimate mental challenge for any soldier, a few weeks spent in the sunshine stabbing bayonets into hanging sacks of hay isn't going to prepare anyone for this most dreaded of escapades. I've spent the majority of my final hours, trying to stare death down and arrest it of it's fear, but the beast can't be tamed, that much I've learned. It will be my chronic companion throughout what remains. In the absence of meaningful hope, the foundation on which beautiful dreams are built, my mangled mind has nestled upon an uneasy acceptance, the life I have and the one I crave to reclaim no longer rests in my hands, that's if they ever truly did. I'm one insignificant number, in a long line of statistics, whose destiny has been viciously wrestled from their grasp. So, in the ugly presence of death, what is a fretful man to do, how does ones impoverished mind squeeze any last droplets of joy out of those remaining seconds?

In the midst of my silent dilemma, all thoughts turn to Rose, a radiant beacon of love who showered glorious light over every facet of my existence. I got to feel the immensity of her love and I've been granted the great privilege of loving her back so completely, this surely is the definitive essence of life. *Oh, Jack Crosby, you have indeed and by no small measure, lived the dream, no amount of shrapnel is going to change that. This grisly final destination bears, but not a hint of resemblance to the beautiful journey love has taken you on.*

"This appears to be it, chaps, one last tango with our foes," utters Sergeant Bevan in a calm, but resigned tone.

"I don't feel like dancing much," replies Joker.

"Me neither" adds Lionheart, "I'd rather be anywhere, but bloody here, down the pub, absolutely anywhere."

"That would be nice," says Bookworm, "or maybe the library."

Oh, Barry, you're a legend, staying true to yourself until the bitter end.

"Yeah, that would be lovely," I interject, "sat around a table in the sunshine, chatting about nothing in particular, while drinking a cool beer."

"Oh, I'll have some of that, boyo."

"Yes, that sounds just the ticket, Jack, splendid."

"Let's do it," says Joker excitedly, "meet up on the other side for a couple of jars."

"Why the hell not," replies Lionheart, "make mine a bloody large one."

"Yeah, yeah, we'll do just that chaps, beers in Berlin"

"Beers in Berlin," we all cry.

Cheer rings out along the line, it's a desperate outpouring of delusion made all the more delicious by its unexpectedness. In the most dire moment, there's nothing like a strand of forlorn hope to cling to.

"Number one, advance forward."

Well, that's gone and killed the mood, some people can be so bloody inconsiderate!

"Gentlemen, prepare to go on my command, and may the grace of God be with you."

How the fuck did I get to this? The point of no return. A life so beautifully laden with infinite opportunity, now offers up only desecrated dreams, sweet resolution can no longer deliver the salvation my sinking heart desires.

"One, two…"

Bang, audible screams of horror echo around the trench, bringing a halt to the countdown. A chap in the first wave has taken matters into his own hands, placing a revolver under his chin and blowing his head off. The ill-timed execution of his last ditch escape plan may have alerted the enemy to our dishonourable intentions, but it's hard to condemn the actions of a decent, but distressful man, callously driven to the brink of insanity. Men standing adjacent and behind are frantically rubbing remains off their bloodied faces while his lifeless body is unceremoniously dragged away. The suicide of one lowly Private isn't going to derail this plan, merely delay the fun momentarily, at all human cost, the show must go on.

"Number one, advance forward." The line quickly reforms, shuffling tentatively closer to the afterlife.

"Gentlemen, prepare to go on my command, and may the grace of God be with you."

We warmly pat their backs in one final display of solidarity, offering up silent prayers for their enduring safety, the first fearful souls forced to engage in this reckless act of sheer folly.

"One, two, three…." his fateful whistle blows.

Any hope we'll catch Jerry napping is swiftly put to bed amidst a crescendo of carnage. Some men barely get out of the trenches, falling back into our line with bullets lodged in their heads, they lay around our feet either dead or slowly dying. The latter are more off-putting, it's impossible to block out their faint cries. Time cruelly denies us the opportunity to cradle and comfort their weakening torsos, they're ghosts now, to be trampled on and forgotten, of no further use and therefore importance to the Great British Army.

"Number two, advance forward."

I can hear the dying screams amidst a hail of bullets raining down, now it's my turn to follow in the footsteps of the dead. The sky turns crimson with the flashing of shells, *fuck, we're standing on deaths doorstep.*

"Gentlemen, prepare to go on my command, and may the grace of God be with you."

One final glance left and right at the brave chaps I've learned to love, their eyes so deeply enriched with anxiety, I can drown in their fear.

"Good luck, chaps, and the best of British," says Sergeant Bevan defiantly, a tower of strength until the frenetic finale.

"One, two, three…" the whistle blows, duty calls.

I've managed to drag myself out of the trench, albeit cutting my arm on the barbed wire, *my God, it's the fucking apocalypse!* Clumps of rugged ground are erupting under a ferocious bombardment of enemy shelling, causing the earth to shake violently as mud intermingled with human residue rains down from the heavens. Injured men, lay strewn across the bloodied earth, begging for water and desperately clutching at my ankles, but I must push on in the hope of minimising future bloodshed, reluctantly leaving their haunting cries stagnating in the breeze.

With eyes fixed firmly on the swollen German ranks, I'm charging through chaotic clusters of carnage with all the mite my pumping legs can muster. The first wave are still bearing the brunt as I witness another comrade succumb to cold steel, his energy banished for all eternity, but others are close to penetrating the German defences and the human fodder in reserve is plentiful. Every stride forward increases the likelihood of a swift demise, but jacked up on adrenalin, I'm too absorbed in the chase to worry. As long as my heavy boots continue pounding the ground, the heart's still beating. The familiar, but harrowing whistle of machine gun fire is ringing in my ears, but I still retain the clarity to realise I've never been closer to death or felt more alive. Even if there's a bullet with my name on it, I won't see it coming. Hopefully I'm rewarded with a clean kill. I couldn't bear to rot away slowly, rats merrily gnawing at my stricken breathless body.

I've advanced further than I could have ever dreamed, although this would make for one disturbing dream. At the horrific cost of large scale human sacrifice, this mission may actually bear some ill-gotten fruit. I'm frightenedly close, to the besieged German trenches, and it appears our latter waves are faring better than their depleted predecessors. I'm firing my revolver sparingly as I don't have the luxury of reloading, it's a necessary evil if I want to distract the Boche from the rather ungentlemanly business of blowing my head off.

A few of our boys lay impaled on the barbed wire, following heroic attempts to infiltrate the German trench, blood drips slowly from their squirming bodies. Some are begging foes to put them out of their misery, but there are more immediate threats for Jerry to negate, namely the rampaging British bulldogs careering towards them on mass. After initially suffering a glut of heavy losses, momentum is shifting in our favour. I'm now close enough to witness the panic in their eyes, it's a sorrowful sight I derive no pleasure from. The poor bastards didn't want this needless bloodbath any more than we did, again in the heart-rending absence of any lessons being learnt, the spilt blood of simple folk will be used to appease the selfish motives of power hungry scoundrels.

Hot on the heels of the brave, I'm fast approaching the coveted dirt we seek to claim, but there's a sting in the tale, while a few of the oppressed abandon their posts and retreat for the hills, others storm out of the trench, intent on stemming the raid by any means necessary. *Shit, now I'm the one being charged at, it's not a pleasant feeling. Hang on a minute, I didn't sign up for this, brawling in the dirt like a savage animal. I'm far more comfortable hiding my deplorable transgressions behind the anonymity of an SMLE Mark 3 rifle.*

Who is this sturdy chap tearing towards me? His enraged eyes lacquered with a threatening shade of bloodlust, who is this man coming for my life? One imagines, before war had it's wicked way with his passive psyche, he lived a humble existence filled with days of decentness. Abruptly plucked from some leafy German suburb, his kindness moulded into killing. The poor soul has more in common with me than he'll ever know. I'm confident that beneath the wide-eyed hate, there resides a fine fellow, but right now his sole intention is to relinquish me of my most precious cargo, the cherished dreams entwined with Rose's future, but I bear no malice, for he is no more the enemy than I am. Yet I have to fuel my heart with enough hate to take his life. All those educating years spent shaping a civilised being must be forgotten, any lingering sophistication extinguished, to permit my troubled conscience to abide by the first rule of the jungle, kill or be killed.

I raise my revolver, but exhibiting the attributes of an ally cat, he's too darn quick, forcing me down in to the aforementioned dirt. The revolver, relinquished on impact, lies close by, but neither of us are willing to give the other a chance to grab it. This is utter madness, we're rolling around like a pair of frolicking teenagers. I'm squirming for my life, but he's a strong bugger, all I get for my considerable endeavour is a few lusty blows across the chops. I can taste blood, it's mine, but he's given up using my head as a punchbag, his hands are now firmly wrapped around my throat. I grab his wrists tightly and try to prise them apart, *fuck me, this big bastard is granite,* he's strangling the last shreds of life from my wriggling carcass. The death reel has started playing inside my head as I gasp for air under the pressure of his vice like grip. It's not the romantic montage grandly portrayed in countless works of fiction, but disappointingly, a series of blurry images lacking cohesion. Wrestling defeat from the jaws of victory, I am quite literally going to die at the bloodied hands of the Germans.

Perilously close to the advent of my death, I summon up the energy to stage one last act of despicable defiance. I wrench away his right arm, pulling it towards my face and viciously sink my teeth in like a scavenging cannibal. He yelps in pain, loosening his grip as I spit out a hearty chunk of flesh. Disgusting, as one would imagine, but my depraved act presents a slither of opportunity for the preservation of life, mine specifically. He makes a desperate play for the revolver, but anticipating his next move I reach for my bayonet, drawing it quickly from the scabbard around my waist and jamming it forcefully into his ribcage. The blade crunches through, persevering until the handle crashes against his punctured torso, I can feel his warm blood running freely between my fingers. If this is what glory feels like, vomit swirling round my mouth and a self-loathing sense of shame, then you can bloody well keep it. The intense shot of pain blistering through his bleeding body causes his eyes to bulge grotesquely as the last effects of life drain from his stricken skeleton, slumping on top of me, he breathes his last.

"I'm so sorry, my friend, so desperately sorry. I'm so very sorry, please, forgive me. Forgive me my sins," I mouth quietly into his ear while cradling his head tenderly.

This death is so much more than a statistic, another needless casualty of war, this is a person who mattered, he'll leave a void in the lives of the many hearts he touched, maybe a loving husband, perhaps a doting father idolised in the eyes of an innocent child. His violent passing is appalling, another tiny piece in the monstrous jigsaw that represents the greatest atrocity mother earth has ever witnessed. Our most enduring tragedy, wholly avoidable and in its entirety, borne out of man's insatiable greed. Undoubtedly his death, one among thousands, will be glossed over and deemed a necessary sacrifice for the greater good, but I'll never forget. Even if I survive, until my hair turns grey and they decorate my chest with the Victoria Cross, the image of his contorted face will haunt me forevermore.

Swarming through the deserted enemy trenches, like a pack of bloodthirsty locust, anyone with a semblance of common sense has had it away on their toes. As jubilant hoards stream past, I'm trudging through the muddy ditch, overburdened with a sagging heart that's riddled with indignity. I'm envious of their joy, but suspect the mood is more a manifestation of relief rather than celebration. The enemy will regroup in some nearby location, for sure, and bolster their ranks. Same stalemate, different field, it's hard to fathom what's been achieved today. I'm standing in a river of German blood that flows through the fringes of a field littered with a battery of lifeless British bodies, we should get the spinless Generals down here, forcing them to observe their handywork first hand. In this trench alone, containing both the dead and dying, the body count is horrific. Alarmingly, one corpse in particular, lying face down, has captured my attention, a burly frame, blond locks matted with blood. *My God, it can't possibly be...not Wilhem, please God, I beg of you, anybody but my dear friend Wilhelm.*

I frantically turn the body over, fuck, another deep crack forms across my already splintered heart. I cradle his head and look ruefully to the skies. "You utter bastard."

I put my ear to his chest, despite blood pouring from a gapping wound in his stomach, there's still breath within his severed body. I press a rag to his overcoat to delay the inevitability of his passing.

"Wilhelm," I say softly, "Wilhelm, can you hear me?"

His eyes flicker ever so slightly.

"Jack, is that you, my good friend?"

"Yes, Wilhelm, it's Jack, I'm here now."

He forces his eyes open, groggy from the heavy loss of blood. "Oh, Jack, it's really you."

"It is."

"How are you?"

"I'm good, Wilhelm, all the better for seeing you."

On the cusp of death, he manages a smile.

"Jack."

"Yes, Wilhelm?"

"Is it over?"

"Over?"

"This silly war, can I go home now?"

"Yes, Wilhelm, it's all over now. You're going home, my friend, back to Freya."

"Wunderbar, wunderbar" he utters, "I love her so much."

I watch his face sweetly succumb to a tranquil state of utter contentment, terminal lucidity, life's parting gift. There is something quite beautiful about death when conducted peacefully, it affords the bearer a serenity that only exists during one's passing. I'll be eternally grateful for being afforded the great privilege of sharing his final journey. Finality, it's a concept all humans struggle with, the fact immortality doesn't exist, a slow burning realisation that the far-flung fantasy of forever lives only in the romantic minds of the permanently delusional.

"Jack," he groans.

"Yes, Wilhelm?"

"I'm cold, ever so cold."

I take off my overcoat and wrap it around him.

"There you go, now rest, close your eyes and rest, Wilhelm."

"Thank you, Jack, you're a good friend, please tell Freya and Anna how much I love them."

"Of course, I promise, now relax, my dear friend."

It's one I fully intend to fulfil, if granted the opportunity, Freya and Anna need to know that Wilhelm spent his last peaceful moments smiling and speaking only of the abundant love he felt for them. He gazes to the heavens in awe and wonder.

"Jack, look at that marbled blue sky, the sun's rising once more."

"I know, it's glorious."

He sighs deeply.

"What have we done to our beautiful world?"

"It's ok, Wilhelm, it's over now," I say reassuringly, tears streaming down my face.

"Why couldn't we all live together, peacefully, under God's liberal sky?"

"I know, but for now, lets just enjoy the sunrise."

"Let's, Jack."

I prop him up, he leans back into me and I hold him, in reverent silence, we witness his final sunrise. Never have I experienced a moment that echoes so loudly of both intolerable pain and imperishable beauty.

"Jack, Jack," he says softly.

"Yes, Wilhelm?"

"Please, reach into my breast pocket."

"Of course."

I pull out his photo, the one that's sustained his existence through all these turgid months. I recognise it instantly, the delightful portrait of Freya and Anna he proudly exhibited on Christmas day.

"Hold it, in front of my eyes," he utters faintly with his dying breath.

I grant his last wish, one of departing this mortal coil while gazing at what he loved most about it. Moments later his head sinks back into my chest, there's no life coursing through his limp body. Wilhelm Becker has passed, his spirit now hovers above the bloodied fields of Flanders in a world left bereft of his presence.

Holding him tightly, I allow myself a brief moment, one wholly dedicated to mourning his death, taking considerable comfort in the knowledge his suffering is over. There is precious little dignity to be had in this muddy grave, but I lay him down carefully and kiss his forehead. Wilhelm's at peace, he's escaped, the untold pain now rests with the broken, those he loved with the utmost passion. Their battle, although of a more passive nature, cruelly affords no ending. For me, the band of war keeps playing it's haunting tune, one rich with rigorous monotony. I look down one final time and smile.

"Goodnight Wilhelm, we'll always have Christmas in Flanders Fields"

Christmastime in Flanders Fields

A poem by Chris Waddington

In Flanders fields, whence Christmas came
Lay a blanket of glistening frost
Hiding one's darkest transgressions
Skeletons of stricken soldiers lost

Mud-lined trenches
harbour rivers of frozen blood
Within minds aching for yesterday
Forlorn dreams of normality flood

Mercifully, the guns fall silent
Heralding dusk on Christmas Eve
Embers of a sacrificed season
We quietly grieve.

Across rugged plains, devoid of glory
"Englander, Englander "they cry
Foes masquerading as merry souls
Too young to die

A portrayal of imperishable beauty
Depicts a sea of blazing Christmas trees
Angelic tones of Silent Nacht
Float serenely on the breeze

Moonlit madness teases
A peaceful tomorrow
Hope infecting hardened hearts
Laden with sorrow

The morning sun rises
On to no man's land, heroes pour
Greeting men they sought to kill
Only hours before

Drinking in a freedom
Inexplicable during war
Sharing hatred for a conflict
Imprisoning us on this shore

Standing in a graveyard of ambition

Where so many dreams died

Amidst a cackle of conversation

Cherished photos are brandished with pride

Excitedly playing football

Like gleeful children in the park

Tastes of sweet liberation

But, it will soon be dark

An ugly black reality descends

Our Christmas is at an end

Fond farewells are spoken

Goodbye, good luck and may God speed you my friend

Despite all that has gone before

I guess we're now at war...

A Note From The Author

Time is our most precious commodity. Heartfelt thanks for devoting some of yours to reading my book, I do hope you enjoyed it.

Please feel free to contact me directly at cjwaddington@hotmail.co.uk with any feedback you have and leave a review on Amazon. Thanks again for choosing Christmas In Flanders Fields.

Kind regards
Chris

Printed in Dunstable, United Kingdom

80140932R00163